BREAKTHROUGH

Ken Grimwood

BREAKTHROUGH

1976
Doubleday & Company, Inc., Garden City, New York

All of the characters in this book
are fictitious, and any resemblance
to actual persons, living or dead,
is purely coincidental.

Library of Congress Cataloging in Publication Data

Grimwood, Ken.
Breakthrough.

I. Title.
PZ4.G8654Br   [PS3557.R497]   813'.5'4
ISBN 0-385-11498-2
Library of Congress Catalog Card Number 75-32012

"The Waste Land" from Collected Poems 1909–1962 by T. S. Eliot. Re-
printed by permission of Harcourt Brace Jovanovich, Inc., and Faber & Faber,
Ltd.

For Rab, of course

PART ONE

The room was cold, glacial almost, frozen in that special keenness of a carefully achieved sterility. The lights were huge and brilliant, but their radiance devoid of warmth or comfort. Their reflection glinted starkly on the smooth chrome surfaces of the devices whose impassive metal bulk dominated the chamber.

Bright beads of nervous perspiration sprang up on the young woman's forehead like tiny crystal mushrooms in an ice-world forest. As they appeared, the man who hovered at her left wiped them away. Only his eyes and bony hands were visible; the rest was swathed and masked in white.

She closed her eyes, trying to control her quickened breathing. What was to come could not be changed, could not be stopped; and there would be no sleep, no dulling of her mind's sharp fear, until the worst of it had happened and been carved into her memory. If, after all, some hint of mind or memory would then remain.

Her throat was thick with dryness, but she was unaware of thirst. The table pressed uncomfortably against her spine, and the muscles of her neck were already cramping from their rigid immobility.

She heard a shuffling and a rustling to her right, and made an automatic effort to turn and look. As she did, the pointed metal rods that held her head in place bit painfully, deepening the four small indentations they had made into her skin.

The rustling she had heard increased, and moved behind her. The sound was like the skittering and scratching of an angry, blinded crab inside a cage of glass.

The others were coming in now. Rubber shoes squeaked on the tiles like chalk, and glimpses of stiff white fabric passed her widened eyes. A line from Eliot flashed perversely through her mind:

> Hurry up please, it's time.
> Hurry up please, it's time.

The unmasked eyes were all around her now, and she blinked as the same long-fingered hand moved back across her face to wipe her brow once more. There was a tugging at her scalp, and suddenly the silence and the murmuring gave way to one shrill whir, reverberating through her cheekbones and her teeth.

She could not see it, but she knew the drill had touched her naked, shaven skull.

They had begun.

The young girl's skirt was slightly longer than it should have been in this fall of 1963, when all her schoolmates' hems had begun their scandalous ascent beyond the knee. Its length might well have been a minor hindrance to her progress up the thickly wooded slope, but the garment and the path were equally familiar.

Her parents owned a cottage by the lake that lay below the hilly forest, and they had come here every summer for the past nine years. She and her mother would stay the season through, joined by her father whenever he could get away from his law firm in Richmond, sixty miles away.

This year's summer was all over now, and this would be their final weekend at the lake before next spring. The fallen leaves crushed crisply underfoot, and Elizabeth surveyed the brilliance of the new Virginia autumn with a practiced eye. Her sketchbooks and collected watercolors held the vividness of four past harvest seasons, and the progress of her skills was visible from year to year. The childish hobby showed clear signs of becoming something more than that.

Now, as she neared her favorite sketching spot, breathless from the steep walk up the hill, Elizabeth could feel a rush of warm anticipation. Her interests, and her work, had changed dramatically within the past few weeks, and the latest of her drawings had been hidden prudently inside a hollow oak.

A bright flush tinged her cheeks as she dropped to her knees beside the tree and snaked her wrist into the rotted bark. She cautiously withdrew the rolled-up paper through the narrow opening. Her "workbench" was nearby, the flattened stump of another tree long since sacrificed to someone's ax, and here she carefully unfurled her drawing.

The masterpiece-in-progress, pressed flat against the tree stump, looked back at her with twice the intensity she had remembered. Elizabeth closed her eyes for a moment, breathing deeply of the cool October air. Only then could she look again, with some small measure of dispassion, on her half-complete creation.

The image there was of a man, dark hair in studied disarray. His plain white shirt was open to the waist, and a heavy, ornate buckle marked the place at which the portrait circumspectly ended. The face itself was only vaguely penciled in; but the shirt, the hair, the buckle, and the eyes were all interpreted with accurate and loving clarity.

The man was no one in particular, no movie star or family friend; but to Elizabeth, his reality surpassed all questions of imagination or existence. What others might perceive as anonymity was to her the very essence of his being: maleness, strength, compulsion incarnate.

She had begun the drawing six weeks before. The eyes came first, not from some rational conception of a subject to be illustrated, but from a desire to visually define sensations that were new to her this year, and very nearly overwhelming. Elizabeth was still unable to allow herself to name the locus of those blissful yet unsettling tremors.

Pencil in hand, the girl set to the slow, delicious task of completing the portrait. Her skirt was slowly pulled higher and higher out of the way, until it bunched unnoticed at her waist. Leaning over the smooth, natural table in rapturous concentration on a detail of angular cheekbone, she wrapped her slender legs firmly around the rough tree stump, hugging it with her thighs as she let her mind be swept into absorption with the forms and shapes and likely feels of abstract masculinity. Bark gently scraped her tender flesh, snagging and pulling at her cotton underpants like eager fingers; and all the while the dark, unblinking eyes she'd drawn regarded her, a handswidth from her own.

She must have worked intently for an hour or more. Then her eyes began to tire, and she set the pencil down, resting her head against the broad tree trunk. Her mind went drifting, as she half perceived the dappled sunlight tumbling through the leaves above her. At first she thought about the new school year, and the plans she had to work in oils; but then the images became more random, more abstract, darting and flashing in concert with the flickering sunlight, shimmering, flashing, breaking, flashing, flowing, flashing, flashing, flashing . . . and then there was a smell of roses everywhere, and everything slowed down.

Nothing like this had ever happened before, neither the roses nor the slowing. It wasn't sexual; Elizabeth had discovered masturbation two months before, and she was familiar with the sweet, quick rush of orgasm, though she'd never heard the feeling named. She knew about the spreading pleasure, and the afterglow; but today she hadn't even begun to do that, and there had been no pleasure or release. Nothing had happened. Only flashing light, and roses, and then this solemn, deadly . . . slowing . . .

Something was wrong, something was terribly, inexplicably wrong.

She heard herself cry out as her body stiffened suddenly, jerking her up and away from the tree stump and roughly tossing her to the ground behind. A large, sharp rock was pressing painfully against her side, and she thought, *roll over*, but nothing seemed to move.

The roses were gone now, and she couldn't breathe. Everything had been too slow, and now everything had stopped, stopped dead. Suddenly she thought of death, and tried to scream; but there was no air there to scream with, no throat with which to try.

As her vision turned to red, then black, she felt the quivering begin, and then the maddened thrashing.

Please, she thought, and *please, please no*, before the universe closed down.

The surgeon sat on a high metal stool behind the thick green drapes. Only the rounded, shaven top of the young woman's head protruded through the curtain: Her face, her eyes, and all the rest of her lay stiffly on the other side, hidden from his direct view. He glanced up at the long and narrow mirror that hung above the table. He could see the patient there, and she seemed subdued, if understandably shaky. The anesthetist was whispering quietly to her and wiping the perspiration from her forehead.

The surgeon looked back down again, considering the work that lay before him. The patient's scalp had been vigorously scrubbed a dozen times or more with antiseptic soap, and it glistened underneath the bright spotlights trained on it.

He carefully injected five cc of procaine along a line that had been marked in red two inches across the gleaming skin. When he was done, the scrub nurse to his right exchanged a scalpel for the long, thin hypodermic. He held the scalpel loosely in his hand, waiting for the procaine to take effect. Neither he, the scrub nurse, nor the first assistant standing at his left spoke to each other.

The operating room was large, and the table was set at an angle in the very center. The young woman's head was immediately beneath the X-ray beam, recessed into the twelve-foot ceiling. Another of the bulky X-ray machines was set into the left-hand wall, aimed laterally at the patient's temple. The combination would afford a three-dimensional chart of the procedures yet to come. The white tile walls were shining in the brilliant light; on one there hung a large sign reading "PLEASE MAINTAIN SILENCE: THE PATIENT IS AWAKE."

The surgeon picked at the edges of the red line with his scalpel, watching the young woman's face in the suspended mirror. There was no reaction; the procaine had numbed the flesh. Slowly, he increased the scalpel's pressure, and made the first incision. There was very little blood, and it was quickly mopped away.

The scrub nurse handed him a small, self-retaining retractor.

He spread the lips of the incision about an inch apart and placed the retractor there, holding them in place. The pure white bone beneath could now be seen.

With steady hands, he applied the whirring electric drill. Within twenty seconds, it had made a hole about the size of a penny in the exposed portion of the skull. The loosened piece of bone was picked away and set aside.

The scrub nurse took the drill away and handed him a tiny, delicate hook and a fresh scalpel. With his left hand he used the hook to lift up the dura mater, the fibrous material that covered the brain, and with his right he cut it open. An inch-long section of the convoluted cerebral cortex was revealed.

A tweezer-like electric instrument was used to cauterize the diminutive blood vessels on the brain's exterior. When this was done, the surgeon punctured the surface of the brain with his scalpel, leaving a tiny hole.

An attenuated rubber tube was inserted through this opening and guided toward one of the brain's fluid-filled ventricles, two inches below the surface. A tiny pump withdrew ten cubic centimeters of the fluid and filled the cavity with air. A clamp was then placed on the rubber tube, holding the air inside the ventricle. This air would create shadows on the X rays, helping to complete the inner map to guide the probes.

The young woman still felt no major pain, since the skull and brain contained no sensory receptors; but a dull headache had started from the pressure of the air inside the ventricle.

The surgeon turned to the thin, hollow probe. He carefully examined it to make sure that it had not been bent in the sterilization process. Several color-coded wires were threaded through the opening, and the slender metal tube was locked in place on its "guide," an instrument attached to the head of the table, which could be swiveled and held in any necessary position. The tip of the probe was then painstakingly aimed at the proper area of the brain, as determined in advance.

X rays were taken from above and from the side, and when the plates had been developed, the surgeon put them on a viewing box behind him. With a sterile ruler and stylet he marked his measurements and chose his target. The shadow of the still-to-be-inserted probe was clearly visible, and its direction toward the target area was carefully appraised.

"Left two millimeters, up one and a half."

The guiding apparatus was smoothly, silently adjusted. Another set of X rays was then taken. The probe's alignment now was perfect, its tip precisely poised above its goal deep in the brain.

The young woman coughed dryly, but the four-pronged holding instrument kept her head completely still. The anesthetist murmured reassuringly, and moistened her lips with a damp sponge.

The probe began its sure descent.

Some time later, how much she had no way of knowing, Elizabeth made the slow return to consciousness. For several drifting moments she simply lay there on her side, letting the sight and feel of rotting leaves against her face fade in and out like a distant television signal.

She soon began to feel the pains, a scattered range of sharpness and severity: sore bruises all along her body where she'd writhed and pressed against half-buried stones, a cramping unpleasantness in her lower belly, and an irritated swelling where her tongue should be.

Her cheek was wet with trickles of saliva, and her first cautious movement was to raise a stiff right arm to dry her face. The sleeve came away flecked with blood.

Clutching at the brittle sheet of leaves, she willed her legs into some semblance of control, pulling them behind her to obtain the leverage to stand. With studied effort she pressed her aching hands against the ground and pushed herself up, slowly, from the waist. As she did, the swimming in her head grew worse, and she grasped clumsily at the nearby tree stump for support.

She never would remember the run back down the hill. All she knew was that she must have overlooked the path, because by the time she reached the cottage her arms and legs were covered with scratches, some ripped across the bruises that already had begun to darken. It was as if the forest had attacked her, slashing out in primal rage with spiking thorns and branches. The world—*her* world, her home, her very mind and flesh and self—had risen up in murderous revolt against her.

Bolting through the open door, she fled to the hopeful sanctuary of her room, threw herself to the floor beside her bed, and tried to quiet the shouting in her brain. The hurts from all the scratches and the bruises were obscured by total numbness and an overriding fear that the force that had attacked her on the hill would soon return, might even now be lurking in this house, this room, preparing to possess her body once again, to seize the reins of her reality and plunge her into sudden, thrashing darkness.

Elizabeth began to tremble, not in wild, strong spasms like before, but in the smaller, more contained convulsions of remembered horror. Eventually her pulse and breathing slowed, and her head began to clear somewhat. The hundred different cuts and bruises made their presence known again, and clamored for attention. The fact of ordinary, present pains drove out, at least for now, the larger fears and questions. There were things that needed doing, wounds to clean and tend to. Thinking had to wait, and for that she thanked the lesser agonies her skin had suffered.

Her father had gone out for a final fishing expedition on the lake, and her mother was shopping in the nearby town. Elizabeth knew the cottage was hers alone for at least an hour.

In the bathroom, she removed her clothes and glumly stared at her full-length reflection, arms crossed unconsciously to hide her chest. Her breasts were unmistakably developing, but for some reason she preferred to ignore the fact as long as possible. She turned away from the long mirror on the bathroom door and began to inspect her face in the smaller one above the lavatory.

There were no bruises on her face, and just one scratch that really might be noticeable. She put a little iodine on the tender red line near the corner of her mouth, and then attached a Band-Aid over it. She could say a cat had scratched her, or a branch had snapped back unexpectedly.

The sore places on her tongue still hurt, and they looked raw and ugly in the mirror, like the times she used to eat too greedily and bite her cheek. Rinsing her mouth with peroxide, she ignored the stinging and hoped it wouldn't sound too funny when she talked. Then suddenly, for no reason at all, she started to cry.

After a shower and shampoo, she put a bathrobe on and returned to her room to brush her hair. It always made her feel good to brush her hair, and she liked to do it by the radio. The station was playing an oldie by the Four Seasons. Their whining falsetto voices always sounded kind of funny to Elizabeth, and this song was called "Big Girls Don't Cry," so it even made her laugh a little. After exactly two hundred strokes, her hair was almost dry and beginning to fill again with its natural body.

Calmer now, she made her way back into the bathroom. Sitting on the edge of the old raised tub, Elizabeth rolled up the sleeves of her robe and began daubing iodine on the scratches on her arms. She heard the front door open and close, heard her mother stacking food away in the kitchen; but even her mother would never disturb her in here. If she wore long sleeves to cover up the bruises for a day or two, no one would ever know what had happened this afternoon.

Shifting position on the tub, Elizabeth moved the robe aside to expose her legs, and started to apply the thin brown liquid to her calves and thighs. There were a few more bruises here than on her arms, but not as many cuts and scratches. By the time she reached her upper thighs, she was humming softly, and had just about convinced herself that nothing really unusual had taken place that day at all.

Then she saw the blood.

Deep, dark blood, some of it already drying to black, but surrounded at the edges by a spreading stain of fresher, redder liquid. Seeing it, she felt it: felt the soggy stickiness, felt the brittle caking. This was no scratch, no minor skin wound; the blood was coming from all the way inside her, and it was coming . . . it was coming from *down there*, it was soaking through her clean white panties in an ugly, angry splotch. She knew what it was, of course, her mother had told her to expect it; but no one could have prepared her for its coming on a day like this.

The next few days, back home in Richmond, were an ordeal of constant shame. Everywhere she went, Elizabeth was sure that anyone who saw her *knew*, could see the bulges of those awful straps and wads that her mother had given her to wear between her thighs. It was impossible to look into the eyes of any male, her father most of all; and every girl and woman that she met was seen now in a new, revolting light of guilt and foulness shared. The pleasure she had begun to find in herself as a female was gone now, totally absorbed by that dreadful day of pain and blood and spasms.

Within a week, though, she was daring to believe that perhaps her torment was not much worse than that of other girls her age. As the bleeding slowed, then stopped, those hopes intensified.

Then all her confidence collapsed at once.

The smell of roses came as she awoke one morning. For a moment, she couldn't quite remember where she'd smelled them last; and then the knowledge gripped her throat with awe, as those jolting, unseen hands closed down again in seeming rage.

After it had passed, she got up from her bed in groggy stupor. Even before she went to mend her bleeding, bitten tongue, Elizabeth knelt down to pray, and was promptly taken with a dry and bitter retching.

Nothing in the normal course of things could hold her interest now. Schoolwork was forgotten, and her lack of preparation or response was reprimanded time and time again. On one bad day, two of her teachers held her after class to ask about this strange decline. Both showed a real concern, and were persistent in demanding whether anything had recently disturbed her; but Elizabeth stared at the floor in frightened shame and swore that all was well.

Twice more that week it happened. Once she was in bed at night, sinking toward a welcome sleep; and then, just two days afterward, it happened at the worst time possible.

English class. Everyone there, all her friends, her teacher, everyone watching as she suddenly collapsed and heaved and spasmed. Nervous giggles, faces turned away. The school nurse coming, wiping away the urine and the bloody spittle. Driving her home. Telling her mother. Epilepsy, she said. Fits. Arrangements to be made. Doctor. Hospital. Tests.

The sedatives they gave her that night did no good, and she lay awake for hours, her eyes wide open but surprisingly dry. Trying not to think, but thinking. Trying not to fear, but desperately afraid.

"All right, now, Mrs. Austin, this is the part where you're going to have to help us out. We're going to be giving you some electrical stimulation at different points now, and if you have any unusual sensations, please let us know."

The young woman tried to nod, and was instantly reminded that her head was locked in place by the four rods.

"Yes. I'm ready."

The microscopic current pulsed from its square wave generator, speeding to the tip of the electrode buried in her brain.

"Have you started yet?"

The surgeon motioned to his assistant at the generator. The intensity was raised to two volts at sixty cycles. The switch was pressed again.

"It . . . yes, there was a tingling, sort of, in my mouth."

The surgeon nodded, and one more assistant marked a number and a note with sterile pen on a drawing of the brain.

The probe descended deeper, entering the Rolandic motor area. The first assistant automatically doubled the voltage on the generator.

Pulse.

The young woman giggled nervously. "I guess you could see that, couldn't you? I mean, I wasn't yawning like that on purpose, it just . . . it just happened."

"That's right, you're doing fine. Now, in just a minute we're going to be asking you some questions, and you answer them if you can. How are you feeling so far?"

"O.K., I guess. My neck's a little cramped, but I guess that's to be expected, isn't it?" She giggled again, incongruously. The anesthetist squeezed her hand warmly and then began to lightly massage her rigid neck.

The probe moved once again, and once again it came to rest.

"All right, now, if you could just start counting from one to ten."

"One . . . two . . . three . . . four . . ."

Pulse.

Her tongue refused to work, although her mouth kept moving. The sounds she made were not a part of any human speech. Then the current was withdrawn.

" . . seven . . . eight . . ."

"Very good, very good. Now, you just hold tight for a minute, and then we're going to show you some pictures and we'll want you to tell us what they are."

The probe pushed farther through the tissue of her brain, sliding toward the fissure of Sylvius, and then it stopped.

This time, the current was maintained for several seconds, as the assistant held up a drawing of a cat.

"That's a cat. A Siamese cat."

The probe sliced deeper, and once more the current flowed. A picture of a hand was held before her eyes.

"That's a . . . you know, it's a part of your body, it's at the end of your arm. You put it in a glove, it's called . . . it's called . . ."

The current stopped.

"It's a hand, a hand. I knew it all along, but I couldn't say it. I just couldn't get the word out."

The slender probe moved down again, and the pulse began. A house was in the picture on the card.

"That's a, you know, it's a place where people live, a . . . oh, my God!"

The surgeon's eyes leaped to the mirror overhead. The young woman's face was full of fear and nausea.

"Are you feeling ill, Mrs. Austin?"

"Yes, I . . . I can't say the word for what's in the picture, but aside from that . . . I can smell the roses now. Just faintly, but they're there."

The target had been struck. Dead center.

The Frances Carson Memorial Neurological Clinic was a blandly modern structure in the northern suburbs of Richmond, an area full of stately homes and winding, wooded roads.

The clinic had been built in 1958, endowed by a tobacco magnate's widow who had died of an inoperable brain tumor four years before. Dr. Lawrence Prentiss, an affable and talented neurologist, had been responsible for postponing the woman's death at least five years beyond the normal expectations. He had been the neurological resident at a major New York hospital when she was first referred there, and the "miracles" that he wrought convinced her that Richmond would greatly benefit from a mind like his. The prospect of a six-million-dollar clinic and complete freedom of research had readily convinced the doctor that his Harvard degrees and New York experience would not be wasted in Virginia. Five years of heading the clinic had not changed his mind.

His office was a comfortable one, designed specifically to instill confidence: deep leather chairs, solid old-fashioned oak desk, dark burgundy pile carpeting, and floor-to-ceiling bookshelves stacked with every medical text and journal since Hippocrates, Dr. Gillespie would have felt immediately at home, as would Judge Hardy with a change of titles on the reading matter.

Dr. Prentiss sat at his desk and surveyed the morning's appointment book. There would be a meeting with surgical staff "A" at ten, to discuss an upcoming tumor operation; then an early, and long, lunch hour was set aside for consultation with the directors of Mrs. Carson's estate. Dr. Prentiss had requested the purchase of a sophisticated, expensive new type of stereotaxic probe-localization apparatus for OR 3, and there were bound to be protests.

The first order of business this morning was something more mundane and yet, in its way, even more important: It was a meeting with a suspected epileptic, a young girl, and her parents.

There was no real reason for the head of the entire clinic to devote an hour of his time to this task, but he believed that these regular reminders of the human realities with which he dealt were valuable, even necessary; they led to a constantly renewed perspective that could soon be lost if one became embroiled in nothing but the abstractions of surgery and the high-level in-fighting for appropriations. Whenever possible, he liked to meet and talk with the external manifestations of those brains he tried to heal.

Picking up a folder from his desk, he scanned the patient's referral record for the second time.

Prentiss set the report aside and lit the first of his self-imposed daily allowance of five cigarettes.

Nothing that he had learned so far seemed to indicate that Elizabeth Chandler would present any neurological mysteries or challenges; this looked like a first-year-textbook case of ordinary grand mal epilepsy. The age was right; almost all epilepsy victims had their first seizures between the ages of twelve and sixteen. It might even be significantly appropriate that the girl had recently begun to menstruate; female epileptics were much more likely to suffer an attack immediately before their monthly period, when their bodies were bloated with menstrual fluid. The reasons for this was still unclear, but the correlation was well established. Before the discovery of convulsant drugs like Metrazol, a common method of inducing seizures in the lab for study was to have the patient simply drink large quantities of water. Somehow, the presence of excessive liquid in the system would often provoke the onset of a seizure. If this girl had, in fact, experienced a previous unreported seizure, it might very well have been brought on by the approach of her first period.

No, there would probably be no difficulty with the diagnosis here; but the social realities surrounding the child presented a complex, if also common, array of potential traumas. This girl would now not only have to face the normally painful experience of early adolescence, but she would also have to do so in the context of a frightening, highly stigmatic disease. Neither she nor her parents would find the probable diagnosis an easy thing to handle. All three of them would have to be approached with sympathy and tact.

```
      10/19/63                    Charles P. Gibbons, M.D.
                                  16 Sumter St., Richmond, Va.


      REFERRAL SHEET: CONFIDENTIAL
```

PATIENT'S NAME	AGE	DATE OF BIRTH	SEX	RACE	HT.	WT.
Chandler, Elizabeth Anne	13	5/24/50	F	Cauc.	5'4"	109

PRELIMINARY DIAGNOSIS

Epilepsy (G.M.)

PREVIOUS MEDICAL HISTORY

Common childhood diseases (SEE attached records)
Onset of menarche within past two months

CURRENT MEDICATION

Valium, 10 mg. 3/day (since 10/19/63)

RECENT TESTS

Standard physical, incl. blood serum, urinalysis,
etc. Patient otherwise in apparent good health
(SEE report, attached)

HISTORY OF CURRENT CONDITION

Patient suffered apparent G.M. seizure 10/17/63,
in school classroom (no accompanying injuries);
attended by Barbara Caine, R.N., Woodsfield Junior
High School. Referred to this physician by Miss
Caine, 10/18/63. Examination conducted 10/19/63.
No reported seizures since the first.

REMARKS

Patient is reticent to discuss own case. Refused
to report whether this was her first seizure,
but Miss Caine notes ''She did not seem surprised
that it had occurred''.

SIGNED, *C.P. Gibbons M.D.*

Fatigued in advance by anticipation of the delicate, emotionally charged meeting to come, Prentiss dug a thick knuckle into his eyelids and stubbed out the half-smoked cigarette.

"Miss Reynolds? Could you show the Chandler family into my office, please?"

She couldn't see, and for a moment she thought she was blind. Then she realized her eyes were closed, but opening them was too much effort, so she didn't.

Her head ached, it really ached like hell. It felt like it was packed with cotton, packed almost to bursting. But that couldn't be, because she wasn't dead. Or was she? What had happened last? Had she had a seizure, had she fallen down? She remembered a whirring, a dreadful roaring in her skull; had she fallen on the subway tracks?

Panicking, she opened her eyes. There was a bright-lit, soundproof ceiling, one of those with all the little holes in it. She moved her fingers and her toes; her body seemed to be there, but she couldn't see it, couldn't lift her head to look. Her neck was stiff, like she'd been sleeping on it wrong.

Someone else was in the room, moaning softly. There was a funny smell, like in biology or in a hospital.

Hospital.

Everything came back to her in a sudden rush: the discussions with Dr. Garrick, and the decision to go ahead, and David's reaction to the idea, and having her head shaved . . . and then the terror of the operation, finally relieved at the very end by the long-awaited sodium pentathol and its lovely, dreamless sleep.

She tried to call out and ask if everything had gone all right, but her mouth was so dry that only a rasping noise emerged. A nurse immediately appeared and offered her a sip of water from a plastic straw.

"Hi there, welcome back. Do you know where you are?"

"Hop . . . hospital. Recover."

"That's right, you're in the recovery room, and you're doing fine. Can you see that clock over there?"

She stretched her aching neck and slowly focused her eyes on the huge round clock. "Uh-huh."

"Can you see what time it is?"

"Twenty. After four."

"It sure is, and I guess that means that you're just about awake enough to go back to your own room now. Would you like to do that?"

But the memories were crowding in too fast, and she had sought the safe retreat of natural sleep.

The girl looked even younger than Prentiss had expected. She sat nervously between her parents, who greeted Prentiss with friendliness but obvious concern. The family seemed proud and prosperous, unaccustomed to dealing with illness or misfortune.

Prentiss heard his own voice, confidently droning. ". . . so you see, this clinic is not at all what many people might assume it is, and you needn't feel in any way ashamed to be here. We almost never deal with insanity as such, and that term certainly has nothing to do with your case, young lady." He smiled, genuinely but carefully.

"But the school nurse said it might be epilepsy; that's a mental condition, isn't it? A form of insanity?"

"No, Mrs. Chandler; there are a number of things that can go wrong with people's brains without rendering them in the least 'insane.' They may just have problems with speaking, or they may have very bad headaches and nothing else, or they may simply lose their appetites, or maybe they sleep more than they ought to. We believe that your daughter just may have a problem with one of those kind of things."

"Yes, but . . . my God, epilepsy!" The woman seemed to shudder involuntarily.

"Mrs. Chandler . . . you and your husband, and especially you, Elizabeth, must all realize that there is nothing really rare or fearsome about epilepsy, in spite of some of the nonsense that people have believed about it in the past. We've learned a lot since the days when it was thought that epileptics were possessed, or cursed, or singled out by God; and the social problems or embarrassment that epileptics and their families used to feel are totally without foundation now.

"A number of very great men and women have had epilepsy, and there have even been theories that the condition might somehow be related to genius or above-average intelligence. Alexander the Great was an epileptic, and so were Buddha, and Mohammed, and Pascal. Flaubert was, too, as well as Paganini, Byron, Napoleon, Dostoevsky, Julius Caesar . . . and it isn't just something that a few people have. About one out of every two hundred people in this country and Europe have epilepsy, so that means a million or more cases in the United States. Thirty to forty thousand right here in Virginia.

"Besides, we still don't even know for certain that this is epilepsy; but if it does prove to be, it shouldn't be a cause of excessive concern to any of you."

"Don't be absurd, Doctor." The girl's father looked slightly indignant. "That would, quite naturally, be a matter of extreme concern to all of us."

His wife nodded worriedly. "Whatever it is, it's only happened once that we know of. Mightn't it just have been an anxiety attack? A fainting spell, perhaps?"

"Have you known your daughter to have fainting spells recently, Mrs. Chandler?"

"Well . . . no, I can't say that I've actually *known* her to faint. But she is at a very sensitive age, you know."

"Hmmh. Yes, that certainly is a possibility that we can't rule out yet, and we'll keep it in mind as we proceed with our tests. One of the reasons I asked was that, sometimes, when a patient does have epileptic seizures, he or his family may describe them as 'fainting spells,' because they can't quite bring themselves to discuss the actual symptoms. The two conditions are not at all alike, however. Would you be interested in hearing about the differences?"

"Yes, of course."

"Well, I'm sure that you all know that one of the main purposes of the human bloodstream is to constantly carry oxygen and sugar to the brain, so it can continue to function." They all nodded, including Elizabeth. "Now, an ordinary fainting spell like you mentioned has a long name—it's called 'orthostatic syncope' —but it's really a very simple thing, just a sudden, drastic drop in blood pressure." Prentiss slashed his pen swiftly downward in illustration. "That may be caused by any number of things, including even just standing up too fast when you've been lying down, or it may result from various kinds of illness or shock. Whatever the cause, it just means that the brain has become suddenly and temporarily anemic, or starved for blood, and several major parts of it simply stop working; that's when you faint."

Prentiss was warming to his topic; he enjoyed lecturing, even on so basic a level as this. If it hadn't been for the even greater challenge of regular practice, and then the clinic, he would've loved teaching. The financial differences had of course played a part in that decision, too; he was honest with himself about that. But now, talking to this child and her parents, he became a dedicated instructor. He wanted to enlighten them, even entertain them; and he wanted the parents to realize that he knew what he was talking about. Their daughter's future was at stake in this little lesson.

"Speaking of the causes of syncope—fainting—I've always found it interesting that so many people faint at the sight of blood. In fact, that's such a common reaction that some scientists think it may have had an evolutionary survival value: We might faint in that instance for the same reason that rabbits 'freeze' when they're in danger, to make themselves less noticeable, or to make it seem as if they're already dead. And when it's the sight of our own blood that we're fainting at, the sudden lessening of blood pressure may even help to reduce the bleeding.

"Epilepsy, though, is a completely different matter. It has nothing to do with the blood, or any other part of the body; it begins and ends in the brain, and the outward effects that we see are only a direct expression of what's happening there. Most of the brain is made up of cells called neurons—ten billion or so of them —and these cells are all interconnected, chemically and electrically. In fact, the entire brain is actually a weak electrical generator, working on chemical principles instead of mechanical. That's what the sugar and the oxygen that the blood delivers to the brain are used to produce. The current involved is very, very small—it's measured in millionths of volts, and the entire brain can only put a maximum of about two volts—but it's that current that allows us to see, and hear, and talk, and move, and think, all depending on where and when it's released within the brain."

Dr. Prentiss turned in his seat and motioned to a large diagram of the brain that hung behind his desk.

"For example, this lower area of the brain isn't very different in structure from the *entire* brains of many animals. This is the part that controls what we call the autonomic nervous system, things like breathing or heart rate or appetite—automatic, simple functions. What makes us different is this large mass up above the lower brain, called the cerebral cortex. Unlike other creatures, man evolved all this extra brain tissue, and it's been specialized into all of our most important abilities as human beings: speech, reasoning, artistic talent, memory, and so forth."

"And where in the brain is epilepsy located?"

"There isn't any one particular spot, Mr. Chandler. What happens in epilepsy is that sometimes, for one reason or another, the electrical system in the brain becomes overloaded, just like a regular electric circuit. This may happen because of too much of one kind of stimulus from the outside, like a strong flashing light or certain types of drugs, or it may just happen spontaneously inside the brain, for reasons that we're not always sure about. There may be some tiny internal injury that doesn't cause any other problems, and isn't really dangerous to the person's health, except that it occasionally causes him to lose control over that delicate balance that exists among the different types of current in the various parts of the brain. When this happens there is—literally—an electrical 'storm' inside the brain, and the *whole* brain starts working at a certain rhythm that is only supposed to be happening in one particular place.

"For example, there is one electrical frequency that's normally confined to the visual part of your brain, toward the back of your head; this is called the Alpha rhythm, and that just means that most of the brain cells there are firing, or sending out little bursts of electricity, ten times every second. The Alpha rhythm, or wave, is linked to the retina of the eye by the optic nerve, and we use it to translate what the eye sees into an image in our brains. The process is very similar to the way a TV camera turns a picture into a series of electronic pulses, and then turns those back into a picture on your TV screen at home. That's a common analogy, and it sounds oversimplified, but it's actually much more accurate than most people think." His mind flashed on the lovely elegance of rasters and scanning waves and interference feedback, and he almost drifted. *Keep going. Keep it simple. Don't digress.*

"Now, in one form of epilepsy, when the person sees a light that's flickering at the same speed as his Alpha rhythm, he loses control over those brain waves, and the Alpha frequency spreads out to take over the rest of the brain for a minute or so. That's why the person shakes or quivers during the seizure: those jerking movements just mean that the brain cells in his motor cortex, the part that controls movement, are temporarily flashing on and off at ten cycles per second. So he's being forced to try to move every muscle in his body at that speed. Do you understand?"

The woman nodded, somewhat hesitantly. "Yes, I think so."

"What I'm trying to get across is simply that anyone—anyone at all—can have an epileptic-type seizure, given the proper chemical or electrical stimulus. In fact, you might even say that a convulsion is the nervous system's normal response to overwhelming stimuli. Some people are just more susceptible to those stimuli than others, and it's that condition of high susceptibility that we call 'epilepsy.'

"In any case, this is all purely academic right now, since we don't even know for a fact that Elizabeth is epileptic. Before we can be sure of that, and before we can decide what sort of treatment, if any, she may require, we'll need to run some tests." He smiled warmly at the girl, who had looked up with an anxious expression. "Nothing painful, dear; I think you'll find it all an interesting experience."

Prentiss pushed back his chair and stood, offering his hand to the girl's father. "Before you leave Elizabeth with us today, we'll also need a complete family medical history. My secretary will introduce you to Dr. Campbell. He's a good man, and we need all the information we can get in order to help your daughter; so try to remember everything you can, and don't hold anything back out of embarrassment."

The mother stopped at the door, a look of sudden awareness on her face. "Do you mean this might be in the blood?"

"No, Mrs. Chandler, not really; there's a small chance that a tendency to epilepsy may be inherited in some cases, but it's a very small chance indeed. There's nothing to be concerned about, I promise you."

The woman nodded slowly. She and Prentiss both knew the hollowness of his "promise." She looked sadly at her daughter. The girl stood with hands straight at her sides, ready to submit to whatever indignities might lie ahead, ready to start the business of learning how to cope with the problems that chance had thrown between her and the rest of her existence as a girl, a woman, and someday a wife . . . and maybe mother. Prentiss knew what the Chandler woman was thinking. He only wished that he could tell her something more.

There were fresh flowers all over the place, and David was there. Everything was going to be all right, really all right.

"David?"

"Hush, honey, you just lie there and rest."

"David, it worked, huh? It did, it worked. They started the whole thing going, and I had my aura, and then . . . they stopped it, they just stopped it cold. Like magic. So I can stop it myself now, anytime I have to. Isn't that great?"

"That's wonderful, honey. That's the greatest thing in the whole world."

"It is, huh? For me, anyway."

"For both of us, angel." He reached out to stroke her face, and she softly breathed against his hand.

"I look funny, don't I? No more hair, just bandages. Think you can love me this way, too?"

"Hush, silly angel."

"Will you bring me my wig? And my sketchbooks, and my charcoals?"

"I already did. They're right over there, whenever you want them."

She smiled and clutched his hand, content now to relax in silence for a moment. The deep headache had started to subside a bit, but her scalp was sore beneath the gauze.

"Did Dr. Garrick say when they were going to start the . . . other part?"

His face went cold, and his hand stiffened around hers. "Never, I hope. You know how I feel about that."

"But I agreed to do it, David. And I think it might be interesting."

"Interesting, hell! Do you know what you're getting into? Does he even know?"

"He's a brilliant man, and as far as I'm concerned, he's restored my life for me. He says it's for the good of mankind, and I trust him."

"*Damn him, and damn mankind! All I care about is you, and I hope you'll change your mind while you still can.*"

She sighed and took her hand away, turning her face to the wall. "*I'll think about it, David. I really will.*"

But she knew she wouldn't. Her decision had been made.

Within a week, the preliminary diagnosis was confirmed and expanded: Elizabeth was suffering from idiopathic *grand mal* epilepsy with lower anterior temporal lobe focus. The seizures were occasionally induced by intermittent photic stimulation, but were more often spontaneous in nature; and they were invariably preceded by olfactory aura.

Dr. Prentiss and the other staff members at the clinic patiently explained the strange terms to Elizabeth and her family. "Idiopathic" simply indicated that there was no obvious physiological cause for the seizures, such as a lesion or tumor or visible injury; there had to be some reason for the periodic malfunction in her brain, but whatever it was was apparently microscopic, and didn't show up on the X rays. "*Grand mal*" meant that the convulsions she experienced affected her whole body, as opposed to *petit mal*, or psychomotor variants of epilepsy, in which only small portions of the body or mind were affected.

Since no gross structural abnormality had been found, it was difficult to identify with any certainty the focal point from which her seizures sprang. There were, however, slight anomalies in certain of the EEG tracings during Metrazol-induced convulsions that drew attention to the lower anterior temporal lobe as a possible site for the problem. This theory was strengthened by Elizabeth's report of smelling roses immediately prior to each seizure.

Dr. Prentiss told the family that a large percentage of epileptics experience some sort of internal warning, seconds or even hours before their convulsions begin; these "auras" might take many forms, but remain the same for each individual. Some patients report hearing bells or other strange sounds, others suddenly feel as if some part of their bodies is being touched or stroked by a mysterious hand, a few see visions, and still others are simply overcome with an inexplicable sensation of dread or sadness. The most common aura, for unknown reasons, is a feeling of excessive gas in the stomach. Elizabeth's phantom roses pointed to the strong probability that the disturbances in her brains had their origin near that area associated with the sense of smell: two elongated tubelike structures called the olfactory lobes. These cerebral organs are located directly beneath the anterior temporal lobes, so it seemed likely that the girl's illness might be centered there.

It was carefully explained that Elizabeth was in no direct danger from the epilepsy itself; there was no chance of death or mental deterioration due to the seizures. There was, however, a possibility that she might be injured if she happened to collapse near a fire, in a bathtub, or in a place where she might fall and strike some hard or sharp object. Since her aura, the scent of roses, lasted an average of ten to twelve seconds, she was merely told to make careful note of its occurrence and to prepare herself for a seizure, preferably by lying down, each time it happened. Certain sports, such as horseback riding, swimming, and bicycling, were potentially dangerous. Other activities, like tennis or volleyball, were not only permissible but therapeutic, since the concentration necessary to participate in them would help ward off attacks.

This factor of concentration was emphasized as quite important, and led to one of the more unpleasant aspects of her condition for Elizabeth: Most epileptic seizures, it seemed, took place while the patient was relaxed and mentally drifting: so from this point on, the cherished act of daydreaming was medically prohibited.

Elizabeth had been away from school for two and a half weeks when she returned. No one mentioned her lengthy absence; in fact, no one except her teachers spoke to her at all. Once or twice, it seemed as though one of the girls was about to approach her with a smile and a welcome; but each time, a look of uncertainty tinged with shame crossed the other child's face, and nothing was said or done. Again excepting the faculty, no eyes met hers directly; and yet, whenever Elizabeth would happen to turn in her seat or look up from her desk unexpectedly, she would catch one or more hastily averted stares. Within a few days, she had learned the meaning of paranoia without ever having heard the word.

No one watched Elizabeth more closely than she watched herself. She had suffered through five purposely induced seizures in nine days at the clinic, and now she apprehensively awaited the arrival of her next "natural" convulsion. The doctors had made it clear that she should not expect the medicine they had given her to immediately eliminate all problems; there was, they said, no such thing as a magic wonder drug for epilepsy, and almost every patient had to go through a period of trial and error with different combinations of numerous drugs before one was found that would leave them relatively seizure-free, with no harmful side effects. Still, each time she swallowed one of the red and white capsules of Dilantin mixed with phenobarbital, she whispered a prayer that she might be one of the lucky ones, that this just might be the right amount of the right substances to let her start her life again.

She never had the opportunity to discover whether the pills would stop her fits or not. To be sure, she lasted six days without a seizure; but she was so grateful for this blessing that she ignored, and even tried to hide, the perpetual drowsiness and occasional double vision that the drugs were causing. Miss Caine, the school nurse, had been alerted to this possibility, and the reports from Elizabeth's teachers were easily put together.

The doctors at the clinic were informed, and her prescription was immediately changed to a smaller dosage of phenobarbital, plus separate tablets of Mysoline. This time, she fought the sleepiness still harder, and was able to present an image of relative alertness in most of her classes. She also learned to control the vomiting to a certain extent, holding it back until between classes so she could lock herself into a stall in the rest room. As the treatment continued, however, the vomiting increased, and within a week she had lost nine pounds. Her gaunt, pale face again attracted the nurse's attention, and her frequent trips to the girls' room were soon monitored. The Mysoline was withdrawn.

A series of experiments with amphetamine compounds, still in combination with phenobarbital, were tried; it was hoped that these might prove effective and simultaneously counteract the lassitude created by the barbiturate. Two days after she began taking Desoxyn, Elizabeth had her first fit since leaving the clinic.

Dexedrine, Atabrine, and Aralen proved no more effective than the Desoxyn; she experienced at least one seizure while using each of these drugs. By Christmas, everyone at the school had witnessed one or more of her attacks. A special assembly was called on a day when Elizabeth was at home, to acquaint the other children with the proper attitudes and procedures to take whenever she was stricken. Several parents demanded that the Chandler girl be removed from the school, if not permanently then at least until her "awful condition" was cleared up. Elizabeth and her family never learned of these requests, and each of the parents involved received a frosty and educational reply from both the nurse and the principal of the school.

During the holidays, Elizabeth was switched to a combination of Ritalin and Librium. The seizures stopped, but she became extremely nervous and irritable, leaving her in a state of quivering emotional exhaustion almost every night. Variations in the balance between the two drugs were tried, but there was no acceptable compromise: On either side of an indivisible line in the balance between the two, Elizabeth would either become very nervous or very drowsy; at no point did they cancel out, as hoped.

By the time school had resumed in January 1964, the clinic's staff had decided to bypass the entire spectrum of tranquilizer/barbiturate/amphetamine combinations in Elizabeth's case and take the slight but genuine risks inherent in putting her on the more potent true anticonvulsants. During the period, it would be necessary for her to have almost daily liver, kidney, and blood tests administered by the GP whom she had originally seen, who was now following the case with intense interest and concern.

Suddenly, as soon as she began taking the three daily tablets of Phenurone, it was as if Elizabeth had never been ill at all. Her seizures completely disappeared, she was alert and attentive in school, and she was more naturally relaxed than she had been in months. A close watch was kept to see whether she developed any of the common side effects of the drug; but no rashes appeared, she gained weight back instead of losing more, the nausea and vomiting she had experienced on Mysoline did not recur, and she remained happy and lively, with no personality changes whatsoever.

That winter, as it became more and more apparent that the seizures were really gone, that they were not going to return, Elizabeth began to emerge from her shell to an extent that would have been unusual for her even before the illness had appeared. Everyone at school was amazed to see her laughing more heartily than she ever had, to watch the lifelong shyness melt away in the light of a new and friendly aggressiveness. If the other students still felt a little funny about talking to her, it didn't matter; now she could talk to them, she could join into games and conversations with the absolute self-confidence of someone who has been condemned and then reprieved.

She set out with a happy determination to make everyone her friend, and the tactic began to work. Gradually, Elizabeth came to be included in all but the cliquiest of the school's social groupings, this in spite of the embarrassing, unspoken memories that everyone had of seeing her collapse and jerk and foam and soil herself at the most unexpected times and places. It was she and she alone who could control the strength of that unpleasant memory, whether in her own mind or in the minds of her classmates; and now that she was facing them with easy, open nonchalance, it began to seem as if none of those things had ever happened.

After three months of this, Elizabeth had even ceased to mind the regular visits to Dr. Gibbons and the once-bothersome rituals of needles and sample bottles they entailed. This was just another part of normal routine, and the tests, with their strange, impossible names, had nothing really to do with her: quantitative urinary urobilinogen and bromasulfein dye retention and icteric index and thymol turbidity and serum glutamic oxaloacetic transaminase determination—they were irrelevant interruptions of her schedule, minor chores to be gone through and forgotten.

Then the results began to accumulate and to show a pattern.

Elizabeth was one of the four people in every thousand whose livers are unable to process Phenurone and its by-products. In essence, she was contracting an artificial, but critical, form of hepatitis. If the treatment were not stopped immediately, she would suffer severe and irreversible liver damage; she would, in fact, be dead within the year.

This susceptibility ruled out even experimental use of the other most effective anticonvulsants like Peganone and Mesantoin; both were known to be related to liver problems, and the chance was too dangerous to take.

The range of available drug types had been exhausted. Only minor variations, such as Valium instead of Librium, now remained to be tried, but everyone knew in advance that the difference would not be that great. The only thing that had really worked, and worked splendidly, had almost killed the girl. Now there were no more miracles left.

During the summer of 1964, a final compromise medication was decided on: fifty milligrams of Ritalin and a half grain of phenobarbital daily. The combination left her slightly dull and drowsy, but the choice had been between that and constant nervousness. The clinic staff, after much debate, decided that Elizabeth could cope more easily with sleepiness, given the already existing difficulties in her life.

The Ritalin and phenobarbital did not completely eliminate the seizures; only Phenurone seemed capable of that effect, but at least the attacks were minimized as far as possible. This meant that she would experience one or two fits per month, usually just before her period. There was no safe method of reducing this number, but at least she now had a good idea of what to expect.

The rest of the country was concerned, that season, with sit-ins and marches and the violent retaliations that they caused. Elizabeth's parents now took their daughter's illness more or less for granted, but she was not so able to ignore the rebirth of her seizures. Her spurt of sociability had been short-lived, and she faced her entrance into high school with well-reasoned apprehension. She secretly began to wonder if the blacks might feel the same way she did, irrevocably marked as strangers in a hostile world.

It was amazing how familiar, innocent remarks had taken on such meaning: "He was so mad he just about had a fit" . . . "Don't go foamin' at the mouth" . . . "You spastic!" Even when she didn't hear them, such comments would be brought to her attention by the blushes and the giggles and the hurried change of topic when everyone remembered who was listening.

Throughout her freshman year in high school, Elizabeth withdrew more day by day. On the rare occasions when she might begin to open up, to make new friendships or present an image of normality, her progress would invariably be stopped within a week or two by yet another seizure, still another setting for humiliation. Once during the pledge of allegiance to the flag, once in assembly, twice in the halls, once in the snow . . . the list seemed endless, yet it grew.

Almost as bad as the fits themselves was the constant dullness that the drugs induced. She was used to being brighter than the rest, but now it was a daily effort just to stay awake, just to remember what was said the day before. Sometimes, for major tests, she'd secretly not take the phenobarbital, or only bite the pill in half; but then she'd be so wracked with nervousness that she couldn't concentrate any better than if she'd been all dopey, and once she had a fit during an examination.

In her sophomore year she was assigned her first male teacher. He had thick, unruly hair, he wore tweed jackets, and he always smelled of London Dock tobacco. When he discussed *Jane Eyre*, she knew he understood the pains of loneliness and womanhood completely. The papers and the tests she wrote for him were filled with secret messages of love, and when he spoke to her in class she thought she saw a subtle look of comprehension and affection.

The inevitable happened in November. He was very good about helping her, keeping the other students in their seats as he held her jerking head: but when she woke and saw her body sprawled in dirty awkwardness, felt the dried saliva and the blood all sticky on her chin, the crush she'd had was over.

It seemed almost as if God was using this disease to wipe out all her femininity, to see that no one ever thought of her in terms of delicacy, of softness, and of grace.

That spring, to her surprise, she found a friend. Karen Purdy was a transfer student from Ohio, who sat next to her during algebra. Neither of them felt at home in that strange jumble of letters and numbers, so they were soon getting together for lunch and homework sessions. At first, Elizabeth was terrified of having a seizure in front of Karen; but when that finally happened, it turned out that Karen had a cousin in Ohio who was epileptic, and she didn't find it strange at all.

At last Elizabeth could talk to someone without fear of embarrassment or misunderstanding. Karen listened with interest and real care as Elizabeth described her life, her dreams, her fears, and the humiliation she felt each time a seizure came in public. The sexually related aspects of her illness were the last to surface in their conversation, and the hardest to express.

Karen, in return, told about her own experiences and fantasies: discovering masturbation, the irrational shame at her first period, the crushes and erotic dreams and images of future loves. Elizabeth found it difficult at first to believe that someone else had felt and done so many of the same forbidden things; but as she listened to Karen's girlish confessions, she felt a renewed confidence in her own essential normalcy.

That summer, though, Karen's father was transferred to the West coast, and Elizabeth was left alone again. The brief friendship had given her, at least, some real respect for the rightness of her own ideas and feelings. The year 1967 was one of sweeping change, though few of the social revolutions had yet touched Richmond. Elizabeth could sense the rise of something different and important, something that in some way still to be defined might touch and color her experience. The radio at night played "Sergeant Pepper," and the passing cars from Washington and other cities carried long-haired passengers with colorful, outlandish costumes. Strange, swirling posters were appearing, and the magazines she read reported weird experiments with drugs and altered consciousness.

These new phenomena were still rejected and derided by the Richmond students, who clung defensively to their own traditions and well-charted expectations. Elizabeth said nothing to refute them; but she felt increasingly, if vaguely, that the world was somehow changing in a way that might include the jagged patterns of awareness and discordance that she knew as life.

The lecture hall was packed with students and physicians, and Dr. Garrick surveyed the crowd with pleasure. He had already described the background of Elizabeth Austin's case, and the tests that had localized her seizure focus near a major speech center, making standard excision surgery impossible. Then he had passed around a plastic card, to which was taped a tiny metal speck. The speck, he had explained, was an electrode of his own devising, utilizing NASA's recently developed "chip" microcircuitry. It was capable, he said, of performing several functions: not only radio-wave reception and brain stimulation, but also simplified brain-wave analysis and radio transmission of that information. Now it was time to explain the unusual uses to which the electrode would be put, and he was looking forward to the task.

"Yesterday morning," he heard himself saying, "following a standard cranial entry and response-mapping procedure, one of these electrodes was placed inside the affected region of the patient's brain.

"With the skull still open and the probe in place, seizure induction was begun by the injection of five cc of Metrazol. Almost immediately, she reported commencement of aura."

He held up a green, oblong plastic box, slightly larger than a pack of cigarettes. There was a row of four black buttons on the box's surface.

"At that moment, one of the buttons on this portable transceiver was depressed. The aura ended, and the seizure never happened. This happy result was achieved by an innovative use of the implanted electrode's transmission capability.

"First, a receptor on its surface perceived the rise in abnormal brain activity that produced the aura and was about to spread into a brainwide seizure. The frequency of that abnormal wave was automatically transmitted back to this unit, which then responded by transmitting a square wave signal of its own, stimulating the electrode to emit a four-milliamp, two-volt current at that same frequency.

"This stimulation, however, although exactly matching the frequency of the original brain wave, was 180 degrees out of phase with the abnormal wave. The interaction between the two pulses was thus one of 'subtractive interference,' resulting in an almost completely flat final wave. The two effectively canceled each other out; meaning, here, that the seizure was stopped before it could begin."

He went on to explain that the electrode was now permanently in place in the patient's brain, and that she would be given her own portable transceiver. Whenever she sensed her warning aura, the smell of roses, she could press the button herself and block the oncoming attack. The electrode was designed for an indefinite period of operation, so there was no reason that the young woman should ever suffer another seizure again in her life.

Then he took a long, deliberate sip of water, savoring the moment. The best, he knew, was coming now.

"As is customary in cases of this type, we also asked that the patient volunteer for certain other tests of an experimental nature, and she consented to this request.

"Therefore, after the seizure-prevention phase of the operation had been completed, we implanted an additional seventeen electrodes in various areas of her brain. This has, of course, been done with many other subjects, and the patterns of response to electrical stimulation of the brain are relatively well known by now.

"In this instance, however, there exist two significant differences. First, the other seventeen electrodes are all chip-circuit modifications of the primary implant; but rather than subtractive interference, they are each designed to produce additive interference. That is, the existing local brain waves and the transmitted signal will be exactly in phase with each other. The result of this will be not a flattening or canceling of the original wave, but a massive increase of its amplitude. No previous electrode has ever been able to evoke such a dramatic response. If there is even a dormant or minuscule brain wave in the stimulus region, it will be magnified far beyond its natural potential."

The second major difference in this experiment, he told his eager listeners, was the choice of target areas. Fourteen of the seventeen additive electrodes, it seemed, had been implanted in the so-called "silent zones," those portions of the brain in which ordinary stimulation elicited no response at all.

"It has been theorized," he said, "that perhaps the silent zones may hold the key to the subtlest, and least understood, processes of human thought. An accurate definition and eventual mapping of the functions of these mysterious 'blind spots' in the brain would be a neurological breakthrough of the first order; perhaps, even, a philosophical one as well.

"We are now presented with our best chance yet to make that leap in the advance of man's understanding of his own mind. The first experiments begin tomorrow, and you will all be regularly informed of their results. Now, are there any questions?"

A dozen or more hands shot up simultaneously, and Garrick selected one at random. The gangly student in the third row continued to scribble furiously in his notebook even as he phrased his query.

"Dr. Garrick, in your own personal opinion, what do you think will happen to the patient when the silent zones are stimulated in this manner?"

The doctor smiled excitedly, his face lit with an almost boyish jubilation. "I have no idea," he said. "No idea at all."

PART TWO

One of the nurses showed her into Garrick's office. She was still a little pale, but her eyes were bright and alert.

"Good morning, Mrs. Austin. How have you been?"

"Great, just great. The transmitter works beautifully. My aura came on day before yesterday, as I told one of your assistants, and I had no problem in blocking the seizure completely. I may even learn to like the smell of roses again, in ten or fifteen years."

Garrick smiled appreciatively and understandingly. "I'll remember to send you carnations next Valentine's Day. Any complaints about the food or service, madam?"

"Well . . . now that you mention it, the lobster thermidor wasn't quite up to par last night, and the Dom Perignon was poorly chilled. Other than that, the London broil and mashed potatoes have been fine. Every day."

The doctor shook his head in mock irritation. "I must speak to the chef immediately. If we lose our Michelin stars, who'll pay our prices?"

A brief smile touched the corners of her mouth, but Garrick could see that it was covering a deeper apprehension.

"You really don't know for sure what's going to happen to me today, do you?"

Garrick had been waiting for the question. "Not precisely, no; but I can assure you that you're in no real danger, and the chances are very small that any of the experiments will be unpleasant or painful. Come with me, and I'll show you the arrangements we've made."

He got up from his chair and led her out of his office and down the corridor, to a white room about fifteen feet square. The only ordinary furnishings were a table and two wooden chairs. One wall was lined with what looked like computer equipment, including several oversized reels of magnetic recording tape. Beside one chair was a stocky machine, trailing wires like colored seaweed. Next to the other was a smooth, self-contained console unit with numerous dials and toggle switches on its slanted top. There was a large mirror on one wall, but the room was otherwise unadorned.

"This is where we'll be working, and you should know some things about how it'll all be handled. We'll sit here, facing each other, and you'll be connected to this device, which is sort of like a more complicated polygraph, or lie detector. Not that we'll be testing your truthfulness, or lack of it; this is just an all-purpose response analysis unit, combining a basic EEG, EKG, and various other measuring instruments, including ones for breathing rate and galvanic skin response. The information will be fed into the computer terminal behind you, and correlated with the specific stimuli, which I'll control from this console. Come around here and take a look."

Elizabeth moved hesitantly to the other side of the table. She had a creepy feeling that the quiet, shiny machine was almost alive, like the insane computer on the space ship in that movie a few years ago. In a sense, it nearly was; soon, this device would be communicating directly with her brain, would even be controlling her thoughts and actions in ways no one could possibly predict. She suppressed a shiver and forced herself to listen to the doctor's careful explanation.

". . . additive interference wave, as I described to you before. Now, the strength of that wave as it is applied to any of the individual electrodes we've implanted is constantly variable by these vernier dials, one for each electrode site. The toggle switches are just the 'off-on,' but the dials will allow us to choose from a wide range of amplitudes.

"Basically, to keep things simple and easily measured, we'll be using a regular series of three different strengths for each electrode. We'll start with 'low,' go on to 'medium,' and end with 'strong'—that is, one, two, and four volts, respectively. If you have an unpleasant reaction to any of the one-volt stimuli, it'll be entirely up to you whether we continue with the stronger inputs. Any questions?"

Elizabeth ran her fingertips along the polished edge of the stimulator console and sighed quietly. "Yes; when do we get started, and how soon do we finish?"

The room behind the one-way mirror was appointed like a small, plush theater, a millionaire's home screening room. The seats were soft and ample, the lighting indirect and pleasantly dim. Each of the twelve comfortable chairs contained a built-in ashtray and fold-up writing surface. Two automatic 16mm motion picture cameras were mounted on the walls, so as not to obstruct the view as they silently recorded the drama to take place on the other side of the glass. Beneath the cameras were two Ampex tape recorders and Altec speakers linked to the hidden microphones in the testing room.

As the invited doctors filed into the viewing chamber, talking and joking among themselves, they found numbered folders on the seats to which they were assigned, each marked with the appropriate name. The folders contained more than a hundred pages of charts, diagrams, and written information. Included were the patient's complete case history, a detailed record of the surgery two weeks before, circuit diagrams of the new electrodes being used, and eight sheets of cranial maps indicating the exact positions of the seventeen electrodes. There were also several blank pages for notes to be taken as the experiment progressed.

There was no grumbling about seat positions, since everyone in the room was well aware of the rigid hierarchies and protocol that had dictated the arrangements. The first row of four seats was reserved for the visiting neurosurgeons: two from Johns Hopkins, one from the Burden Institute outside London, and one from the Clinique Nationale de Recherche et de Chirurgie Neurologique in Paris. The center seats of the second row were occupied by Dr. Graham Crandon, head of the neurology department at the university to which the hospital was attached, and Dr. Lois Beatty, a colleague of Garrick's. Her own experiments with electrode implantation in the human pain control centers had alleviated the suffering of dozens of terminal patients without clouding their final months of awareness in a haze of drugs. Drs.

Crandon and Beatty were flanked by the first and second assistant surgeons who had attended the operation on Elizabeth Austin.

In the last row sat three of the young neurological residents at the hospital, and the only nonphysician in the group, Gene Templeton. Templeton was a fourth-year medical student who showed unusual promise in the field; even as an undergraduate, he had played a major role in the development and execution of a brilliant series of experiments on the visual/spatial co-ordination system in the brains of cats, opening a line of investigation that might someday result in an electronic method of restoring vision to the blind.

There was a gentle rustling of papers as the assembled observers reviewed the data on the case before them. Through the glass, they could see a nurse attaching the last of the recording electrodes to the exposed left arm of the young woman who sat stiffly at the table. When the nurse had finished, she gave a signal to Dr. Garrick. He nodded his thanks and turned to the console at his right. Above the heads of those in the faintly lit viewing room, the cameras began to softly whir.

"All right, now, Mrs. Austin, we're going to start off with stimulation of some of the areas that we're already fairly familiar with, basically to test the equipment. We have a pretty good idea of what you'll experience with these electrode sites, and there shouldn't be anything unpleasant, so just relax and let me know what happens. Would you like a glass of water before we start?"

"No, no, that's all right. I'm ready, let's just go ahead."

"Fine. I'll be starting off with five-second bursts, and each time we'll work our way from the lowest power to the highest. Here comes No. 1."

Elizabeth felt constrained in her movements by all the wires that trailed from her head and arms and chest and fingers, and the band around her diaphragm that was measuring her breath rate was a little too tight. She was sure Dr. Garrick meant it when he said these first few wouldn't be bad, but still, it would've been better if he'd told her more about what to expect. She knew it was silly to be nervous now, after all she'd already been through, but it was so weird to think of those tiny bits of metal and wire inside her head, all connected by radio to that machine he was fiddling with. This was unlike anything she'd ever . . . no, familiar. It was suddenly very familiar. That was odd; right now it didn't seem strange at all.

"Mrs. Austin?"

"Yes? Yes, I'm ready, you can go ahead now."

"You didn't feel anything at all just then?"

"No, I . . . you mean you did it already? That was the first one?"

"Yes, on the lowest setting. You felt no effects, not of any sort? No physical sensations, no unusual thoughts?"

"Well, not really; the only thing, sort of, was that I was thinking how strange all this was, and then it seemed kind of . . . more familiar, somehow. That's all."

Garrick smiled and nodded. "O.K., then, we'll give it a try at the next level. Pay attention now, and tell me if you feel anything peculiar."

She could see his hand move back toward the console, and she glanced away to look at her reflection in the mirror on the wall. She really looked a mess with her wig off, and all those wires and things . . . but all of a sudden she knew that she'd seen herself looking *exactly* like that somewhere before, and she'd seen somebody's hand move exactly the way Dr. Garrick's had, and she'd been in this very same room some other time . . .

"Well?"

"Again, the only thing was just this . . . very strong feeling that I'd been through all of this before. This experiment, I mean, in this room. Did we ever do any of the other tests, before my operation, in here? I didn't think so at first, but now I'm not sure."

"No, unless you were sleepwalking and found the key, you've never been in here before today. Anything else?"

"No, nothing. But I was so sure I'd been here. I could've sworn . . ."

Without warning, Garrick moved the dial to its highest setting and pressed the switch again. Elizabeth's mouth and eyes went wide with a look of shocked surprise.

"My God, I just . . . it's as if *all* of this has happened before, every word I speak, everything. I know it hasn't, but I know it *has*. My God, I'm getting goosebumps."

Garrick released the switch, and she slumped loosely in the chair, shaking her head in consternation.

"Haven't you ever felt like that before, Mrs. Austin? When you saw someplace for the first time, and all at once you felt that you had been there previously? Or that a conversation you were having had already taken place at some indefinable point in the past?"

"Yes, of course, I know what you mean. It's called *déjà vu*, and it's always eerie when it happens, but it never . . . not like that, not that strong and certain. But how could the electrode be causing that? I thought a *déjà vu* was a memory from a dream or something."

"No, actually there's a specific center in the brain that causes the sensation; no one knows why, it doesn't seem to serve any useful purpose. Delgado discovered it, years ago, during surgery similar to yours. Whenever that area is stimulated, the patient automatically has the overpowering impression that whatever has been happening during those few seconds has happened somewhere, sometime, before. There's a possibility that the ordinary, spontaneous *déjà vus* are the result of cosmic rays accidentally striking that area. Odd feeling, isn't it?"

"Odd isn't the word for it. It was *freaky*."

"Unpleasantly so?"

"Not completely, just . . . just really, incredibly bizarre."

"Well. Shall we move on to the next site?"

"Would you mind if I had a cigarette first? That kind of shook me up a little."

"Of course, go right ahead. I'll get you a glass of water, if you'd like."

"Thank you."

She sipped the water and dragged deeply at the burning cigarette, recovering her composure. The electrode's effect had been totally different than anything she had imagined or expected. She wouldn't have been surprised if her foot had felt tingly, or if she'd heard a strange sound in her head; she had experienced a few electrode stimulations like that during the operation, and of course she was used to the weird way her mind would knock her out when she had a seizure; but the *déjà vu* had crept up on her from behind, as it were, and she wasn't sure how to react. There was something so *personal* about it, so chillingly deep and total in the way that it had twisted her innermost perceptions. She extinguished the unfinished cigarette and turned to Dr. Garrick.

"We can go on now, if you'd like."

"Are you sure? It could wait until tomorrow, if you'd prefer a rest."

"No, I'm sure. Let's keep going."

The next electrode was less unnerving, a simple muscular control reaction. At the lowest amplitude, she felt an urge to straighten her right arm, but was able to restrain the movement. As the stimulus strength increased, she found herself spontaneously jerking the arm out from her body, the fingers spread wide and stiff.

By the time they were prepared to test the third electrode, Elizabeth had perceptibly relaxed, and was chatting freely again with Garrick. The experiments weren't so bad, nothing really dreadful was happening; even the *déjà vu* was fading in her mind, and seemed less disturbing now.

"Ready for No. 3?"

"All set."

. . . *blue T-shirt, and the doll won't fit right in its chair. Mashing it down, and then the leg snaps and* . . .

"Anything?"

"Yes, I was remembering something that happened when I was a child; nothing important, just a time when I broke one of my dolls. I hadn't thought of that in years, though. As a matter of fact, I'm not even positive that I remembered it at all before, but I do now."

"Let's try it at two volts."

. . . *blue wrinkly T-shirt that scratches, and it's a bad doll that won't sit up in her pretty red chair with the ducks, and mashing on her fuzzy yellow hair and her stubby leg goes crack! and* . . .

"The same thing, exactly, only it was a lot clearer this time. It started and ended at the same place, but I could notice a lot more details."

"Once again now, at four."

. . . *faded blue wrinkly T-shirt that scratches, and one white sock falling down like it always does, and the floor is cold, and it's a bad old doll, Mommy wouldn't get a new one, if it doesn't sit right in the red duck chair mash its ugly little head straight down and then mash harder and CRACK, there, now Mommy will have to get a new one* . . .

"Oh, wow. That was unbelievable, it was . . . it wasn't like it was a memory at all, I was really *there*. I was going through the same motions again, but I could absolutely feel everything and see everything, and I knew exactly why I was doing what I did. I even felt angry at my mother for not getting me a new doll. I was breaking that one so she would. I was a pretty mean little kid, huh? I didn't know I was ever that conniving."

Garrick smiled. "I'm sure you were a regular terror. Did all of your senses seem to be intact within the memory?"

"Yes, entirely. I could smell the Lysol that my mother was spraying in the kitchen, and I could see the finest details in the whole scene. I could even feel the tension in the plastic when the doll was about to break, and the satisfaction that it gave me. It was just like reliving it."

"And the incident was a minor one? You weren't severely punished afterward, or anything else that would cause you to remember the event under normal circumstances?"

"No, nothing like that. I recall that I did get a new doll shortly after that, but the old one was still around for years, with its leg taped up. If you'd reminded me of that, I don't think I could have told you how it ever got broken in the first place; I'm sure my mother passed it off as an accident. Does that kind of thing happen a lot with electrode stimulation, reliving things like that?"

"Yes, quite often. Usually a specific, random moment in the past; always extremely realistic. The existence of those memory traces has altered several of the old theories about the mind. It seems strange, in ways, that an entire experience, with all the related sensory perceptions, should be stored in a single spot within the brain; but that's the way it seems to happen. If you'd been eating a sandwich in the trace, you would've tasted every bite and clearly felt the texture as you chewed. Or if you'd been slicing onions, it would have brought tears to your eyes. But whatever it might be, a memory trace is strictly limited in duration, and usually repetitive, like an endless film loop. It's handy to have one located; it can help us to calibrate and verify results with the other electrodes."

The mention of other electrodes reminded her that there were other, possibly stranger, tests to come now, tests about which Dr. Garrick couldn't be nearly so reassuring and knowledgeable, and couldn't compare to previous results with other patients. Whatever happened from here on out was going to be her experience, and hers alone. She wanted another cigarette badly, wanted a Valium, wanted a drink; but there was no point in stalling.

"Can we go ahead with the rest now?"

Garrick hesitated, fiddling unnecessarily with the dials on the console, rechecking the sensor connections to the young woman's body. He was just as aware as she of the totally experimental nature of the second phase. Anything or nothing might occur, either of which could be disastrously embarrassing for him. Unlike his subject, he knew all about the twelve invisible observers behind the mirror, he was fully conscious of the humming movie cameras. This whole thing had been his idea, it was he who had spent months fighting for the huge expenditure required to develop and manufacture the new electrodes. His career was on the line today.

He held his arms close at his sides, so no one in the viewing room would see the dark stains of perspiration that were soaking through his white lab jacket.

"Yes, well. If you're ready. Phase 2, electrode 1. Stimulus at one volt. Begin."

". . . just like I was *there*, David, living through those few seconds all over again. I even felt like I was in a child's body, with everything all small and chubby and close to the floor. It was fascinating!"

David grunted, his eyes fixed on the water pitcher on the bedside table. His fingers were rotating a cat's-eye marble that he'd picked up in the hospital corridor.

"Oh, David, cut it out. You look like Humphrey Bogart in *The Caine Mutiny*, the way you keep frowning off into space and playing with that damned marble."

He dropped the tiny crystal sphere into a water glass and brushed a lock of sandy hair back from his eyes. "It's dangerous, having things like that lying around on the floor, particularly in a hospital. Doesn't anybody keep an eye on the children around here?"

"Oh, I don't know. And if you're so safety-conscious, why'd you put it in my water glass? Would you rather I swallowed it?"

He grunted again, and poured the marble into the wastebasket. It hit the metal bottom with a sharp noise that resounded in the silent room, bounced twice, and then rolled to rest at the side of the green container.

"Honey, why do you have to act this way when you come to visit? Aren't you interested in what's going on, don't you want to hear about what it all feels like?"

"The only thing I'm interested in is the fact that you're cured now. They've taken out the stitches and you can stop your seizures every time they begin. The doctors have done their job, and they've done it very well, but it's finished now. You can come home and we can live a perfectly normal life, no more worries. That's what interests me, not Dr. Garrick's crazy experiments with your mind. You say they're fascinating; but they scare the hell out of me, and they're totally unnecessary. Can't you understand that?"

The anger in her face softened, and she reached out to take his hand. "David, it's wonderful to know that you love me, and that you're concerned about me; but I'm all right, really I am. The experiments aren't hurting me in any way, and I honestly think they're important. It'll all be over soon enough."

They were interrupted by a nurse who brought Elizabeth's dinner on a tray that she set up on the bed. Elizabeth removed the metal cover and laughed. "Surprise! London broil and mashed potatoes. God, will I ever be glad to get back home to some good food." She gave her husband a sly look and an impish grin. "Among other things, of course."

"Then, damn it, why don't you just check out of here? Let somebody else be the guinea pig; you've been through enough."

Elizabeth handed him the paper cup of coffee he had ordered, and began to pick at her food without enthusiasm. "Please, David. This is getting to be a bore. I appreciate your concern, and I really am anxious to get home, but I promised I'd finish this first. I *want* to finish it."

David took a sip of the weak coffee and put the soggy cup down in disgust. "You mean you actually enjoy letting that man play with your mind that way? You like having him push a button and jerk you around like a puppet on a string?"

Elizabeth sighed in exasperation and pushed the tray away, reaching for a cigarette. "It's not like that."

"You told me yourself that it was, the way your arm just leaped to attention. You couldn't control it, you said, it was like your arm didn't belong to you at all."

"But that was no big thing, and that was only with one of the electrodes. The other two that worked were interesting sensations, more like having a dream or something; and the experimental ones that you're so worried about, the ones in the silent zones, didn't do anything at all. Nothing."

David jumped up from his chair and started to pace around the long, narrow room. "But those were only the first eight! There are nine more of those things in your head, and God knows what they might do to you!"

"I doubt if they'll do anything, either. I'm afraid that Dr. Garrick's experiment with me is going to be one big flop, but I certainly can't back out now, not before he knows for sure. Do you know how long he's worked on this idea?"

"Well, let him go work on somebody else. Let him experiment on his own wife, for Christ's sake!"

"That's a silly thing to say, David. Silly and stupid, even if you are just trying to spare me any unpleasantness. Like you said, the electrodes are already in my head; the least I can do is let them fire the things up and see what happens. What if the Wright brothers had built their first airplane, and then just let it sit there without ever trying it out? Do you have any idea how much those electrodes cost?"

"No, and I don't . . ."

"I know you don't care, and neither do I, really. But they are valuable; I must have a hundred thousand dollars' worth of electronics in my skull right this minute, and the care and devotion that went into designing all of this are worth ten times that, in human terms. This isn't just some meaningless game, you know; the things they learn from this may save somebody's life someday, or at least relieve their suffering somehow.

"What if there's some little girl out there right now, going through the same kinds of torment I went through, and this experiment turns out to be the only thing that could have helped her? I know what that's like, David, I've been there; and no matter how much you love me, you can never fully understand. I'm sorry, honey, but my mind's made up: I'm seeing the experiment through to the end. It'll all be finished in a few more days; I'll be home by the end of next week, probably. Then we can forget all about this. In the meantime, let's not argue anymore; please?"

He sat back down in the bedside chair and rested his head in his hands. "You know I only want what's best for you, angel; that's all."

She crushed out her cigarette and touched his arm. "Then look up here and smile, you old grumpus. We've got a lot of smiling to do, now."

Garrick watched the nurse fixing the last of the sensor wires to Mrs. Austin's arm. Just to look busy, he made several unnecessary adjustments to the controls of his console, and then moved them back to where they had been in the first place.

The young woman looked calm and collected today, not at all nervous about the experiments any more. Garrick resented her relaxed demeanor. Aside from the standard memory trace, *déjà vu,* and motor cortex electrodes, the tests had so far yielded no results. Five different sites in the silent zones, and no response. Nothing. Garrick knew the odds he was working against, and he knew that he never should have expected immediate results. There were still nine electrodes left to test, anyway. It could all be different today. Maybe.

He tried to force an attitude of detachment and resignation on his rushing, jittery thoughts. Most forays into uncharted territory didn't work, that was what science was all about; but, hell, he wasn't most scientists! He *knew* there was something going on in the silent zones, knew that they weren't just superfluous tissue. He'd fought for that belief for years, and this was his chance to prove that he was right; perhaps his only chance. If he drew a total blank, there'd never be another grant like this one; there were dozens, hundreds, of other researchers with other, more popular theories, all begging for the money to try them out. He'd only been given the opportunity to see his own through this far because of his unblemished reputation as a careful, rational investigator. If this turned out to be a flop, that reputation might be blown for good.

Well, Garrick, you know, he was a good man, but he went tilting after windmills. I always thought he had a first-class mind until he got involved with that business about the silent zones. On foundation money.

He bit his lip, remembering that his frustrated expression was visible to the unseen watchers in the room behind the mirror, and was even being filmed. He didn't really want to continue, he wanted to put the rest of the experiment off to another day; but there was no excuse that he could use. Everyone would see it for what it was: chickening out, losing faith in his own concept. Damn!

"Ready, Dr. Garrick."

"Thank you, Miss Fenman. Mrs. Austin? Are you comfortable?"

She smiled easily. "Oh, yes, everything's fine. I'm really eager to get going today."

Damn her smugness, she *knows* nothing is going to happen. What difference does all this make to her, anyway? It's not her experiment, not her career. Garrick flushed with sudden embarrassment at his own thoughts; it might not be her career, but it was certainly her brain. That made quite a difference to her, indeed.

"All right, then, we may as well begin. Phase 2, electrode 6, one volt."

He watched her face as he pressed the switch. Her expression never changed.

"No, nothing that time. I kind of felt a little itch on my left leg, but I think maybe that was there before."

"Two volts."

She looked pensive, as if concentrating hard to notice anything different.

"No. As a matter of fact, the itch went away, so I guess that wasn't it."

"Four volts."

The young woman was concentrating intently again, but after a moment she smiled apologetically.

"I'm sorry, Dr. Garrick. There just really wasn't anything at all, not that I could tell."

"Very well. Electrode 7, one volt."

She ran her tongue across her lips and looked thoughtfully at the ceiling. "I got a little thirsty that time."

"Would you like a sip of water?"

"Yes, please."

He handed her the water, and she drank.

"Want to try two volts now?"

"O.K."

He could see her moving her lips experimentally, testing for dryness. She swallowed once.

"Thirsty again?"

"Well . . . no, not actually. To tell you the truth, I don't believe it was the electrode after all." She looked almost embarrassed, and quickly added, "At least I don't think it was. I'm not absolutely positive one way or the other."

"All right, then. Four volts." There was no need for him to be so curt with her, he knew that. She was trying to help, she was acting like a confused little girl who wants to please her parents somehow but doesn't know exactly what to say. He felt like a real bastard, but he couldn't help letting his irritation and disappointment show through. Surely she must be feeling *something*. He felt an irrational urge to boost the transmitter up to eight or ten volts, but repressed it.

"Anything at all that time?"

She shook her head, avoiding his questioning eyes. "Nothing. Sorry."

His palms were getting damp as he reached for the next dial. He was making a fool of himself, he thought, in front of his colleagues and his rivals. Blakeley and Charnier had flown here from Europe just to watch this, and all they were going to see was him screwing up. He'd never live this down, never; but there was no way to back out now. He had to finish what he'd started. Christ, why hadn't he stuck to the idea about mapping relative types of mathematical ability in the left hemisphere?

"Electrode 8. One volt."

Her sudden, piercing scream froze him in his seat, and for a moment he didn't even think to take his hand away from the toggle switch. Before he could release it, the scream had evolved, sirenlike, into a wail of grotesquely rasping laughter, her face contorted into a death's-head grimace. As quickly as the scream had come, the laughter changed into a deep and anguished sobbing, and the tears flowed down her face in streams. His hand turned off the switch, and she was quiet again, but breathing fitfully and trembling all over as she clutched her arms around her chest. The entire episode had lasted about seven seconds, but had included every element of severe, prolonged hysteria. Garrick was still too dumfounded to react, but the nurse was rushing to the young woman's aid.

He lit a cigarette with shaking fingers and extended the pack to Mrs. Austin. She nodded gratefully but seemed to have some difficulty in releasing the protective grip in which her hands had reflexively reached to hold herself. The nurse wiped her tears away and lit the cigarette for her, holding the tip to her mouth and taking it away again when she had inhaled a deep lungful of the acrid smoke.

She and the doctor smoked together in silence for several moments before he spoke, quietly and gently. "Are you feeling any better now, Mrs. Austin?"

Her voice was surprisingly calm, and he found it difficult to believe that this attractive, composed face before him had, only a minute or so before, been stretched into a torturous mask of pain and horror.

"Yes, thank you. I'll be all right. That was . . ." She struggled to find the words to describe her experience.

Garrick probed the subject delicately. "Were there any specific images or thoughts?"

"No. No thoughts at all, it just . . . came on me like that. It was just a chain of straight emotion, starting out with . . ." she closed her eyes and breathed deeply.

"Take your time, there's no rush. Just try to remove yourself from what you were feeling, and tell me about it objectively."

"Yes. All right. I was trying to say that the whole thing started with an awful . . . fear. Just that, fear."

"Fear of anything in particular?"

"No, it was kind of like fear of everything and nothing, all at once. The closest thing to it that I can remember was when I was ten; my family took a vacation to the Gulf Coast, and we were having a picnic on a beach on Santa Rosa Island, in West Florida. It's a long, thin island, and there aren't many hotels or tourists there; we were the only people you could see for a mile or more in either direction. It was a beautiful day, warm and sunny, but then all of a sudden I looked up and there was this tremendous, thick fog moving in from the gulf. It was almost like a wall: There was a place where there was no fog, and then a place where there was *only* fog, rolling in like wet cotton over the surf. My parents gathered up the picnic stuff and started walking through the sand dunes to the car on the highway, while I was shaking the sand out of the blankets. But I didn't fold them up fast enough, and the fog . . . caught me. Before I even knew what was happening, it was swirling all around my arms and legs and face, cold and wet, and the sun was blotted out, and then I was right in the middle of it, I couldn't even see the path where my parents had walked off toward the car. I knew the fog couldn't hurt me, and I knew I'd find the car if I just walked straight away from the sound of the surf; but all I could do was stand there and scream. No words, just screaming, and then I dropped the blankets and fell down in the sand, still screaming, until my parents found me and took me to the car.

"The whole world had just changed so fast. I'd never imagined that everything could change that fast, and that completely. I guess I kind of felt the same way the first time I ever had a seizure. The world just turned scary and awful, but not for any reason." She shivered and looked away at the mirror. Garrick felt a twinge of guilt, remembering the dozen faces that were back there, watching her go through this.

"Mrs. Austin, would you like to take a break for an hour or so before we resume? Or if you'd prefer, we could even put the rest of the tests off until tomorrow."

"No, that won't be necessary. I would like to move around a little, though; maybe go to the cafeteria for some coffee?"

"Of course. I'll meet you there in about half an hour, and you can decide then whether or not you feel like continuing later."

She began pulling the wires away from her body and laying them carefully aside. "I'll be ready. I just want to get my breath back. One thing, though—"

"Yes?"

"I know it's important, but—you said before that if anything was really bad, we wouldn't have to go on to the higher voltages. Would it ruin your experiment if we didn't step this one up any stronger?"

Garrick couldn't even reply for a second. He had been so horrified at her unexpected reaction to the one-volt stimulus that it had never even occurred to him to repeat the trial, let alone increase its effect. The idea nauseated him, called up images of Nazis experimenting on their prisoners. He had always felt light-years beyond those madmen, ethically; now, having caused what he had caused, he wasn't so sure. He had prayed for a response, any response at all, to salvage and to boost his own career. He had gotten his response.

"There's no question of that, Mrs. Austin. No question at all. After what's happened here this morning, I wouldn't be surprised if you wanted to quit the whole thing, and I wouldn't even try to dissuade you from that. But in any case, that electrode will never again be activated."

"Thank you, Dr. Garrick. And, no, I don't want to stop the experiments; I know how important they are, and I'll do my part."

She walked out the door, looking frail and helpless in her hospital gown with the thin robe over it. Garrick stared after her, then gathered his papers together and walked out the side door of the lab. The observing doctors were leaving the viewing room at the same time, and he met them as they began to file out, headed for their own coffees and lunches. Blakeley, the man from London, was the first to speak.

"Congratulations, Doctor. Frankly, I wouldn't have believed it possible, but you've proven your thesis: There is activity in the silent zones, or at least it can be provoked. A daring and brilliant experiment."

The others added their agreement, several of them admitting their own previous doubts as to the feasibility of the idea. Dr. Beatty, a thin, attractive woman in her late thirties, was already beginning to speculate on possible uses of the new type of electrode in her own work. She was interrupted by Graham Crandon, the department head from the hospital's affiliated university.

"Excellent work, Peter. Very bold, and very cleanly executed. What do you think will happen when site 8 is stimulated at two and four volts?"

The question caused an immediate silence in the group. Garrick and Lois Beatty looked at the balding professor in amazement.

"I don't plan to try that, Graham. You saw for yourself what happened in there."

"Well, yes, it didn't seem as if the young woman was having the best of times; but still, she knew what she was risking when she volunteered, didn't she? You can't stop now, not when you've just begun to get results."

"That result has been achieved. And besides, there are still six more electrodes."

"But, my God, man, you'll make a mess of all the graphs and calculations. You'll be working with incomplete data."

Lois Beatty started to speak, her face livid. Garrick caught her arm before she could begin an argument.

"I'll control the progress of my own experiment, Graham. I appreciate the influence that you exercised on the foundation for my grant, but I believe that the data on electrode 8 are more than sufficient at this point. Now, if you'll excuse us, Dr. Beatty and I have a luncheon engagement."

The sandwiches had been stale, and the iced tea full of too much artificial lemon. Garrick's ulcer ached, and he swore for the hundredth time that tomorrow he would start bringing his own lunch to the hospital.

The young woman was completely silent as the nurse covered her again with the tangled wires. Not so calm as she had been this morning. With good reason.

"You're quite sure that you feel up to continuing today, Mrs. Austin?"

"Yes, I'm sure."

"Well, I just want to say that the chances are very, very small that there will be a repeat of anything like what happened this morning. There probably won't be any further response from the other six electrodes, and even if there is, the results will most likely be either neutral or even enjoyable. Maybe we'll strike it lucky and hit a pleasure center; then we could give you a button for that, too, and you wouldn't go away from here mad at us."

Elizabeth smiled, relaxing a little. "I don't know how my husband would feel about that, Dr. Garrick. He likes to think he's the one in control of my pleasure centers."

Garrick chuckled, happy that she seemed to be recovering from the emotional trauma of the morning's incident. "Maybe you're right. We had a mouse here who could stimulate his own pleasure center; he pushed the button an average of three thousand times an hour."

"So much for experimental cruelty to animals. He must have had a good time."

"He did, for a while; then he starved to death. Forgot to eat."

"Hmmh. You ought to patent that, Doctor; you could open the world's most popular diet clinic."

Garrick laughed again, and finished his readjustment of the switches on the console.

"O.K. Last chance. Want to call it quits and go home?"

"Nope, I'm in for the duration."

"All right, then, Phase 2, electrode 9, one volt."

The current pulsed inside her brain, and she smiled slightly. "Nothing at all; but this time, you're not going to catch me apologizing for that."

Garrick grinned back at her. "Two volts."

They went through three electrodes quickly in succession, and none of them elicited a response. Garrick didn't mind that now; he'd shown his theories to be true with the eighth silent zone stimulus, and he'd rather finish the series with no further results than have a repeat or variation of that experience. Further grants, and more work on other patients, was assured now; this young woman had been through enough, and he'd be happy to be able to leave her in peace.

"Electrode 12, one volt."

Elizabeth was about to shake her head "no response" when she heard the music. It was very faint, but it sounded like it might be a piano. Something classical. Haydn? Mozart? Just as she was on the verge of identifying the piece, she was suddenly aware of something moving before her eyes, something white, like lace. Then the stimulus abruptly ended, and the image and the music went away.

Garrick looked up and saw her staring into space, her lips pursed and her brow furled in concentration, like someone working out a math problem. "Anything?"

She hesitated a moment before answering, as if reluctant to leave the problem unsolved. "Yes. Yes, there was. Music, and then . . . I saw something white, and soft, moving."

Garrick raised his eyebrows a bit, interested. "Music? What kind of music?"

"Piano music. Something classical, I'm not sure what. That's what I was trying to remember."

"And the white thing?"

"I can't imagine. It was very dim, and it only came in toward the end. It was sort of like—like I'd had my eyes closed, and then suddenly opened them. But not very wide, apparently." She laughed.

"Well, shall we try to see if we can't open them a little more?"

"Sure. It's driving me crazy, trying to figure out what that music was."

"O.K. Two volts. Listen carefully."

The music was stronger this time, and the visual element was clearer. The vaguely perceived white objects came into focus, and she could see that they were smooth white sleeves, ending at the wrist in a puff of delicate lace. Below the lace, she could see and feel her fingers moving across the piano's keyboard.

"Well?"

"It was a lot sharper that time. The music was plainer, and I could see that the white things were just my . . . my arms and hands. Playing the piano."

"Could you remember the name of the music this time?"

"I'm still not positive. Maybe it was Mendelssohn, I don't know."

Garrick looked at her curiously. It was odd enough to find a memory trace in a silent zone, but if it was as vivid as she had said, she should have also remembered what she was playing. An electrically stimulated memory trace, as Elizabeth had learned when they'd hit the one about the broken doll, was more like reliving the incident than just recalling it; and how could someone be playing the piano without knowing what the music was?

"Why don't we move on to four volts?"

"O.K."

He moved the dial and pressed the switch, sending the heightened signal flashing to the electrode buried in her brain. As he held the switch down, she sat across the table with a look of involvement and enjoyment on her face. Whatever the memory was, it was obviously evoking a very different sensation than the other one, this morning, had. Garrick was glad to see that; she deserved a little pleasure today.

"Well, was it Mendelssohn?"

"I still can't tell. It's moved on to another part of the piece."

"What do you mean, another part of the piece?"

"When I first heard it, it was *moderato*; now the melody has changed, and the tempo has picked up to *allegro*."

Garrick's pulse began to race. She was wrong, she had to be. This was obviously a memory trace, and they were always repetitious. Like endless film loops, as he'd told her.

"And you still can't remember what the name of it is? Where were you when you usually played this?"

She was quiet for several seconds, as if she didn't want to answer. When she did speak, she looked down at the table. "To be honest, I don't think I ever have played it before. I was always more into Chopin and Debussy."

Garrick's sympathy for the young woman began to fade. She must be angry about the negative reaction he'd sparked this morning with the eighth electrode, and now she was deliberately trying to make fun of him and the experiment in front of his colleagues. But no, she didn't even know they were there behind the mirror. And she wasn't the type of person who'd seek revenge in a mean, sly way like that. Then what the hell was she up to? Was she just trying to please him, making up a second silent zone response so it would look better on his report of the experiment?

"Let's try it one more time at four volts, shall we?"

"All right."

She closed her eyes this time, anticipating the visual effect and wanting to shut out any outside interference. As Garrick pressed the switch, she smiled slightly, and then a look of sudden surprise crossed her face.

"Well? Was it the same music? Was it fast or slow this time?"

She still looked vaguely shocked, and definitely confused. "Neither one. It ended."

"You mean there was no response this time?"

"No, I mean the music ended. I—I finished playing the piece, whatever it was. It was over."

"*Over?*"

"Yes, and then . . . then I looked up over the top of the piano, and there was someone standing there. A man, smiling down at me."

Garrick's mind was doing double time. She had to be making this up, she simply had to be. And yet there was an expression of genuine bewilderment in her eyes, and her halting voice was filled with unmistakable sincerity.

"Who was he? Your husband? Your father?"

"I—I don't know who he was. I've never seen him before, ever. He had a mustache, and he was wearing . . . some kind of a costume."

"What do you mean, a costume?"

"Like he was dressed up for a play. An old-fashioned kind of suit, and a fancy shirt, with ruffles. He was just standing there, smiling at me, and then he started to lean over the piano, like he was about to kiss me. You know?"

The question was rhetorical, but the pleading in her face showed that she was asking Garrick for some explanation, some support. He couldn't think of a thing to tell her. Worse yet, he was already starting to worry about what he was going to tell the other doctors at the conference to follow.

The meeting room was comfortably furnished, and there was a large window at one end to let in whatever New York sunlight might be available. For now, the curtains on the window were drawn, and the only light in the room came from a flickering projector that had been placed on the long, oval table. Everyone who sat at the table had turned his or her chair to face the wall at the other end of the room. On the wall, a screen had been lowered, and on the screen Peter Garrick and his lovely young patient faced each other. Their voices emanated from a speaker underneath the screen.

"... I'm not absolutely positive one way or the other."

"All right, then. Four volts."

Garrick sat in the darkness, watching himself watch her. He was keyed up with anticipation of what was coming. On the screen Elizabeth Austin was looking sheepishly apologetic.

"Anything at all that time?"

"Nothing. Sorry."

Garrick could see the tight frustration that the camera had caught in his face, and hoped that no one else had noticed the expression. His projected image reached back to the console.

"Electrode eight. One volt."

The tiny speaker could not convey the full force of her scream, but its sudden anguish was still chilling. Elizabeth's face contorted again with terrified hysteria as the thirteen people watched in silence. At last the segment ended, and Garrick switched off the projector as an assistant turned up the room lights.

"What you've just seen, of course, is a replay of that surprising and rather unnerving moment at which we were all present yesterday morning. I speak in all modesty when I say I believe the moment to have been a historic one, as it marked the first recorded instance of an artificially induced response in one of the so-called silent zones of the brain. Now, are there any comments? Dr. Blakeley?"

The rotund Englishman brushed a spot of ashes from his coat

and worked his jaw in a circular motion, as if winding up his larynx. "Obviously," he said, "the most striking element of this response is the raw, undiluted nature of the evident emotion. The young lady herself described the subjective sensation as one of pure, unrooted fear. Not a memory of something that had frightened her in the past, but the absolute impression of fear itself, as a self-contained entity. This, I believe, is something quite new."

There was a general nodding of heads, and one of the Johns Hopkins men cut in. "Certainly new in my experience, and in all my reading, though, God knows, I'd consider myself well informed if I could read a tenth of everything that's being published in the field these days. I'll work on the assumption that, among them, the rest of my colleagues here may have made a dent in the remaining 90 per cent." There was a ripple of understanding laughter.

Jacques Charnier politely raised his hand, and Garrick nodded in his direction. The Parisian's English was flawless and without accent. "It seems to me that perhaps there might be some type of correlation between this response and the nightmare state. As you know, a true nightmare—the deep, almost primordial sort, the kind that forces you awake in a cold sweat—has been shown to be quite distinct from the ordinary dreaming pattern. Most dreams, even the unpleasant ones, take place in a sleep phase that is marked by a relatively high degee of activity, with short, spiking waves; but genuine nightmares occur during the deepest periods of sleep, when the brain is dominated by slow, looping delta waves. Dr. Garrick's discovery of a basic fear response in one of the silent zones may well point us toward an answer to this phenomenon."

The other doctors around the table murmured their interest, and several were jotting down notes as Charnier spoke. There would probably be a sharp increase in the number of delta sleep investigations over the next year or so: dozens of different lab assistants scattered around the world, sitting up through the night to watch their sleeping subjects, and eagerly awaiting the moments when those subjects dreamed of headless beasts pursuing them across unbroken, burning plains. The scientific scrutiny of Hieronymous Bosch.

Garrick smiled and rose, nodding his gratitude for the doctors' remarks. "Thank you very much. Are there any further questions or comments?"

For the first time since they had gathered at the table, Graham Crandon spoke. "I think not. Why don't we move on to the other . . . response?"

"Very well. Charles, would you get the lights, please?"

The young assistant reached behind him with a long arm, plunging the room back into darkness. Garrick touched the projector switch, and the screen was lit with countdown numbers from the spliced-in leader film. The reel had already been edited, and the unproductive trials removed. They would be going immediately into electrode 12. Garrick cleared his throat and swallowed.

Elizabeth Austin's image appeared on the screen again, looking intent and curious. Garrick heard himself speaking.

"*Anything?*"

"*Yes. Yes, there was. Music, and then . . . I saw something white, and soft, moving.*"

The conference room was completely still as the film progressed. Garrick looked around and saw that the only person making notes now was Graham Crandon.

"*. . . It's moved on to another part of the piece.*"

"*What do you mean, another part of the piece?*"

Garrick sat uneasily in the dim room, watching the flickering reproduction of his own earlier consternation. God, he really did look uptight on the film. That wasn't good. He glanced again at the shadowed figure of Crandon. The professor was still scribbling away.

"*. . . then I looked up over the top of the piano, and there was someone standing there. A man, smiling down at me.*"

Garrick began to chew on the top of his ball-point pen. Crandon was still writing with his, but continued to watch the screen as he did so.

"*Like he was dressed up for a play. An old-fashioned kind of suit, and a fancy shirt . . .*"

Almost over now. Garrick simultaneously longed for the film to be finished, yet dreaded its ending and the resumption of the discussion. What was he going to say? What *could* he say? He was still trying to figure that out when the screen returned to blinding white.

No one in the room spoke as the lights were turned back on and the curtains opened. A cold November rain was running in tiny rivulets down the window that faced the gray New Jersey Palisades.

Lois Beatty broke the palpable, uneasy silence. "Well. That was very—interesting."

"But what exactly do you think it indicates, Peter?"

"I don't really know, Graham. There are, of course, certain unusual features to this response, as I'm sure we're all aware."

"Why don't you go ahead and sum them up for us."

Garrick sighed resignedly. "All right. At first, the response from site 12 seemed to be an ordinary memory trace, like the doll-breaking incident at site 3 in phase 1. A memory trace in a silent zone would seem rather odd itself, but not unthinkable. However, that hypothesis seems to be ruled out by at least two factors: (a) that the subject reports no actual memory of such a scene, and (b) that the perceived events were not repeated on successive stimuli, but appeared to continue in real time.

"We are then left with the alternative, and superficially likely, explanation that the response was purely a hallucination. This is still a strong possibility, but its validity would seem to be weakened by the fact that the site in question is in the region of the frontal lobe, far removed from the visual or associative centers whose activation is required to produce realistic hallucinations of this complexity. I do expect major results from our work with the silent zones, but I must in all candor admit that I'm skeptical about their ability to produce full-fledged, highly organized hallucinations. We thus seem to have encountered something of a conundrum."

"Perhaps. Perhaps not."

"What do you mean, Graham?"

"Isn't it true that this young woman has been under considerable emotional stress for quite some time?"

"No more than any other epileptic, or any other person who's recently undergone waking neurosurgery. I don't think anyone in this room could have lived through those things without a certain degree of strain and upset. But if you're implying that she's insane, I must emphatically disagree. All of her psychological tests, both pre- and postoperative, have been quite normal, considering the circumstances."

"I'm not disputing that, Peter. But isn't it also true that the patient has been made fully aware in advance of the details of this experiment, including its 'pioneering' investigation of the 'mysterious' silent zones? And don't the records also show that she is an exceptionally bright young woman, of recognized artistic and creative abilities? In short, that she is a highly . . . *imaginative* person?"

Garrick's palms were sweaty, and he reached for one of his infrequent cigarettes. "Graham, are you accusing . . ."

"Please, Peter. I'm not accusing anyone of anything. I only meant to anticipate what I'm sure would soon have been your own suggestion: that the remaining experiments with this subject be rigorously designed to avoid the possibility of even accidental or unconscious error."

Garrick had to concede the point. If it had been anyone else's experiment, he'd be saying exactly the same thing Crandon was saying now.

"What sort of controls did you have in mind? I wouldn't want to leave any loopholes for later objection, so let's be thorough."

Crandon sucked wetly at his pipe, ticking the requirements off one by one on his fingers. "Random order restimulation of the electrodes; elimination of warning signals to the subject; random time intervals between stimuli; random stimulus strength; and physical separation of subject and experimenter. In fact, complete physical isolation of the subject might be best. And, of course, periodic rotation of the experimenter's duties. We have several competent young lab assistants eager for work."

"Fine. Anything else?"

"Yes, one small point, but an important one: I'd like to see the original experiments completed as they were intially scheduled."

"What exactly do you mean by that?"

"Electrode 8. We were never given an opportunity to compare its effects at two and four volts."

"My God, Graham! You saw for yourself, both live and on film, how negatively she was affected by that electrode, even at one volt! She specifically requested that it not be used again, and I think we have a moral obligation to honor that request."

"Yes, of course; but in the perhaps unlikely event that Mrs. Austin is shown to be faking her response to electrode 12, how can we assume that the results obtained at site 8 are any more valid? How . . ."

Garrick's deep baritone intruded sharply, drowning out the rest of Crandon's sentence. "Christ, man, do you honestly believe that young woman is capable of *pretending* to suffer through that kind of agony? Do you think she's such an accomplished actress that she can spontaneously run through all the symptoms of severe hysteria—in *seven seconds?*"

Crandon frowned and shook his head. "Peter, this isn't necessarily a question of pretense or purposeful fakery. The young woman has been under considerable strain, and who's to say whether it might not have affected her more deeply than it might another patient in similar circumstances? These things don't always show up on psychological tests, you know. You also can't deny that she must sense a strong pressure to "succeed'—that is, to produce noticeable results of some sort—in these experiments. The combination could very easily have provoked an unconscious mimicry of what might seem to her to be exactly the type of 'mysterious' responses you've been searching for.

"Now, I don't want to downgrade what you seem to have achieved, and I also don't want to subject Mrs. Austin to any unnecessary torment; but your published results will be subjected to the closest scrutiny, in universities and other research centers around the world. Not only you, but the university, the hospital, and the foundation will be held accountable for the veracity of your reports and papers. There's too much riding on this to allow it to be endangered by shoddy experimental techniques, however worthy or humanitarian the motive. Am I correct, Peter?"

He was, and he knew he was, and he knew that Garrick knew he was. It wasn't pleasant, but it was strictly proper procedure, and God knows this experiment was going to be too controversial to settle for anything less.

Garrick slumped a little in his seat. "I'll have the stimulator console moved into the viewing room. It should be ready by tomorrow afternoon."

Elizabeth sat by herself in the testing room, waiting for something to happen. Dr. Garrick had explained the new procedure, and had told her that a microphone and speakers would be installed so she could communicate with him whenever she wished. Unless there was an emergency or a question unrelated to the experiment, however, she would hear nothing in response from him, and there would be no warning before each stimulation. They wouldn't even be activating the electrodes in the usual order, so she would have no way of knowing from moment to moment what, if anything, might come next.

She had been sitting there for almost ten minutes now, and there had only been one mild flashback to the doll-breaking sequence. She knew that feeling well enough by now to be fairly sure that it had been at two volts today: not vague, but also not as strikingly clear as it had been at other times, with four volts.

She looked around the room in a slightly bored curiosity, hoping that they would soon get back to the electrode that had started the piano-playing episode three days before. She wondered whether the sensation would be repeated again today, perhaps beginning back at the start of the musical piece, or if it would pick up where it had previously ended, with that costumed, dark-eyed man smiling and leaning toward her. Then again, maybe it wouldn't work at all this time; Dr. Garrick and the others seemed to have some doubts about that electrode, almost as if she'd made the story up. She hadn't made it up; or at least, she didn't think she had. She was strongly aware now of the strange tricks of awareness and perception that her mind could play on her.

There was absolutely nothing in the room to hold her interest; the wall of computer equipment was a cold and unfathomable mass of tapes and wires and controls, and if she stared at it all day she'd never understand a bit of it, or find it a pleasant thing to look at. The other walls were almost perversely featureless—stark, uninterrupted white. The least you'd think they'd do would be to paint them; but even if they did, it would probably be that dreadful hospital green. Better white than that.

Her eyes were drawn back to the mirror again, even though she hated seeing herself done up like this with all these wires. Why should there even be a mirror in . . . of course. Obviously, they weren't just going to listen to her on some speaker somewhere, without seeing her reactions and expressions. There had probably been someone back there all along, even the times when Dr. Garrick had been in the room; maybe even several people. The thought sent an unwanted chill across her back, and she hurriedly looked away from the mirror. *He should have told me. I wouldn't have objected, but he really should have told me.*

She was growing irritated, tense with waiting, and the knowledge of those people, however many of them there were, hiding behind the mirror didn't help her mood. She angrily lit a cigarette, and then on impulse shot a brief but purposeful glare at the mirror, blowing a little cloud of smoke in its direction as she did so. *What was taking them so long? Why didn't they get down to trying out electrode 12?*

The minutes passed, and still there was nothing. *She should have brought a book to read. She should have—*

God, no! The room was alive with menace, with loathsomeness, with blinding, raging terror reverberating from the very walls, with . . . *no, they couldn't, he said they wouldn't do this again! He said, he said—*

Garrick stared at Graham Crandon with unconcealed fury. Through the window of the viewing room, they could see the nurse who'd rushed in when Elizabeth had fainted. Crandon's pipe was out, unnoticed, and he stared into the testing room in chastened silence.

"All right, Graham. That was two volts. Shall we try for four? Eight, maybe? Ten?"

"I didn't expect . . ."

"No, you expected that she wouldn't even notice it, because she had no way of knowing that was when she was supposed to start faking. Well, I didn't tell her; did you notice anyone else telling her? Did you happen to see one of my assistants walk into the room and hand her a note?"

"Peter, please. Obviously, I was wrong. I don't think we'll need to go on to four volts, after all."

"Thank you. Now, I'm going to see to my patient and try to explain this ugly surprise to her. If she's all right, and if she's willing, we'll resume again in an hour or so."

Elizabeth was still extremely shaky, and less interested in the outcome of the experiment than at any point so far. She had been shocked at the unexpected reactivation of the eighth electrode, and the experience had been hideous. Afterward, Dr. Garrick had patiently explained; he told her everything about Dr. Crandon's insistence that it be tried again, without warning, and the reasons behind that. He assured her that now even Dr. Crandon was willing to let the matter rest; but then, he had also assured her that it wouldn't be used again after the first time. A fine line of trust had been breached, and she knew now that she would never feel entirely secure as long as the experiments continued. She had downplayed the original fear response to David; she thought it best if she didn't mention this one to him at all.

They had been back at it for about twenty minutes now, and so far there was still no response, except for one more activation of the doll-breaking scene, this time at a clear four volts. Boredom was no longer an issue, though; Elizabeth was tense and expectant, not quite trusting them to leave the eighth electrode dormant.

The room had taken on a different quality now; its blank white walls seemed to mask a terrible array of waiting torments, and she was unable to forget the eyes behind the mirror. Maybe they'd already tried electrode 12 and found out that it didn't work anymore; maybe the whole thing was a flop, except for that fear thing, and she could go home soon. Maybe . . .

She was suddenly aware of brilliant sunlight and of being carried forward with a rhythmic, rushing speed. Green all around her, blurring past like streams of emerald meteors, and . . . it went away.

"Dr. Garrick?" She leaned a little closer to the microphone. "Dr. Garrick, could we try that one again, at a higher voltage? I'm not quite sure how to describe it, but something was definitely happening."

In the viewing room, Garrick glanced down at the sheet before him, and entered a question mark in the blank response space. He raised an eyebrow and turned to look at Crandon. "Well? Do you think we should do as she asks?"

"How many more trials until we come back to No. 12?"

Garrick leafed through the sheets with their computer-printed list of electrodes and voltages. "It comes up again in nineteen trials, at four volts."

"I think we should stick with the random order. But don't tell her, one way or the other."

Garrick nodded. "Fine. If we are getting a response, I don't want there to be any question about it later." He reached for the console and touched the switch for another of the previously unsuccessful electrodes.

Elizabeth was unaware of their decision, and she patiently awaited the return of that strange sensation of movement and color. Nothing happened. After a minute or more had passed, she began to be puzzled; she had been so sure that something unusual was going on. She leaned into the mircrophone and shook her head apologetically. "I'm sorry; I don't know how I could have been mistaken."

After about five minutes she had another *déjà vu*, and informed the silent listeners of the sensation. It was a distinctly unpleasant feeling now, in this room, and she hoped they wouldn't hit that site too often. Then another wave of nervousness passed over her, and she wondered again if they might go back on their word a second time and press the button that would send her into that pervasive, waking nightmare. God, she wanted this all over with!

She was preparing herself to wait another twenty minutes for the next response when all at once it came upon her, with astonishing force and clarity. She was in a rich green forest, riding toward—*riding!* There were leather reins in her hands, and a muscled horse heaved and galloped between her legs, headed for an open clearing up ahead. She could see a field of yellow daisies in full bloom beyond the clearing, and the wind that whipped her hair was warm and clean. Then her eyes moved to her left, and she glimpsed another rider catching up to her, on a huge brown horse that—

The blank white walls came back, and the ever-present mirror. Speechless, still enveloped in the exhilaration of that speeding, graceful freedom, she breathed deeply, trying to regain her senses.

For the first time, she noticed the taste of the air in the room: stale and chemical, recycled city air. She realized that she was already missing that unexpected, brief aroma of greenery and flowers.

The speaker above her head came to crackling life. "Mrs. Austin? Are you all right?"

She shook her head to clear away the remembered vision. "Yes, yes, I'm fine. Just startled. There was a very clear response that time. Very clear. It was . . . lovely, and strange."

"Could you tell us what was happening? Was it the music?"

"Oh, I'm sorry. It's just hard to get it out of my mind so quickly. No, there was no music. I was riding a horse, very fast, through some woods. I could see fields ahead of me, where the forest ended; there were lots of flowers, and everything was very green, and fresh. Sunny, and the air was like it used to be sometimes back home, in Virginia. Just before it ended, I was looking around behind me, and there was someone else on another horse, keeping up with me. I don't know who it was, I didn't have time to see." She sighed, and shook her head again.

Garrick and Crandon looked at each other, expressionless and silent. Garrick turned to the microphone that sent his voice into the testing room. "Is this a familiar episode to you? Do you recall having ridden before in the place that you were seeing?"

"No, I don't think so. It wasn't as hilly as Virginia, and of course I've never ridden since then. Not since I was twelve. I couldn't, not with the epilepsy." As she spoke, she looked straight toward the mirror. Obviously she knew that they were back there. Garrick felt like a fool, and a cheat, somehow.

"How do you know you weren't eleven or twelve in this scene?"

Elizabeth smiled amusedly at the mirror. "Dr. Garrick, when I was eleven or twelve, horseback riding didn't make my chest bounce."

Garrick flushed slightly, and behind him, Lois Beatty laughed. "And you didn't get a look at this other rider at all?"

"No. It shut off just as I . . . just as my . . ." She stopped, a look of bewilderment on her face.

"Just as what?"

"Sorry. I was having trouble phrasing it, and that made me realize something kind of funny. Funny peculiar."

"What was that?"

"When the stimulation ended, I was turning my head to look behind me; but *I* wasn't doing it. It was like my head was just turning by itself, or . . . like somebody else was controlling the movement."

Garrick cleared his throat nervously. This was sounding weirder all the time, and Crandon wasn't looking happy. If she *was* lying, then why didn't she at least come up with something more believable? Then again, the possibility of it being completely a lie seemed terribly remote; that was the whole purpose of this rigamarole about the testing conditions, and the random order stimulus. Garrick wished she'd stop going on like this, but she kept talking.

"As a matter of fact, now that I think of it, that fits perfectly with the thing the other day about the piano. I could see and feel my fingers on the keys, as surely as if there'd been a piano in this room; but it wasn't my thoughts that were moving them. I was just . . . watching, somehow; from inside, but also from a distance. I don't know how else to describe it."

"And you never feel that way in the memory trace, the doll-breaking incident?"

"No, whenever that comes up I'm completely into it; I go through exactly the same thoughts and emotions that I did when I was ten, and it's *me* doing the breaking; it's my own decision, as I remember making it. Not with these others, though."

Garrick nodded, his eyes closed in exasperation. "Well, Mrs. Austin, I think that's all we need for today. Why don't you—"

She interrupted his attempted escape. "Aren't we going to try it again? Don't you want to find out who the person on the other horse is? I do."

His reply was unnecessarily sharp. "What makes you think we could find that out by repeating the stimulus?"

"Well, I don't know—the other time, with the piano, it seemed to keep on going from where it started, and I just thought that it would probably do the same thing now. That seems logical, doesn't it?"

Garrick was watching Crandon out of the corner of his eye. The department head was sitting well back in the soft seat, his fingers steepled underneath his chin, and his face an unreadable mask. He waited patiently for Garrick to make a deicision, to say something.

"Mrs. Austin, *nothing* in this case seems logical to me at the moment. If you insist on trying this electrode once more today, I have no objections; but I think you're being awfully premature in predicting the outcome."

Through the glass, Elizabeth smiled and shrugged, still staring directly at the spot on the mirror behind which Garrick sat, as if she were looking right into his eyes. He didn't like the sensation, and he wanted this whole day done with. He placed his hand back on the console and moved the switch for electrode 12, still at four volts.

Elizabeth hadn't expected the stimulus so quickly, but she adjusted to the sudden change in her perceived environment immediately. The horse she rode was standing still now, breathing heavily beneath her. The other horse stood quietly beside hers, but no one was in his saddle. They were in the open clearing she had seen before, just at the edge of the flowered field. She could hear someone moving in the tall grass nearby, outside her range of vision. She tried to will her head to turn and look, but her eyes remained stubbornly fixed on the woods through which she had been riding earlier. Then her eyes swept up, seemingly of their own accord, to take in the almost cloudless azure sky. The footsteps in the grass approached her, and she felt a hand reach up and grasp her arm. She—

The bare white room returned.

"Dr. Garrick, please, turn it back on! Don't stop it yet!"

Her eyes were pleading, and she searched the mirror frantically, as if trying to re-establish the earlier, accidental, and unknowing eye contact she had had with Garrick. He felt a surge of pity for her, and curiosity at the eagerness with which she wanted to continue the stimulus.

"What was the response this time?"

"I'll tell you later, let's just give it a few more seconds!"

"Perhaps, but first I'd rather know what happened."

She told him hurriedly, the words running together in her haste. "It was the same place, the horses were stopped out in the field, and I still didn't get a chance to see who the other person was, but I'm sure I could now. Please, just one more time? Just for a few seconds?"

There was no denying her earnest desire to return to the hallucination, or memory trace, or whatever it was. Everyone in the viewing room could see the fervent intensity in her expression, could hear the urgency in her voice. Lois Beatty broke the hush. "Go ahead, Peter, it can't hurt. There's no reason to frustrate her like this."

He shrugged and nodded, glancing once again at Crandon. The older doctor sat as impassively as ever, saying nothing. Garrick sighed and pressed the switch.

The change in Elizabeth's face was instantaneous. Garrick held the tiny lever down for ten full seconds, twice the ordinary time, watching her absorption in her mind. When the time was up, she smiled off into space and touched her fingers lightly to her lips.

Garrick was tired and perplexed, and the young woman's beatific, almost secretive enjoyment of these troublesome experiments was beginning to irk him. He bluntly broke her reverie. "Well? What was that all about?"

She looked back at the mirror, continuing to smile as she answered. "Silly. So simple, really, but . . . it was a picnic, of all things. I haven't been on a picnic in years. There was a beautiful linen cloth on the ground, and a real wicker basket full of food and stuff. There was even one of those old antique picnic sets, in a leather case lined with velvet; you know, the kind that has everything all in silver, right down to marmalade spoons and egg slicers and silver wine goblets. He was pouring the wine, and I was eating some paté. Very good paté."

This was getting to be too much for Garrick to put up with, but he carefully controlled the irascibility in his voice. "What do you mean, 'he'? Who are you talking about?"

Elizabeth looked vaguely startled, as if the answer should be obvious. "Why, it was that man. The same one who was there when I was playing the piano. But I still don't know who he is."

With only a brief nod to Garrick, Crandon stood up and left the viewing room. Garrick watched him go, and then reached up to rub an unpleasant knot of tension that was forming in his neck. Lois Beatty smiled sympathetically.

Garrick turned back to the microphone. "All right, Mrs. Austion, you can go back to your room now. I think we've had enough for today."

The tests resumed at nine o'clock the following morning. Elizabeth seemed to be feeling chipper today; through the mirror, Garrick could see her laughing and joking with the nurse as the sensor wires were attached to her body. She was obviously looking forward to the session. Her cheerfulness rankled him a bit, but at least she seemed to have lost the fear and distrust she had built up over the episode with the fear center electrode. Better a happy subject than a nervous, suspicious one, even if her mood did clash with his.

The sensors were all in place, and the nurse was leaving the testing room. Garrick spoke into his microphone. "Good morning, Mrs. Austin. Ready for another day of this?"

She beamed happily at the mirror. "Ready when you are, C.B."

Good humor was one thing; bad jokes were another, particularly at this time of the morning. Garrick ignored her try at jocularity, and nodded to the lab assistant who was taking his turn at the console.

The computer-ordained preselection of electrodes to be tried was different today. Many of the previously unproductive sites had been eliminated to save time, so that the bothersome twelfth electrode would be activated on an average of once every six trials. Like dice, Garrick thought; like playing dice with my project and my career.

The *déjà vu* was first today, and Elizabeth duly reported it. Then there was a long stretch of nothing electrodes, interrupted only by one doll-breaking memory trace at two volts. Finally, at twenty past nine, electrode twelve came up. Twice in a row, first at one, then at four volts. Garrick held his breath as the plump young assistant moved the switch. Elizabeth's expression didn't change.

"No, nothing yet."

Garrick refused to raise his hopes too high, not yet. After all, it was only one volt, she could have not noticed that. But now it was scheduled for four. The assistant changed the setting on the dial and began the stimulus again. Still, no visible change in her face.

"Nothing at all so far."

Garrick's excitement mounted. Could this really be the end of it? He had hoped so much for some magic elimination of this damnable mess that he hadn't really thought about what the results might be if it finally did stop. The apparent realization of his hopes now threw a dash of cold water on his resurging confidence. Actually, this might end up showing that she *had* been lying all along. Maybe she'd just been incredibly lucky in guessing when the twelfth electrode was on yesterday, and today her luck had left her. But that still didn't erase the record of those times when she claimed to have those absurd flashes, horses and picnics and pianos and all that; if that was proved to be made up, then the whole experiment would be in serious doubt, and not just by Crandon. At the very least, they'd insist on going back to the fear electrode, probably several more times; and if the Austin woman refused to put up with that, as she had every reason and right to do, then Garrick's reputation would be in shambles, it would be a worldwide medical joke. Catch-22: damned if it works, damned if it doesn't. There was nothing he could do but wait and watch.

Another fifteen minutes were occupied with irrelevant electrodes, and then the twelfth one was up again. Two volts; no response.

The morning went on that way. Every time site 12 was stimulated, she reported zero reaction. Blank, just like the others. As the pattern repeated itself again and again, Garrick's anxiety was almost overcome by a growing curiosity: If she had been lying about the earlier responses, why wasn't she doing the same thing today? Why hadn't she pretended to have even one of those supposed experiences, whether she picked the right electrode or not? Maybe she had realized that her responses were in question, and was scared of missing. And yet, she looked increasingly puzzled herself, sitting at the table in that barren room. Shortly before eleven, she brought the subject up.

"Dr. Garrick? Why haven't you tried electrode 12?"

If this was all an act, at least she was good at it. He didn't know what to tell her, and by now he wasn't so sure that he trusted her motives himself. It would be better if he didn't say anything specific; she could be trying to trap him somehow.

"The sites to be stimulated have been selected at random. I can't discuss them with you while the experiment is in progress."

Elizabeth frowned, disappointed. She couldn't understand why they were ignoring the only really interesting part of this whole thing, and she was miffed that they were depriving her of an opportunity to satisfy her own curiosity. Then it occurred to her that perhaps they *had* stimulated that site this morning, that those disturbing but fascinating visions might be gone for good. The prospect saddened her; the flashes had been so clear, and pleasantly intriguing. The one yesterday had really been nice: that sudden, dashing ride through the forest had genuinely thrilled her, and the oddly elegant picnic scene had been delightful. It would be too bad if all that just turned out to have been some temporary aberration, a fluke of her own imagination or something.

The rest of the hour dragged interminably on. Elizabeth had been so excited about today's experiments that she had hardly touched her breakfast, and now she was bored and tired and hungry. If they gave her another *déjà vu*, she thought she might throw something through that damned mirror. She looked at her watch and gratefully noted that the noon break was only twenty minutes away. If this afternoon's session was anything like this one, she'd just have to sit through it somehow, but she'd deal with that later.

The body sensations took her by surprise, although their onset wasn't sudden. There was a gradually building sensory awareness, mainly textural in nature: something soft and smooth against her skin, and although her arms were in fact crossed upon the table in the testing room, she now could feel them lazily moving, stretching, flexing. The movement emphasized the texture she had felt, and now she recognized it as silk, fine silk spread out across her naked arms and thighs and breasts. The sliding cloth caressed her body as she felt herself turn slowly over on her side, her nudity enveloped in a sea of warmly scented softness. The visual part came unexpectedly and all at once: whiteness everywhere around, and slanting sunlight delicately scattered through gauzy curtains. Unwilled, her eyes moved to her right and rested on the darkly rumpled hair of the man she'd seen before, now breathing peacefully beside her. A breeze from the window—

"Only five more to go now, Mrs. Austin, and we'll stop for lunch."

"No, wait! I got something that time!"

Garrick reacted as neutrally as possible. "What was it?"

"I think I know now why there haven't been any other results this morning. You *have* been turning on that electrode, haven't you?"

"I told you before that I'm not able to discuss that, Mrs. Austin. Now, if you did feel some response this time, could you please simply describe it for the record?"

Elizabeth smiled, serene and sure again. "Yes," she said, "I just woke up."

The curtains were open on the window in the conference room, revealing the bleakness of the season's first early snow. The edited films of the last two weeks' experiments had already been shown, and one of the assistants was packing away the 16mm projector. Garrick glumly surveyed his colleagues and prepared to open the final meeting on the experiment.

"Well, you've all seen the films, and you've read the transcripts. Any comments?"

Jacques Charnier politely waited for the others to speak, and when no one did, he opened the discussion. "At the very least, I believe that we may all agree that we have been privileged to witness a most unusual experiment." He looked deliberately at Graham Crandon. "I think I can also safely say that every possible safeguard has been met to establish the validity of Dr. Garrick's results. There was no opportunity for any type of conscious or unconscious cheating in this experiment, either by the subject or by the experimenters. There is no question but that results *have* been achieved in the stimulation of silent zone areas. However—" The pause was evident, and everyone in the room waited to hear how he would phrase this next part. "However, we are faced with a highly puzzling response at the twelfth electrode site. The only possible scientific explanations are that the results have been due to memory trace or hallucination, yet there are compelling arguments against either of these interpretations. I must admit that I myself have no theories to offer in this regard, other than the remote possibility that this portion of the silent zones may constitute a redundant and normally dormant association cortex. I would welcome an alternative to this idea, or an extension of it.

Everyone around the table seemed to have something to do: making notes, inspecting a pen, examining a skull chart, filling a pipe, or rubbing an eye. Lois Beatty obviously wanted to help, but didn't know how. It was all up to Garrick.

"I'm afraid there are no alternatives, Dr. Charnier; at least, none that can be hypothesized or supported at this point. The explanation you've offered is obviously unlikely; but then, this entire experiment has been unlikely. It seems as though the grudging, silent consensus of this group is that we have uncovered a new hallucinatory center in the brain, located in a most improbable area."

Crandon was stirring to life. Here it comes, thought Garrick. "That does seem to be what we are left with, Peter. And yet—" It quickly occurred to Garrick that his discovery might be forever known as The However And Yet Factor. He brushed the cynicism from his mind and listened to Crandon.

"Even when the known associative centers are stimulated, the hallucinations that are induced bear little resemblance to the ones this subject has reported. Both electrical stimulation and the psychedelic drugs evoke a wide range of different subjective experiences, perceptions, and thought patterns: There are often a dozen or more highly variant hallucinations within a matter of minutes, and the majority of these take the form of ideational or attitudinal changes. Very few involve *complete* alteration of the subject's perceptual set. Even dreams go off in numerous and often seemingly unrelated directions with great fluidity and rapidity.

"Mrs. Austin, however, has claimed to experience an ongoing, serial group of total sensory hallucinations, all apparently closely interwoven, and all fitting into a constant imaginary reality: horses, picnics, carriage rides, classical piano music, servants attending her, a mysterious man in period clothing who regularly appears . . . this has continued for a full two weeks now, without variation. It's as if the woman is watching, or rather living, an incredibly extensive and idyllically romanticized motion picture of her own devising.

"Now, the double-blind nature of the experiment over the past ten days has assured me that there is certainly *some* perceived response from electrode 12—at least she knows when it's being activated—but I find it impossible to accept the factuality of such an extended and well-organized hallucination, particularly in an area that under normal stimulation produces no results at all. The fear response is well documented, and is supported by the weight of logic, as Dr. Charnier has pointed out; it is the type of reaction one might well expect to find within the silent zones, something deep and indistinct. But an astoundingly complex, thoroughly well-integrated, two-week-long hallucination? In the vernacular, Peter: no way; no way at all."

The two men looked each other in the eyes for several quiet moments. Then Garrick looked away and slowly nodded.

"You must realize, Peter, that this does not invalidate your whole experiment; far from it. I am prepared to accept the fear response as genuine, and the other electrode, as I said, at least alerts her to its activation in some fashion. I'm not necessarily even accusing Mrs. Austin of purposeful fabrication; hypnosis provides enough examples of the unconscious lengths to which a subject will go, quite innocently, in order to please the hypnotist. The young woman may not even realize that she is making all this up, so she might well be blameless; but I do think it's obvious by now that there is nothing useful to be learned from further stimulation of this electrode. You've made your case with the fear-induction stimulus; the hospital, the university, the foundation, and I personally will stand behind the verity and importance of those results. Provided, of course, that these experiments are—properly presented."

What the hell, Garrick thought; show me the hoop, I'll jump. Properly. "Meaning?"

Crandon smiled in a way that was at once comradely and authoritative, a subtler version of the Rooseveltian grin, with a pipe instead of a cigarette holder. "Well, of course you wouldn't want to muddle up your report of an important experiment like this with the meanderings of an imaginative and highly suggestible young woman's fantasies, would you?"

Garrick swiveled slowly in his chair and stared out at the thickening snow. It looked like this was going to be a long and heavy winter. The Hudson might even freeze south of Poughkeepsie this year.

"No, Graham, I wouldn't want to cause any confusion about my experiments. So how would you suggest I handle my report on the twelfth electrode?"

Crandon looked around the table at the other doctors. Whatever he said, they all knew better than to protest: His influence carried a long way. Besides, in all likelihood he was right. It was probably for the best. Not a cover-up, really, just . . . protecting the valid results of a respected colleague. Looking out for one's own.

"Well, now, even a brief description of all that stuff she told you would turn out to be quite a bother. The mass media would have a field day with it, and some fool or other would be bound to try to make some kind of crazy 'supernatural' claims about the whole thing; Bridey Murphy, and all that. Your reputation would be endangered, and Mrs. Austin herself would be at the mercy of the press. So, in everyone's best interest, I think it might be appropriate if your paper on this simply made some passing reference to 'brief and ill-defined hallucinations.' I'm sure everyone here would go along with that."

There was an embarrassed general agreement. Yes, it was really for the best. No need to start a scandal or an uproar. Why spoil someone's perfectly good experiment?

Garrick continued to stare out at the snow. "And the films? The transcripts?"

"I'll leave that up to you, Peter. But it doesn't seem to me as if they're really crucial documents to keep around. Not the ones on electrode 12, anyway."

Garrick nodded, wanting the meeting over with as soon as possible. "What about Mrs. Austin? What shall I tell her?"

"If I were in your place, I believe I'd say that the experiments were . . . valuable, but inconclusive. You might even go so far as to imply—not really say outright, but strongly imply—that this work might have some type of government applications, and request that neither she nor her husband mention anything about what's happened. Would she go along with that, do you think?"

"I believe so; but she has become unusually fascinated with that electrode, and she may question why we're just stopping it cold. I think it'll also displease her not to be able to try it out anymore."

"Then offer her some bait to keep quiet about it. She'll be given a portable transmitter to stop her seizures, anyway; why not install a second button for the twelfth electrode, and let her play with it at home? It can't harm her. Pretend that you want her to keep a secret diary of the results. Would she go for that?"

"I'm sure she would. I can have the circuits installed in her transmitter right away."

"Good, good. I guess that about covers it, then; unless you had something else to say, Peter. After all, this is your conference."

"No, I think that's it. Anybody else want to comment?"

No one said a word. Garrick shrugged and nodded, and the doc-

tors all began to put their papers away. Suddenly Gene Templeton, the only student who had been permitted to attend these sessions, raised his hand. "Dr. Garrick, Dr. Crandon? I just have one
question that nobody seems to have considered at all."

"Yes?"

"Well, I know it sounds ridiculous, but—what if she's not faking, consciously or unconsciously? What if those experiences are
somehow . . . real?"

They all ignored him as they left the table and headed for the
door. The look on Crandon's face made it plain that Templeton
was going to have a very rough time with his final exams this year.

PART THREE

It was strange to be back in her own apartment again, after everything that had happened in the past six weeks. Elizabeth had expected a brief period of readjustment; but now, as she sat in the living room trying to relax while David mixed the drinks, she started to wonder if anything at all would ever seem the same as it had been before.

Some things had definitely changed for good, she thought, her fingers running idly over the surface of the transmitter Dr. Garrick had given her the day she left the hospital. "The Problem," that ever-present and seemingly eternal element of her life and her relationship with David, had suddenly and amazingly disappeared. Never again would their daily existence and their plans for the future be affected by that abiding, awful fear. They could go sailing now, or camping in the mountains, or anything they chose to do. Thanks to Dr. Garrick and this shiny little box, their lives could be as normal as any other couple's.

Except, she thought, except . . . guiltily, she glanced into the kitchen and saw that David was still busy crushing ice. She turned the voltage dial to its midrange setting and pressed the oblong yellow button, the extra one they had installed just before she was released.

Another set of sights and sounds was immediately superimposed on her reality, like a frame of film that had been randomly double-exposed. She shut her eyes to block the image of the apartment's living room, and then she could clearly see the pages of a thick, leather-covered book. By now she was accustomed to the way her "other eyes," as she had come to think of them, moved on their own and not by her desired control; her vision now moved carefully across the finely printed pages, more slowly than she normally might read, resting briefly on each word in every line instead of moving smoothly down the center of the page.

> . . . *some verses he had been making that*
> *morning, in which he informed himself that*

> *the woman who had slighted his passion could*
> *not be worthy to win it: that he was awaking*
> *from love's mad fever, and, of course, under*
> *these circumstances, proceeded to leave her,*
> *and to quit a heartless deceiver . . .*

She couldn't place the lines; something from Dickens, perhaps, or maybe Thackeray? She tried to make out the title printed at the top of the page, but it was lost in the blurred edges of her peripheral vision, and her "other eyes" refused to break their steady, plodding progress.

> *. . . that though to him personally death*
> *was as welcome as life, and that he would*
> *not hesitate to part with the latter, but*
> *for the love of one kind being whose hap-*
> *piness depended on his own . . .*

In the background, she heard David pouring the martinis from the shaker, and she released the yellow button. The phantom book was gone at once, and she was back in the Sixty-fifth Street apartment. Nothing had changed; and yet she felt, not for the first time recently, that something very basic in her life was being subtly but irrevocably altered. Whether for good or ill, she couldn't say. She tried to shake the feeling off, and forced a smile as David carried in the drinks.

She had met him in her sophomore year of college, her alert but shy demeanor a perfect complement to his quietly aggressive nature.

The experience of college, up to then, had brought less of a change for her than she had thought it would. She'd imagined college life in simple terms of independence vs. life at home, new friends instead of old; but there were unexpected gaps that she suddenly found difficult to bridge.

The drug thing was one of the hardest. It seemed that 1967 was the year that marijuana was invented, or at least mass-marketed. Everything she read or heard about it fascinated her, and the psychedelic chemicals, like LSD and mescaline, intrigued her even more. She was majoring in art, and constantly absorbed in her visual imagination, so the idea of a substance whose effects could transform sound and touch into a swirling flow of vivid, brightly colored images was like a fantasy come true. For her, though, it was to remain a fantasy; her epilepsy was still only partially controlled, and the risks of powerful and unfamiliar drugs were just too great to take.

It should have been a minor issue, if not irrelevant; but that was a time in which sharp lines were being drawn, and there was no such thing as in between. Every aspect of her personality and interests drew her to the creative, experimenting crowd of students; but their every waking moment seemed to be defined by one drug or another, and their vocabularies were filled with terms for which she could have no personal reference. She was relegated, by default, to socializing with the minority of campus anachronisms who drank beer, joined things, and planned dull careers and duller marriages. She preferred to be alone than to spend her time with most of them.

Her painting and sketching flourished, since she had plenty of time by herself in which to practice. Then her interests began to center more and more on a field she had discovered during senior year in high school, when a counselor suggested that her college applications should mention at least one extracurricular activity. She had chosen to design the sets for the senior play, and had been immediately captivated by the challenge. She would've loved the chance to act or sing or dance onstage; but since that was impossible, at least she could create the world in which the others would appear. The play was only *Li'l Abner,* and the production was of a standard high-school quality; but the sets she did were genuinely outstanding, full of life and color and an essential sense of the imaginary environment they were intended to convey. The local paper had praised them more than anything else about the play.

A place in the college drama group was assured by the photographs of those *Li'l Abner* sets, and she approached every production with relish and vigorous originality. For *Oedipus,* she designed stark, jagged sets and all-white robes and masks with great black eyeholes; her version of the candidates' impersonal hotel suite in *The Best Man* was done with a coolly plastic super realism, and she put together a dusty, truly claustrophobic attic for *The Diary of Anne Frank.* An obscure Shaw play called *The Shewing up of Blanco Posnet* was distinguished by her crazy, abstractly comic western street scene; and she created a nostalgic, lovingly evocative turn-of-the-century living room and porch for O'Neill's *Ah, Wilderness.*

She had, in fact, been making a Tiffany lamp from onionskin and watercolors for the O'Neill production when she met David. He was then a senior in the architecture school, and the director had enlisted his advice in the construction of an onstage "front porch" that would support the weight of several actors. He sat down beside her and wordlessly helped put the prop lamp together; when it was finished, they had turned off all the lights inside the empty theater and stood hand-in-hand, smiling at each other in the cheerful red-and-yellow glow. Within a month she had dropped all pretense of living in her dormitory and was staying with him in his off-campus studio apartment.

David was the third man she had been to bed with, but those other fumbling, semi-obligatory sexual experiences bore no resemblance to the feelings she soon had for him. Unlike all the other students, who seemed obsessed with publicly declaring which side of the social fence they'd chosen, he was neither "straight" nor "hippie," but an individual with enough self-confidence to pick and choose from the best aspects of all the different styles available. He smoked grass, but never bothered to question Elizabeth's refusal of it; he was planning a serious career in architecture, but was intent that it remain an avenue for his own integrity and self-expression, not just a path to status or security.

In the first few weeks they were together, Elizabeth was terrified of the inevitable time when, despite her daily medication, she would have a seizure in front of David. Every day, she promised herself that she would tell him about her condition, and every day she found another reason to wait until the next. It finally happened, in what seemed to be the very worst of circumstances. They had just made love, and were lying underneath a pile of woolly blankets on the floor before his one-log fireplace; David rose to fetch some wine, and as she lay there gazing dreamily into the fire, the scent of roses slowly overcame her, and the attack began.

When it was over, she sat huddled in the blankets, weeping uncontrollably, embarrassed and ashamed to even look him in the eyes; but he gently reassured her, and they sat up all that night and half the morning, as she described to him the inner torments she had faced ever since she'd left her childhood. He was more than understanding: There was no hint of condescension or false sympathy in his attitude, only strong and honest caring. Even still, it took three months and four more seizures before Elizabeth could really believe that he loved her as a total human being, and didn't simply feel obliged or pitying because of her condition.

She was afraid that all that might be lost when he graduated that June, but they spent most of the summer together, first in Virginia and then at his own parent's home in Connecticut. In the fall he entered graduate school at another university, but it was only three hours away by train or car, and they visited each other almost every weekend. As the decade ended, he took his master's degree in architecture, and they were married the week after she received her own diploma. There were two idyllic weeks in St. Croix, and they settled into an apartment on Bank Street, in the Village.

New York was an exhilarating place for both of them. David found a good position with an energetic new architectural firm, a job that enabled him to pursue his desires to create true living spaces in Manhattan rather than more glass and steel monstrosities. Elizabeth, through her impressive portfolio of college plays, was soon immersed in designing for the off-off-Broadway stage. The budgets were often even less than she had worked with at school, and her pay could not have supported her alone; but she liked the work, liked the people that she met, and felt more vitally alive than she ever had before.

Then the difficulties started.

The seven years that she had lived with her epilepsy should, she thought, have thoroughly inured her to the problems that it raised; but the initial flush of happiness at seeming to have overcome them through her work and through her love for David gradually gave way to the depressing realization that her problems, hadn't, wouldn't, simply go away.

The medication that she took still made her drowsy, and on several occasions she had had to make excuses and leave a party or an evening on the town just as everyone else was starting to enjoy the get-together. Her excuses were unnecessary, since their friends all knew about her illness; but, somehow, their understanding smiles just made it worse. She also knew David well enough to see the disappointment beneath his own insistence that it really was all right, that he didn't care that much for nightlife, anyway. It slowly sank home to her that she would have to take those drugs for the rest of her life.

Even with the medication, the seizures continued to happen occasionally, without warning. She tried to limit her schedule as much as possible for a week or so before each menstrual period, but the interference that that caused with her work and with their social life became increasingly intolerable; and besides, there was no assurance that the attacks would always come at that time of the month.

New York seemed to offer a whole new catalog of places where she might collapse: at work, at dinner parties, in a nightclub; there had been one particularly humiliating incident in a discotheque, when a pulsing strobe light had been suddenly trained on the dance floor. It had sucked her inexorably into its jerky rhythm and crumpled her into an awkward, twitching heap there on the polished floor at the center of the club. She had come to to see herself surrounded by the curious, stoned faces of strangers who had stopped their dancing, while the music still blared on.

Their activities together were maddeningly restricted: Before they'd met, David had been a very active man, eagerly involved in a wide variety of sports, from skiing to swimming to sailing. Now, because of Elizabeth's condition, he had given up these pursuits so they could share their leisure time together. It literally wasn't even safe for her to ride a bicycle. Tennis was allowed, and they played frequently; but it was obvious to her that he missed all the other familiar forms of exercise and relaxation.

These things were minor, though, in comparison with the deeper, subtler effects that intruded on their relationship in spite of Elizabeth's efforts and David's best intentions. Neither of them wanted to start a family right away, but when they did think about the future possibility of having children, it was impossible to ignore the difficulties that her illness might impose. If she were to suffer a seizure at the wrong moment it might result in a miscarriage, or, later, the risk of serious danger to an infant that she might be holding or caring for.

There was a more immediate issue, too, and it worsened as the months went on. At the age of thirteen, Elizabeth had been told that she should avoid letting her mind drift freely into daydreams or the like, since this state of loose awareness was most conducive to a seizure. As much as she disliked it, she had trained herself to always keep an attitude of focused, rational attention. Now, this necessary habit was having highly negative effects on her sexual life. It was almost impossible for her to relax, to let her thoughts range freely into fantasy and unencumbered delight in pure sensation. She was in constant fear of losing control, and obsessed by the hideous potential image of a seizure happening while she and David were in the act of making love. She could enjoy the closeness, and appreciate, to an extent, the simple physical pleasure to be found in sex; but she could not let go fully, could not quite bring herself to enter the encompassing release of raw, unthinking emotional and physical response.

For the first few months, she had pretended orgasm; but when David realized what she was doing, he insisted that she never fake her feelings for him again. He had been patient, understanding, and as helpful as he knew how; but the mental block was too ingrained to break, and eventually he'd almost given up. The awful associations that she had with "letting go," and the real fears that it caused in her, seemed too strong to change. There was no way she could redefine the experience as potentially pleasurable, not as long as the danger of another attack remained.

They made love less and less, until by the fifth year of their marriage, their sex together was rare and self-consciously perfunctory. They both pretended that it didn't really matter, but of course it did. The strain was gradually causing the bright dreams that Elizabeth had had since meeting David to go sour in every respect, even in her work. She was too strong to give way to simple self-pity; but there was a growing element of bitterness, a realization that she was doomed to spend her life as an emotional cripple, someone constantly and incurably "different" in an embarrassingly unpleasant way.

The letter from Virginia came in the early summer of 1976. Dr. Prentiss still wrote to her every year or so, informally, just to find out how her life was going. She usually sent him back a short but cheery note, sometimes including photos of her latest set designs. This time, though, the letter arrived on one of her bad days, just after she and David had had one of their quiet but acrid arguments. It was raining outside, and her period was due in a few days, along with the possibility of yet another seizure. The letter that she wrote to Prentiss was uncharacteristically depressing, a pouring out of all her frustrations and concerns.

She regretted sending it almost immediately, but the following week Dr. Prentiss replied, expressing at length his sympathy and understanding. At the end of the letter, he asked whether she would consider an unproven and maybe even risky chance at alleviating her condition for good. She didn't mention this to David, but wrote back that she would try almost anything if there was a real possibility that it might enable her to lead a normal life.

Prentiss sent her Dr. Garrick's name, along with a note explaining that what Garrick was doing was, at best, highly experimental. She might not even prove to be an appropriate candidate for the procedure, he said, but he definitely thought the possibility worth investigating if she was still willing.

Only then did Elizabeth mention her correspondence with Dr. Prentiss to David. At first he was upset that she hadn't told him about it, but his tone softened as he saw her face grow lighter and more animated, discussing a possible final cure for her condition. He agreed to come to the hospital with her and talk it over with this Dr. Garrick.

There had been another battery of tests, more thorough than all the ones she'd undergone in the years before: hour after hour of EEG recordings, dozens of X rays, seven Metrazol-induced laboratory seizures . . . and finally, two months after they had first met, Dr. Garrick told her she was an ideal subject for the operation. He was willing to go ahead with the surgery right away if she and her husband were still interested. At that same meeting, he made his first request for the additional electrodes in the silent zones.

After all the hopeful excitement, David's feelings became mixed when he learned about the other electrodes. He pointed out that brain surgery was a dangerous step even in the best of circumstances, and reminded her that there was no guarantee that this would work at all. For hours on end, he played the devil's advocate, trying to talk her out of going through with it: They could make another go at learning to live with her condition, he said, and maybe it would be better to try psychoanalysis to overcome her sexual problems. Finally, however, it was apparent that her mind had been made up long before. She had no intention of letting this opportunity pass by, dangerous and chancy though it might well be. Reluctantly, he relented to her wishes, but he never stopped expressing his strong reservation about the experimental electrodes.

The surgery was scheduled for the first week in November. Suddenly one morning her head was being shaved, and then she was lying wide awake on an operating table, listening to the grating sound of an electric drill . . .

Now everything was done. Successfully. Their seemingly impossible hopes were all fulfilled, her epilepsy cured by a tiny, incomprehensible box full of transistors and capacitors and metal chips. They could go on now, they could live and grow together without the cancerous problem that had seemed about to destroy their marriage . . . but, ironically, the experiments that had accompanied her miraculous cure had now become a new source of division between her and David. His original opposition to the tests had only increased as they progressed. Even now, he shared none of Elizabeth's excitement at the curious results electrode 12 produced. Her continued, growing fascination with its effects only irritated him, and whenever she mentioned it he would scowl and say she shouldn't be so eager to escape reality.

Perhaps, she thought, that's all it was: just an escape, a self-induced hallucination, a temporary and hopefully benign form of madness; but whatever it might be, Elizabeth could not resist returning to it time and time again.

Those first few flashes in the testing room—the music, the horses, the sunlit morning—had been intense but absolutely mystifying. Then the experiment was halted, abruptly and with little explanation, just as a pattern seemed to be emerging.

Now her own hands held the means to spark those visions; and not even David's angry, almost petulant silences could stop her inner voyage of exploration and discovery. The journal that Dr. Garrick wanted her to keep would be regular and thorough; and she was determined that, eventually at least, that journal would contain the answers to a thousand questions that absorbed her now.

THURSDAY, NOVEMBER 27

11:00 P.M.

This was my second day at home. I didn't get a chance to start
this until now, what with moving back into the apartment and everything, but there wasn't much to report yesterday anyway. I
only tried the electrode once, at two volts; there was an image of a
book, and my eyes just stayed on the page. The print was small
and close together, and it felt like a fairly heavy book, with
leather binding: a lot like the old first editions in rare book stores,
only crisp and new-smelling, and not faded at all. I couldn't see
the title, but it seemed to be some old-fashioned novel or other,
and it was printed in English.

I tried to be a little more consistent today, and tried out my
"new toy" three times. The first time was at ten this morning; I
didn't get anything at all, like that time in the lab when the
whole effect seemed to have disappeared.

Then I tested it again around two in the afternoon, and everything was back to "normal" (?!). I seemed to be sitting alone in a
small but elegantly furnished room, with a bow-window overlooking a little garden. There was an old-fashioned chaise longue in
the middle of the room, and two or three fragile-looking chairs.

The whole place had a sort of pleasant, lived-in feel about it. It
was comfortably cluttered with all kinds of random objects, but
not really messy. There were five or six silver trinket boxes around,
full of shells and miniature china things, and in one corner there
was a big rush work-basket lined in blue satin and stuffed with
scraps of different kinds of cloth.

There didn't seem to be any one prevailing style; everything
was just sort of mixed together, very colorful, but it all fit somehow. A couple of the things in the room looked oriental: There
was a tea table that might have been Japanese, and a miniature
ivory pagoda, and at one side there was a tall embroidered screen
with storks and cranes in the design.

I was sitting on the chaise longue with a pillow on my lap and a
box of different-sized pins beside me. On the pillow itself there
was a large piece of paper with a rough sketch of a little girl holding a bunch of flowers. I was filling in the details of the sketch by
using various pins to prick tiny holes in the paper. At one point I
picked up a little tool, set in a bone handle, that had a wheel with

sharp points along the edge; I rolled that along the paper to make the outline of the girl's dress.

That was all. I kept the stimulus going for several minutes, but nothing else happened. I checked back about four this afternoon, and it was the same scene, except that the pinprick picture was almost finished, and the door to the room was just closing as I turned the transmitter on. There was a tray of sandwiches, with the crusts cut off, on the tea table; so I guess it must have been someone bringing those in.

FRIDAY, NOVEMBER 28

10:30 P.M.

Checked the electrode seven times today. The reason I did it so much was that I started out at ten-thirty this morning, and again there was no response at all, just blankness and silence; so I decided to try it again every half hour, and see if I could find out when it "switches on" or whatever.

There was nothing at eleven or eleven-thirty, but when I checked back at noon, there it was, in full color and stereophonic sound.

I was standing beside that big canopied bed that I mentioned in the lab, getting dressed. I don't know if this "other me" is a late sleeper, or what; but anyway, it definitely seems as if all those blank spaces just mean that I'm asleep.

Unless something changes, I'll make it a habit to do all my testing in the afternoon now, and make do with game shows or something in the morning!

The clothes I was putting on were just as "costumey" as the things I've been wearing all the other times, only this time I got a look at the underwear. All I can say is, there certainly was a lot of it.

I got a better look at the bedroom I was in this time, too: It's very airy, light, and sunny. The bed is huge, covered with a canopy and surrounded by draped curtains, all in white. There were matching drapes on the windows, and the walls were covered with a simply patterned paper, red and pink ribbons on a light cream background.

There wasn't a lot of other furniture in the room: just a chest of drawers, a wardrobe, and a couple of small chairs and tables. The room was quite large, with a very high ceiling, and the lack of too much furniture really gave it an open, spacious feeling. There were some chalk and water color landscapes hung on the walls; one of them looked like it might be of the Alps or the Rockies, and another one was definitely Italian.

It's still bothersome, not being able to look where I want to look; I miss a lot of visual details that way, but no matter how hard I try, I still can't force my eyes to move where I want them to. The pattern of attention makes it seem as if I've seen these same places and objects a thousand times before, and have long since stopped bothering to look at things I know so well. I do the same thing in my own apartment; but, damn it, I *do* know everything in here! None of these other scenes are even vaguely familiar to me; there's no sensation of *déjà vu*, or anything like that. Maybe I can work on building up the strength of my curiosity; but in the meantime, I'll have to be content with seeing whatever happens to be in front of my eyes, as if somebody else was aiming them, like a movie camera.

All this has made me very conscious of the limits of vision: When you're trying hard to make out some details about an object at the edges of your sight, and you *can't* look directly at it, you realize how narrow the eyes' field of focus really is. This is particularly maddening to me, because I'm trying to look at these images with a set designer's eye, to get as much information about them as possible. I'm not used to being forcibly limited in that respect. Oh, well. I ought to be used to frustrations by now, but I'm not.

When I tried the electrode again around two-thirty this afternoon, I was walking through still another room, a huge one this time. There was a massive Persian carpet on the floor, and enough furniture to fill a large antique store, but it wasn't crowded at all. The walls were covered in fluted silk, with gilt molding around them. There was a tremendous fireplace with a beautiful white marble chimney-piece. A large, gold-framed mirror was hung over the mantel, but I was too far away to see it closely.

At one end of the room were three floor-to-ceiling windows that looked as though they opened out onto a terrace. There were several separate groupings of sofas, ottomans, and chairs (Chippendale? Hepplewhite?), most of them upholstered in green damask. The curtains were silk damask, too, with a deep gold fringe. There was a grand piano, with a *harp* next to it, but I'm sure this was a different piano than the one I was playing that time in the hospital, on the first electrode test. There was also a splendid chandelier hung at least fifteen feet from the ceiling, with fresh candles in it, and well over a dozen paintings on the walls. I didn't get a good enough look to be sure (damn!), but I could swear I saw at least two Raphaels and one Tintoretto.

I was only in that room for about twenty seconds, walking through. Then I opened a door and went into the same room that I saw yesterday, where I was making the pinprick picture. I checked back twice again later, hoping to get another chance to see those paintings; but both times I was still in that little boudoir, reading the last few chapters of the book I saw the day before yesterday. I still don't know what the novel is, but it drives me crazy to read so slowly.

I was about to try once again, late this afternoon, but David came home just as I picked up the transmitter. He saw me with it, and asked if I was in any trouble, if I was starting to have a seizure. I told him I wasn't, and he just gave me a tight look and stormed into the kitchen to mix a drink. As I'm writing this, he's gone to sleep.

Over dinner, I tried to talk with him about what I'd seen today, to describe that incredible room with all the silk and paintings, but he got very gruff and said he didn't want to hear "any of that crap." I don't understand why this upsets him so much, but until he calms down about it I think I'd better keep my little "excursions" between me and this journal. And Dr. Garrick, and whoever else ends up reading it.

SATURDAY, NOVEMBER 29

SOMETIME AFTER MIDNIGHT (*so I guess it's really Sunday*)

David came home too early this afternoon for me to get any tests done. He was very tense, and I think he could tell that I was eager to try out the transmitter again, although neither of us brought the subject up.

To take the edge off the evening, he suggested that we go out to dinner and a movie; but the dinner was only mediocre, and the movie turned out to be worse. So much for trusting Pauline Kael.

We ended up at P. J. Clarke's, just drinking and not talking very much. I hate it when we get like that; I can't even get drunk along with him, because I've never been allowed to have that much alcohol, what with the epilepsy.

Question for Dr. Garrick: Can I get safely smashed now that I've got these little magic supertransistor things in my head? As long as I stay sober enough to find my transmitter? Pretty please?

SUNDAY/MONDAY, NOVEMBER 30/DECEMBER 1

1:30 A.M.

David was impossible today, as he always is when he's hung over. He can be such a baby. Sometimes that's endearing, but most of the time it isn't. He never acted like that when we were first living together, or even during the first year or two after we were married; I guess it dates from when my epilepsy started getting to be more of a problem than we thought it would be. But that's supposed to be all over now, and nothing has changed!

To be fair, I have to admit that maybe it's my fault, partially. We've only made love twice since I got home from the hospital, and neither time was as great as we'd been building ourselves up to believe it would be. And, too, I guess I've been kind of neglecting him in general; but I still don't see why he can't accept my interest in the effects of the electrode, why he doesn't share my curiosity. Maybe he thinks I'm making it all up, like that Dr. Crandon did; or maybe he thinks I'm going crazy.

For all I know, maybe I *am* going crazy. I certainly can't explain what's happening to me, and neither can anybody else. I try not to think too much about causes and explanations right now; that can wait until I know a little more, subjectively, about what it is that I'm experiencing. Till then, I'll just think of it as an entertaining dream, or maybe my mind's way of making up for all those LSD hallucinations I was never able to try.

We stayed home all day today, reading the Sunday *Times* and watching a couple of specials on Channel 13. I didn't get a chance to try the electrode again until after David had fallen asleep, around midnight. This was the first time I'd ever done it at night, so I was really curious to see what happened.

What happened was I ate dinner. Or part of it, anyway; I only stayed around for a bite or two of veal, because I was worried that David would wake up and get mad because I was using the transmitter.

The food seemed to be delicious, and there was a lavish amount of it; again, though, I couldn't help but see everything as if it were somebody else's fancy stage set that I was checking out; so I paid more attention to the surroundings than to what I was eating.

I was in a dining room, of appropriate scale to match the size of that roomful of paintings that I saw on Friday. There were five people at the table besides me, one of them the same man that I saw in the horseback riding and picnic scene. The other people were two couples, one in their fifties, another in their early thirties; I've never seen any of them before. Everyone, including me, was formally dressed, in nineteenth-century period clothes, as always. I'm still trying to place the decade, but offhand I'd say it was somewhere between 1850 and 1880.

There were also at least three servants, two women and one man, all in uniform, and all ostentatiously busy with cut-crystal wine decanters and serving dishes and carving utensils. When I first "tuned in," everyone was laughing at some joke I'd apparently missed, and then for the rest of the thirty seconds or so that I was there we were all concentrating on our eating. All except the servants, of course.

The furniture was all massive, heavy mahogany. Aside from the large table and solid chairs, there was an imposing sideboard that seemed to dominate the whole room. The walls were covered with dark crimson paper, and the curtains were maroon with gold trim. There was a carpet—Brussels, I think—and an odd but probably logical touch: a large square of linen cloth underneath the table, apparently there to catch dropped crumbs and spilled wine.

I find it interesting that I always seem to be waking up around noon, and that I was in the middle of dinner when it was actually after midnight. Could this mean that I'm maintaining a constant time difference in these flashes, one that's always off by a few hours from the actual time of day?

I hope to find out more about all these things this week, while David is back in his office. That is, if I can manage to do something besides sit in that boudoir and read and make pictures!

Resolved: that, starting tomorrow, I will make a *firm* (firmer?) effort to take control of this weird dream. After all, it's my dream, isn't it?

MONDAY, DECEMBER 1

11:15 P.M.

Well, maybe it isn't my dream, after all. At least, not mine to direct as I see fit. I have a terrific headache tonight, but that's about the only tangible result of my "firm efforts" today to go where I wanted to go and look at what I wanted to see. For the moment, I'm going to give up on that resolution and go back to just seeing where events take me. As if I had a choice.

Mindy called this morning. She wanted me to come over for coffee and a chat, but I told her I still wasn't quite up to doing much socializing. I felt a little guilty after I finished talking to her, so I spent part of the morning phoning various friends and promising that we'd all get together soon. I was dying to tell some of them, especially Mindy, about what's been happening; but Dr. Garrick said absolutely no one was to know about it, so I didn't say anything.

I started checking out the electrode at two this afternoon. This time I was sitting in the little garden that I'd noticed from the boudoir window. I wasn't doing much of anything, just sitting there, watching a pair of humming birds dart around among the flowers. It was quite warm, and sunny again. I kept hoping I'd turn my face up to the sky and bask in that bright sunlight, but I spent the whole time sitting under a lacy parasol, with my face fully shaded, as if the sun were something to be avoided instead of relished. I also would've preferred to be wearing a bikini, or at least something short and backless, but I just sat there and sweltered, covered up in layer on layer of velvet and chintz. I could feel the sweat trickling down my sides and back, but I never even loosened a button.

In any case, it was nice to be warm and outside. The streets of New York are covered in an early slush right now, and we've been doing Con Ed a favor by holding the thermostat down to sixty-eight. If my mind is structuring some kind of summer fantasy in response to the cold, though, I do wish it would at least take me swimming.

I tried again around five-thirty, just before David got home. Everything was blank, like it usually is in the mornings. I can only guess that my alter ego was taking an afternoon nap. After sitting in the sun in all those clothes, I wouldn't be surprised.

David and I had a quiet dinner in, and then he worked on some blueprints while I read. No arguments tonight; but then, no great love scenes, either. After he went to sleep I tried the electrode once more; this time I was playing backgammon with the "mysterious mustached man," as I've come to think of him. He looks to be about thirty-five or thirty-six, tall and slender, with thick, dark hair and very striking eyes. I'm certain that I've never seen him anywhere before, although I can't say that I really *mind* having him around in this dream. The backgammon set was beautiful, with inlaid ivory points and solid ivory pieces. David rolled over and seemed to be waking up in the middle of the game, though, so I never found out whether I won or lost.

TUESDAY, DECEMBER 2

11:30 P.M.

TODAY I SPOKE! In all this time, I've been quiet as a mouse every time I happened to turn on the transmitter, but this afternoon I pressed the button and immediately I was talking, in midsentence. Not that I was saying much of anything; I was speaking to one of the maids I saw fluttering around the dinner table the other night, giving her the third degree about some gold brooch that I claimed to have lost. We were both speaking with noticeable British accents: hers sort of a restrained cockney, mine very crisp and correct. She seemed to be embarrassed and a little scared, all "Yes, mum" and "No, mum"; but finally she suggested a certain box that it might be in, and I abruptly changed my tone, saying "That's a possibility, Marie. I'll look there later."

If it had been someone else talking, I would've gotten the impression that they had suddenly remembered where they'd put the thing, but didn't want to admit outright that they'd been wrong. I didn't feel any of that, though, no sudden memory and no guilty pangs; my mouth was moving, and I could feel the words vibrating in my throat and sounding in my ears, but nothing I was saying had any connection to my thought processes. It was like my mind was completely separate from the rest of me, and my body, including my voice, was acting entirely on its own—the same pattern I've noticed before, but it was much more striking today when it was combined with actually *speaking*.

This is all very confusing; even in my dreams, whenever I do or say something, it's *me* doing it . . . but this all seems like there's some entirely different person involved, and I'm just . . . along for the ride, so to speak. A silent partner.

I've been trying to avoid thinking about the possible implications of what's been happening to me; but they get more and more difficult to ignore as this continues. It's hard to be as blasé and objective about it as I was in the beginning. I don't know what to think, and I'm almost afraid to try.

WEDNESDAY, DECEMBER 3

11:00 P.M.

I tried to have a serious talk with David about all this tonight. He got peeved again, and told me I was just trying to escape into a fantasy, that I was avoiding the responsibility of working out my life now that I don't have the epilepsy as an excuse and a crutch to lean on. He said I was making up for years of lost daydreaming time, but that I was getting to be as bad about it as any hippie acid freak.

I guess that's basically the conclusion I've been keeping at the back of my own mind ever since the experiments started: that the electrode just hit some kind of hallucination center, or sent me off into a long wish-fulfillment kind of fantasy—there's no denying that everything has been extremely pleasant so far—but I'm finding it more difficult to relax with that assumption. This doesn't seem like any kind of dream, waking or sleeping, that I've ever had before; and it doesn't sound like any drug experiences I've read or heard about. Everything is just too damned *consistent*, for one thing; and it also doesn't fit with that weird kind of mind/body separation that I feel every time. I don't think Dr. Garrick was ever comfortable with the "hallucination" explanation, either; but there's no way that I can get across to him, or to David, or to anybody else, how totally, constantly *real* these experiences feel to me. I've had a few dreams that were almost this strong, but never any that continued so long or came back again and again this way.

Unfortunately, that doesn't leave me with much else in the way of rational explanations. I'm sure Mindy would take it all as proof of some past life or something, but I've never really been able to believe in reincarnation, or time warps, or doors into other dimensions, or any of the rest of that kind of thing.

Which boils it down to one thing: that I'm insane. Stark, raving nuts.

But I'm not. I *know* I'm not.

THURSDAY, DECEMBER 4

11:00 P.M.

The hell with it. Whatever's happening is happening, and I'm not going to run away from the most interesting thing that's ever happened to me in my life just because I can't figure it out right away. Even if I am crazy, I want to find out as much about my craziness as I can, if only so I can describe my symptoms better when they put me away one of these days soon. And anyway, how do you draw the line, how do you define what's insanity and what isn't? Whatever the explanation, there's no getting around the fact that when I push that button, I am, quite literally, "out of my mind." The only question is: Just whose mind am I in?

Actually, that's not quite accurate; whether this "other me" is a hallucination, or a dream, or some past life that I've lived, or whatever, it's not a *mind* I find myself in, but another body. I've been totally unable to connect with any set of memories or emotions or thoughts other than my own. Every physical sensation comes through clearly and fully, but that's it.

Today I tried something new: Instead of just holding the button down for fifteen or twenty seconds at four volts, I tried setting it at two volts and leaving it on for about ten minutes. That way, while the images and sounds were all clear and identifiable, they were only partially superimposed on the things I was really seeing here in the apartment (when my eyes were open). Nothing out of the ordinary happened during that time—I was just walking around in the garden, picking flowers—but I was able to drink a cup of coffee here while I did that, and pay attention to both actions. If I really want to find out what's going on in these flashes, it might be best to keep doing it that way: pressing the button down for as long as my thumb will hold out, and only turning it up to four volts if something interesting starts to happen.

David apologized for the things he said last night, but then he started talking about how we should get back to spending more time with our friends, and he suggested that I start planning a big Christmas party. Obviously, his opinions about all this haven't changed; but he is honestly concerned about me, so it's hard to stay mad at him, no matter what he thinks of the experiments. I told him I'd get together with Mindy soon and that I'd think about the party.

FRIDAY, DECEMBER 5

5:20 P.M.

I've got to write this fast, because David will be home in a few minutes, but I couldn't wait until tonight to put it down on paper.

I looked into a mirror today.

Only it wasn't me.

I was holding the button down for as long as I could again, at two volts. It started off very innocuously, I was doing some kind of shell arrangement in the cluttered little boudoir; but then all of a sudden I felt myself standing up and walking into that larger room, the one with all the paintings, so I turned the voltage up to the highest setting. I walked right past the paintings, though, and headed for the white marble mantelpiece set in the center of one of the long side walls. When I got there I picked up a shell that was on the mantelpiece, as if I'd remembered it was there and planned to add it to the arrangement I'd been making; but as I reached to pick it up, I could feel my eyes move to glance at the mirror, and then they held there for at least twenty or thirty seconds and my hands moved up to straighten a lock of hair that was out of place. I didn't care about the hair, though; I was looking at the face, and the eyes that were looking back at me weren't the same eyes I was seeing with. I had—*she*, whoever she was—had long ash-blond hair done up into a cluster of ringlets, and a light, smooth complexion. Her cheekbones were high and delicate, and her face was a slender oval, with full lips and a small, straight nose. She was very lovely; but she definitely wasn't me, or anyone I've ever seen.

The eyes were the strangest part—not that they were strange in and of themselves, they were a deep green and quite attractive— but I've never experienced anything so unreal as that, looking at those completely unfamiliar eyes and yet . . . looking at them from *within* them.

The face in the mirror didn't show the slightest sign of surprise or confusion. It was as if, as far as . . . *she* was concerned, she had no idea that I was there.

"There." Inside her head. Behind her eyes. O God, please, what is happening to me?

David will be coming in the door any minute now, and I have to put this back in my dresser drawer before he gets here. We have tickets for a play tonight; a friend of mine did the sets, and it's his first big break. But I don't want to go. I just want to have a chance to think.

SATURDAY/SUNDAY, DECEMBER 6/7

2:00 A.M.

David insisted that we have dinner and go dancing tonight with a friend of his from the office, Bill Hartwell, and his wife, Sandra. David really seems intent on keeping me occupied, but I wasn't able to relax anymore than I did at the play on Friday night. Craig's sets for that were magnificent, but I just couldn't concentrate, and we didn't even go backstage afterward.

I'd only met David's friend Bill twice before tonight, and I'd never met his wife. They must have thought I was terribly reserved, because I don't think I spoke a dozen sentences the whole evening. I guess they know about the operation, although they didn't mention it; but I'm sure David hasn't mentioned anything about the experiments to them.

The only thing that held my attention at all was Sandra; she doesn't actually resemble the woman whose face I saw in the mirror Friday afternoon, but she does have hair like hers. I kept watching her all evening, watching her dance and drink and smoke and talk . . . I suppose I've always noticed other girls and women, watched the way they looked or dressed or carried themselves; all women do that, and men notice other men, too. But tonight I concentrated on thinking about what it would be like to *be* Sandra Hartwell, or Mindy, or David, or any other person. It really struck me that there truly is a whole separate pattern of awareness and perception in everyone's brain; that other people have similar but totally disparate and distinct subjective feelings, exactly the way I do.

That's so obvious that it seems trivial, and yet that knowledge has never been 100 per cent *real* to me before. I guess almost everybody operates on the basic premise that they're the one and only true individual in the whole universe. We're all solipsists at heart, just waiting to have our inner convictions confirmed by our own personal version of Twain's Mysterious Stranger.

But all of a sudden, I find those automatic feelings challenged, if not destroyed. I've made—somehow, I've *really made*—the absolute and quintessential leap between realities, between one isolated self and another: the leap that Sartre dreamed of, and Buber, and Kierkegaard.

I have looked through someone else's eyes. Touched with another's hands. Tasted through her mouth.

I have been—and can be again, whenever I choose—*two*.

And I don't even know who she is.

MONDAY, DECEMBER 8

11:30 P.M.

I went—*she* went—shopping today. There were so many intriguing sights and sounds that I can't possibly describe them all. I must have held that button down for a total of an hour or more, in five- and ten-minute stretches.

She took the young maid, Marie, along as a companion, maybe to make up for half accusing her of stealing that brooch the other day. The girl seemed ecstatic at the opportunity, and somewhat nervously proud to be out and about in such high style.

It started with a closed carriage ride over cobblestone streets, past rows and rows of immaculate white town houses, all very similar from the outside; but I'm sure they all concealed interiors at least as elegant as the one I've been getting to know these past few days. We passed by a large, well-kept park, but there didn't seem to be many people around. There was a heavy iron gate at the entrance to the park, so it may not have been for public use at all. Then we rode past an enormous enclosed and guarded building and out onto a long, wide, and shaded mall, and I knew exactly where we were.

London.

I've never been there, but I've seen enough photographs of Buckingham Palace to recognize it. There were no cars on the streets, only other carriages and horse-drawn hansom cabs, and I never saw a single building over four or five stories high. I refuse to speculate on what it means, but this was definitely not the London of the 1970s; probably not even of this century.

I've been more or less assuming that since the beginning, because of the clothes and the accents, but it was almost overpowering to have it confirmed on such a dramatic scale. I'd practically begun to think that there was nothing outside that house and garden that I've been in; now I know that there's a whole city out there, a whole country . . . a whole world. But which world? And whose?

Anyway, the carriage finally pulled up in front of a building that had a sign identifying it as "Mr. Thomas Liberty's Regent Street Emporium." The young girl, Marie, and I (damn it, I can't stop saying that!) got out and went inside the place. It was a large building, almost as big as one of the major Fifth Avenue department stores; but there were no escalators or elevators, and the lights were all coal-oil lamps, hung in profusion from the ceiling. There were rows and rows of merchandise, all of it fascinating to me: thousands of different types of buttons, and molded candles, and complicated toys, and hundreds of other things. There were no racks of clothes, though, and no mannequins; I guess there wasn't any such thing as ready-to-wear yet.

I didn't get a chance to see as much as I wanted, because we headed straight for one section that was done up as an oriental bazaar. It was full of figurines, and ivory chess sets, and silk screens, and huge displays of beautiful fans, and painted bamboo and wicker furniture. I (or she, or we, or whoever) bought a small but perfect carved teak box.

Then we went back outside, where the carriage was still waiting (nobody seems to pay any attention to double parking here, either!). It took us on to another, smaller shop, not three blocks from the first. This was a millinery shop, and my "hostess" spent half an hour or so looking at hats. This gave me a chance to look in a mirror again, at length this time. She seems to be about my own age, and awfully sure of herself: Her eyes are very strong, very knowing.

Her eyes! I still can't get used to seeing them in a mirror, particularly when she's looking straight at them, too; I get a shiver of fear that I'm going to get lost in some kind of perceptual black hole, a well of internalized infinity . . . or, worse, that she's going to suddenly, somehow, *see me in there*, looking back at her, looking with her, looking into and from and through her deepest self.

Friday afternoon, I wrote that I wanted a chance to think about all this, to try to reach some definite conclusion or at least a workable theory. Now the only way I can go on is to purposely *not* think about it. There are too many strange implications, none of which I like or can accept or feel comfortable with.

I wish I could talk to David.

TUESDAY, DECEMBER 9

11:45 P.M.

I have a name!

An invitation to a dinner party was delivered to the house this afternoon; it was addressed to "Mrs. Jenny Curran, 24 Eaton Place, Belgravia, London."

Jenny, Jenny Curran. *Mrs.* Jenny Curran. That, therefore, implies that I have not only a name, but a husband as well; I assume (I hope!) it's that same man I woke up in bed with when we were doing the experiments in the hospital.

The only reason I happened to catch that piece of mail was because of a trick I started using today: I set the voltage dial on the transmitter at two volts, and put a piece of tape over the activator button, so it would stay on without my having to hold it down. Everything that happens ("to Jenny," I can say now!) keeps going on in the background, and I can turn it up whenever something worthwhile, like the arrival of that invitation, happens. I spent most of the afternoon practicing walking around and doing minor chores and stuff while I continued to "monitor" Jenny's perceptions. It'll still take some getting used to, but I don't think I'll have any real problem. The only slip-up today was when both of us happened to be walking through a room at the same time; I focused on the room Jenny was seeing, instead of the one in my apartment, and ran right into the living-room wall! After a few days' practice, I think I can keep the two sorted out, though.

WEDNESDAY, DECEMBER 10

MIDNIGHT

I used the tape on the transmitter button again all this afternoon. Nothing particularly interesting happened, except that I finally got to define the daily time difference. At one point, Jenny was looking directly at a big rosewood grandfather clock in the drawing room; it was a beautiful piece of machinery, with a color-fully painted extra dial behind the clock face, one that apparently revolves to display the changing phases of the moon. Anyway, it was eleven-fifteen in the morning for her, and it was about five till three for me. That means we're out of synch by approximately three hours and forty minutes. Plus a hundred years or so. But I promised myself not to think about that.

THURSDAY, DECEMBER 11

11:40 P.M.

It occurred to me today to test the range of the transmitter; I put the tape over the button while Jenny was having breakfast, and set the unit down in the far corner of our bedroom. Then I walked into the kitchen, as far from the bedroom as I could get. There wasn't any change; the image and the sound (and the taste of the grapefruit) all remained just as clear as they are when I'm holding the transmitter in my hand or when I leave it in my pocket. I tried putting it in a closed drawer, under a pile of clothes, and it was still as strong as ever.

Just out of curiosity, I tried leaving the apartment entirely; the effect shut off when I stepped into the elevator, and then came back again, faintly, when I got off in the lobby of our building. It faded away completely when I'd walked about two blocks down the street. Then I suddenly panicked at the thought of a seizure and not being able to get to the transmitter, so I hurried back home. Apparently, though, it works for a distance of at least a few hundred yards; I guess it was the metal in the elevator that blocked the radio signal.

This means that, if I can get used to acting perfectly normal while Jenny's experiences are superimposed on mine at the two-volt level, then I can keep monitoring them even when other people are around, and no one will ever know that I'm not "all there" (love the innuendo!). If I'm careful enough, I might even be able to leave it on after David comes home from work, instead of shutting off every day at five-thirty my time and around 1:50 P.M. Jenny's time. Then I could start seeing what happens to her in the evenings, instead of being stuck with that same four or five hours in the morning and the early afternoon, when the most exciting thing that ever happens is a shopping trip.

Maybe I'll even try that tomorrow; just for a few minutes, to see if David notices anything. If he knew what I was doing, he'd be terribly upset.

FRIDAY, DECEMBER 12

11:30 P.M.

Well, I did it; I fooled David. That sounds horrible, as if I were doing something malicious or really sneaky to him; but it's not that way at all. I have a perfect right to see this thing through to my own satisfaction, no matter what he thinks. He's not the one who's been through all this, from the epilepsy to the surgery to everything else; I am. I'm sure he thinks I'm getting hooked on this somehow, but I know myself better than that. This isn't any kind of obsession or sickness with me, it's just an intellectual fascination; and it's not just for my own idle curiosity, either, it's for a serious scientific purpose. Or is that rationalizing?

I only checked the electrode a couple of times this afternoon; by now I know Jenny's morning schedule pretty well, and there don't seem to be many real surprises (How strange that this has become so natural for me; this time last month, just getting an image, any image at all, was a surprise. Now I'm actually starting to get bored with hanging around the house every day!).

David came home on schedule, around five forty-five. We talked about a new project he's been working on for the West Side, and neither of us mentioned my experiences with the transmitter at all. Then I started dinner, and while he was making the salad I went into the bedroom and taped down the button on the transmitter at two volts. I didn't say anything when he wanted a third martini before dinner; I figured it might make him less apt to notice if I got confused or stumbled over a chair or something.

Whether it was his drinks or my acting ability, he didn't notice a thing. The transmitter just sat there in the dresser drawer, beaming its little waves at my brain, all through dinner. Jenny was having tea served in the garden, and I got the giggles as I tried to alternate her sips of tea with my bites of steak, but David just laughed too and asked if I'd sneaked another drink myself. I told him I had.

At one point, Jenny popped a sweet pastry in her mouth while I was chewing a mouthful of asparagus. I could feel both my mouth and her mouth moving at the same time, and the tastes and textures of the two foods were all mixed together; it was a disgusting combination, but an interesting sensation. I just sort of picked at my food after that.

It was pleasant, though, to look out the window at the sleet falling on our terrace-*cum*-fire escape, and be able to close my eyes for a moment and have a clear, uninterrupted view of Jenny's garden in the summer sunlight, with bumblebees buzzing around the violets.

I still wish I could know what's going on in Jenny's mind; even if it turns out that she's only a fantasy, a figment of my own imagination, I've really come to think of her as an authentic, separate person. In a way, she's literally the closest friend I've ever had; at least, I've certainly never been right inside someone else's head before, if you could call that "friendship." But I'd like to have access to her memories, to her emotions and opinions and thoughts about the future. Maybe it's crazy of me to assume that those things exist at all, that she's a separate entity with her own mind; but I do have a strong feeling that she is, in *some* way or other, a different person, in spite of our partially shared perceptions. I know that some of her reactions haven't been what mine would be: the way she reads, for example, and some of the things that she chooses to look at or ignore, and her aloof manner with servants in her house. I feel that there's an awful lot that I still have to learn about her and her life, and I wish I could learn it by somehow communicating with her directly, instead of just spying on her world through her eyes and ears. It does feel like spying, too; she doesn't ever seem to notice that I'm there "with her" at all.

Maybe if I try hard enough, I can make more direct contact with her. I wonder how she'd feel about that—knowing that she's not alone.

SATURDAY/SUNDAY, DECEMBER 13/14

1:00 A.M.

David was home again this afternoon, completing the blueprints for his West Side project. I pretended to spend the day reading, but I actually had the transmitter on most of the time. I kept thinking, "Here I am, Jenny, here I am" as hard as I could; but she just went right on with the things she was doing, and never reacted. Maybe I'll have to wait until during the week, when I can go back to four volts.

I shut it off during dinner (we went out to Sign of the Dove, to celebrate David's finishing his design), and then turned it back on when we came home, about ten-thirty. Jenny was laughing and talking to the "man with the mustache." It seemed as if *he* had just come home, too; he was telling her something about a shipment of porcelain from Holland, and it sounded like he was discussing his business day, but concentrating on the parts that she might find interesting or funny.

He's apparently involved in import/export, and from the way he was phrasing things, he either manages or owns his own company. Judging from the looks of that house, he owns it. Oh, yes, he also made some remarks about things that had happened "at the country place," so I'm sure I was right about the piano that time in the lab being in a different house.

There wasn't much more information to be gotten from their conversation; mostly they just talked about people they knew, and they seemed to know a lot of people. I kept waiting for her to call him by name, but she never did, not while I was there. They seemed to be very comfortable together, very informal and familiar with each other. Jenny's a lucky lady, real or not; her husband's awfully handsome, and he has a good, quick wit, although some of the stories he told didn't mean anything to me.

I bet David would even be a little jealous if he could see him.

MONDAY, DECEMBER 15

11:30 P.M.

Yesterday was a typical lazy Sunday, just lying around the apartment reading the paper as usual. David wanted to go play tennis at the indoor courts on First Avenue, but I didn't feel up to it.

I put off using the transmitter until late last night. I'm sure David doesn't notice when I have it on at two volts, but I left it off anyway, just in case he's noticed me seeming to drift or anything recently. I thought it might be good for myself to take a day off, too.

David went to bed early, though, and I couldn't sleep, so I finally turned it on around midnight. They were eating dinner, and I was already stuffed myself, so I switched it back off and watched an old Fred Astaire and Ginger Rogers movie on TV. Then I went to bed, but I still couldn't get to sleep, so I rolled over quietly and tried the electrode again a little after two.

I've never turned it on that late before, and the result was a little embarrassing, in a way: Jenny was taking a bath. I've never seen her naked, and for some reason I was too fascinated to be discreet and turn the transmitter off. She was in one of those old, funny-shaped tubs, with no faucets and no shower attachment; I guess the servants must have had to fill it up with hot water. I've gotten used to taking showers in the past few years, and I'd almost forgotten how relaxing a leisurely hot bath can be.

It was kind of eerie, touching another woman's body like that, and at the same time feeling the touch both on my fingers and my flesh—touching myself-but-not-myself. She has a beautiful figure, with long, slim legs, and breasts that are slightly larger than mine, but firm and well shaped. She really seemed to luxuriate in the bath, and to genuinely enjoy touching herself; there were all sorts of delicately scented oils and lotions that she massaged into her skin, and the bathroom itself was very plush, full of ferns and mirrors and candles.

When she got out of the bath she slowly powdered her whole body, looking at herself in the mirror all the while. Somehow I couldn't bring myself to leave the scene, to back away and give her the privacy she thought she already had.

I've never quite been able to relate to my own body in the way she seemed to; I guess it was the epilepsy that made it difficult to be proud of my femininity, to think of myself in that way and to really like my body. It always seemed almost like an enemy, something separate from the real me, something that might betray me at any moment and turn very ugly and spastic and be disgusting to other people, strangers even. But Jenny acted like she was . . . *friends* with her body. It felt good.

While she was powdering herself, there was a voice from the next room, asking her if she was almost finished. She answered back, "Right away, Phillip," so I suppose that's her husband's name, Phillip. Phillip Curran. She must have been getting ready to go to bed with him.

I shut the transmitter off then, but it took me a long time to get to sleep. When I finally did, I dreamed about swimming in a clear blue river, and then lying warm and naked on the grassy riverbank. I looked up and saw a man standing over me, looking at me, his hair haloed by the sun; and it was Jenny's husband, Phillip. But I wasn't Jenny in the dream, I wasn't in her body. I was me.

I think I'd better type these entries tomorrow, and call Dr. Garrick.

Peter Garrick had a lot on his mind. Christmas was coming, and he still hadn't started the shopping for his wife and their three children. Two of the children were in that age period where it's impossible to know from week to week what might make them happy: Should he get Karen toys, or a stereo system, or a separate phone line? Would Paul be satisfied with a short-wave radio, or was he old enough for a Kawasaki?

These questions were a nagging, constant undercurrent to Garrick's preoccupation with the Austin case. His paper on that was almost complete now, and it would appear in the *Journal of Electroencephalography and Clinical Neurophysiology* immediately after he had presented it at the conference that was now scheduled for January 6 at UCLA. As he had promised Crandon, the paper concentrated on the fear center electrode. He had already planned his evasive tactics in case anyone pressed him for more information about the passing reference to "brief, ill-defined hallucinatory responses" at the twelfth electrode site.

The films, tapes, and transcripts of that portion of the experiment had already been destroyed. Of the few who had seen them, the only person who might disclose their contents to outsiders was the student, Gene Templeton; but Garrick was confident that Crandon could exercise enough academic pressure to keep him quiet. Even if he did speak out, no one would believe him; Garrick's and Crandon's denials would quickly squelch any such rumor.

Lois Beatty would be accompanying Garrick on the California trip, and that was also weighing on his mind. Should they or shouldn't they resume the affair that they had briefly enjoyed when she first joined the hospital staff? For four years now, ever since they had broken it off, he had maintained a friendly but businesslike relationship with the attractive young specialist. They had recognized that there were too many complications, too many dangers involved in continuing what they had so eagerly begun. But now, the excitement and the pressures of the Austin experiment had driven them back into a situation of closeness and mutual dependency. She was the only woman who fully understood the extremes to which he had been pushed in the past two months, who knew that he had been spinning in confusion at a crossroads that led to either professional disgrace or eminence; and it was largely her support, her understanding, that had sent him on the difficult, but manifestly proper, path. There were emotions there that couldn't be ignored, and he now felt that the outcome of the week in California had nothing to do with shoulds or shouldn'ts, but simply would they or wouldn't they. It had gone beyond cool reason, and the choice was probably no longer theirs to make.

He thought of all these things, and more, as he sat across the desk from Elizabeth Austin, skimming over the twenty-five or thirty neatly typed and bound pages she had brought for his perusal. The story they contained was ludicrous, a wild scenario for some Hollywood production of the mind: life among the upper classes in Victorian England, mysterious strangers, a voluptuous young blonde naked and bathing by candlelight . . . it was all an absurd, involved extension of the tales she'd come up with in the lab, a complicated fantasy that she actually expected him to *believe*.

He glanced up from his reading and surreptitiously looked at her again, trim and attractive in her well-tailored winter clothes. An expensive light-brown wig covered what he knew would be the still-sparse growth from her recently shaven scalp.

Neither of the obvious alternatives were fully acceptable: She had no reason to be doing this as a deliberate hoax, and his long experience with disorders of the brain told him that this earnest, composed young woman was a highly unlikely candidate for treatment by his psychiatric colleagues at Bellevue. If she were mentally disturbed, he shuddered to think of what a thorough examination would bring: This whole experiment, and, worse, his selective cover-up of its results, would be revealed. No, referring her to a psychiatrist was out of the question.

There was no apparent need for that anyway, he rationalized. This fantasy is her only departure from reality, and she seems to have it well under control. It isn't likely that she'll suddenly jump out of a third-floor window or start babbling incoherently to strangers on the street. There's no reason for anyone to think she's anything but normal; and besides, he thought, the possibility still remains that this is a purposeful attempt at fraud. A ridiculous, and unsuccessful, practical joke on him and the hospital; or an idle, if powerful, wish-fulfillment fantasy from an imaginative woman whose daydreams have been bottled up for years. It was one or the other of those, for sure.

Still, he had to tread lightly; he had to make sure that she kept this to herself, that she didn't run selling her fake or imagined "reincarnation" story or whatever to a publisher or a newspaper. Could that be her motivation? Had she planned this all along, for profit? But no, she didn't seem to be that type; her husband was moving up swiftly in the architectural field, and she herself had seemed involved and content with her work in theatrical set design. A sensational cock-and-bull story like this could wreck their careers as well as Garrick's, and she must be aware of that.

He took off his reading glasses and rubbed the bridge of his nose, where the spectacles had left two pink and tender indentations. The young woman across the desk looked up, anxious for his reaction to the journal she had given him.

"Well? What do you think, Dr. Garrick? Isn't it weird?"

He slipped his glasses back into their leather case. "Yes, Mrs. Austin, it is. Very weird, indeed. Do you have any theories of your own about these . . . events?"

She seemed to flush slightly, and looked away from his gaze. "Well, I know what my husband thinks. He thinks I'm going crazy."

"Have you discussed this with him at length? Has he read this journal?"

"No to both questions. He still doesn't want to hear anything about it. It makes him angry when I tell him I've been using the transmitter. He'd really go through the ceiling if he read those notes and knew how often and for how long I've been doing it, even when we're together and he doesn't know what's going on. But I haven't been going out of the apartment much at all, almost never by myself anymore, and I know he can tell when I'm excited or confused about something that's happened in the experiments. I almost wish he'd go ahead and start a screaming, yelling fight about it; even that would be better than his condescending silence, and that look of distaste he gets on his face."

"Perhaps you should get out more often; maybe even think about getting back to your work soon."

"I couldn't possibly get enthused about working on a play, not while all this is going on. Not until I've been able to come up with some satisfactory answers or explanations, anyway. I was hoping maybe you could help me with that."

Christ, he thought, she wants me to put a scientific seal of approval on all this! Best to try and sidestep the issue for now, not tell her what he really thought.

"Frankly, Mrs. Austin, I'm not at liberty to do that. I'm afraid I would be forced to consult some other individuals and organizations before I could discuss our theories on your case in detail."

"Do you mean the government, or something? Is that what you're talking about? Is that why you told me not to say anything about this to anybody?"

"I'm sorry, Mrs. Austin. I really can't discuss it."

She looked bewildered and a little angry. "That's the most ridiculous thing I've ever heard! What could any of this possibly have to do with the government?"

"I never said it did, Mrs. Austin. I only said I couldn't discuss the results, or their possible ramifications, at this time. But you must be aware that all forms of behavioral and perceptual modification techniques may have eventual uses that go beyond ordinary treatment of patients, or purely scientific experimentation."

"What do you mean by that? Is the Army planning to kidnap enemy soldiers and put electrodes in their heads so they'll wander around the battlefield thinking they're in nineteenth-century England? That's absurd!"

"Perhaps. At any rate, I'm afraid I simply can't discuss our theories about the effects you've been experiencing. I'm sure you understand."

"No, I don't understand, Dr. Garrick. I've trusted you from the very beginning of all this, and I'm extremely grateful to you for curing my epilepsy. Now I just want to find out what's been happening to me, and why. After all, you're the one who started it, and I'm the one it's happening to. Don't I at least deserve a straight answer?"

"Mrs. Austin, I sympathize with your curiosity and your confusion. I honestly do. For the moment, though, there's really nothing I can tell you. I appreciate your co-operation in all this, and I'm sure this journal will be of tremendous help to us. You and

your husband haven't discussed it with anyone else, have you?"
He tensed slightly as he waited for her answer.

She sighed dejectedly. "No, of course not. You told us to keep
it to ourselves, and we have. Do you have any idea of when you
might be able to tell me what you think is going on in my head?"

"Soon, I hope." His face was gravely sincere. "We haven't even
completed our own analysis of these effects yet, but when we do,
I'll try to make sure that you're among the first to know what
we've discovered."

She nodded, disappointed. "All right, whatever you say. I'll
keep up the journal, and I won't mention anything to anyone."

He rose from his chair, offering her his hand as she prepared to
leave.

"Excellent, excellent. You're making a splendid contribution to
our studies, and I'm very pleased to see that your recovery has
been so swift and thorough. Remember, if you encounter any
complications or difficulties whatsoever, I'm always here."

He thought he could detect a twist of dubious sarcasm in her
smile. "Sure. Well, if nothing goes wrong or anything, I'll see you
again in about a month, Dr. Garrick. Thanks again."

When she had left, he opened a compartment in his bookcase
and poured himself a double shot of Chivas Regal. Thinking back
over the meeting, he decided he'd handled the whole thing pretty
well.

He glanced back over a few of the pages from the journal she'd
brought him, shaking his head in amazement at what a runaway
imagination could convince itself of. As he ripped the typewritten
pages into long, thin strips, it occurred to him that sometimes a
hospital had just as much use for a paper shredder as ITT or the
White House did. Maybe they should invest in one.

Then, in one quick rush of decision, he settled on the stereo set
for Karen and the ham radio for Paul. And the week with Lois in
California for himself.

The talk with Dr. Garrick hadn't satisfied Elizabeth at all. She had hoped that she could finally talk freely to someone, and at least get some hint of a logical explanation for the things she'd been experiencing. Instead, she had been put off with what she definitely felt was a fabricated excuse. Dr. Garrick had never hinted at any government connections with this experiment before. The more she thought about it, the more she was convinced that he was simply giving her a brush-off, and one that insulted her intelligence besides. But, then, was her journal any more believable than his excuses?

Maybe that was it, she thought. Maybe he didn't believe what she'd been seeing. David didn't take it seriously, and neither had Dr. Crandon. Maybe everyone thought she was making it all up, or imagining it. She knew she wasn't making it up; but could even she be sure that it wasn't a product of an overactive imagination?

Riding home in the cab from the hospital, she took the transmitter from her purse and pressed the button again, at a full four volts. Immediately, the cab and the New York streets disappeared, and she was in the library of the London house, a high-ceilinged room dark with wood and leather, surrounded by huge shelves full of red-spined books. There was a carved-wood mantelpiece supporting a bronze candelabra and a French gilt clock. All around the room were gilt-rimmed oil lamps with green-glass shades, throwing warm circles of light on reading desks attached to thick, low-legged leather chairs.

She was sitting at a large round walnut inlaid table on a pedestal base, leafing through a travel book. There was an unmistakably masculine feel to the room, a leftover scent of brandy and cigars. As Jenny idly turned the pages, pausing over woodcuts of Rome and Florence, Elizabeth was dizzily absorbed in the recent presence of Phillip Curran, could readily imagine him wandering from shelf to shelf beneath the busts of Shakespeare, Scott, and Dante, could see him dozing in the softened glow of the burning lamps.

Her heart sped with the excitement of being an intruder, both on this obviously male domain and also within the unsuspecting mind and body of its owner's wife.

Breaking the contact, she lit a cigarette and began extracting the cab fare from her purse. No, she thought; no, my imagination couldn't be that strong.

But what, then, could be?

Elizabeth had always loved December in New York, despite the deepening cold weather. There was still a leftover autumn crispness in the air, unlike the frozen humidity of January and February, and the gradual approach of the holidays gave a sense of joyful purpose to the otherwise harried speed of life in the city. She even took a childish pleasure in the spectacle of the tree at Rockefeller Center, and the intricate displays in store windows and airline offices along Fifth Avenue. This December, though, Elizabeth seemed to be serving a self-imposed solitary confinement in her apartment.

Since the abortive meeting with Dr. Garrick, and the realization that even he probably didn't believe what she'd told him about the electrode's effects, she was determined to document those experiences as thoroughly as possible. This time, her journal would be so complete, so full of factual detail that she could have no way of making up, that he, and David, would have to take her seriously, would have to offer her their support in solving this strange riddle. For the moment, though, she knew that she would have to carry on her investigation of Jenny Curran's world alone, with no advice and no one with whom to share what she might learn.

There were also certain other reasons for her daily, almost continuous use of the electrode. Ever since that night when she had found herself sharing Jenny's luxurious, languorous experience in the warm bath amid the shimmering reflections of the candles and the ferns, she had recognized that Jenny's personality differed from her own in some basic and important ways. This other woman she had found within and yet outside herself seemed to possess a natural sensuality, an openness to personal pleasure, that Elizabeth had long ago stifled out of fear and shame and a hundred other reasons.

She couldn't forget the way Jenny had touched herself that night in the bath, caressing and savoring the responses of her own soft flesh, the oils and powders smoothing and warming every inch of her, her nipples erect beneath her own self-knowing, self-loving fingers, and then the same long hands moving firmly down between her thighs in expectation of the night to come . . . and Elizabeth had been there too, touching and being touched by Jenny, by herself, by touchingness itself, abstract and undefined: acting, yet being acted upon, leading and following, dominant and passive, a participant/observer in helpless fascination at the cliff edge of sensation and desire. Feeling, learning; feeling how to learn and learning how to feel.

And there was Phillip.

Handsome and successful, witty and gentle, strong and full of eager spirit . . . and more, still more than all the sums of all those things. There was a look of wondrous, intimate *knowing* in his eyes when he looked at her, at Jenny, at the both of them together in their divided sameness. Sometimes, she was sure that he saw *her*, saw Elizabeth, in there; that he somehow recognized that Jenny had become more than whatever she had been before . . . that there were three of them where others would see only two.

Still, Elizabeth maintained a careful discretion regarding Jenny's husband, a circumspect appreciation of his special human worth and kindness, but no more. She had come to focus her attention and her inexplicable presence on the early London evenings, over dinners alone or with the Currans' friends, over games of backgammon and chess while David checked his blueprints or the television droned unheard or a book was propped before her elsewhere eyes.

Twice now, Phillip and Jenny had impetuously embraced and kissed while Elizabeth was with them; but she had carefully avoided using the transmitter at those times when they would most likely be together in more intimate ways. That would have been . . . too strange, too much a shattering of privacy and human boundaries. Even when Elizabeth lay sleepless in the early morning hours, David lost and dreaming in the bed beside her, she forced herself to stay away, to dull her mind into an eventual, lonely sleep.

Elizabeth woke up later every morning now, the mornings being empty of everything but her own increasingly unnoticed life. Her days would typically begin at noon, with breakfast on the sunny terrace in Belgravia, and slowly build to 8:00 to 9:00 P.M., when Phillip would come home.

She was wonderfully adept now at feigning attention for David, while the hidden transmitter kept her mind where she preferred to be. She could prepare and serve a meal in the apartment while Phillip told her tales of Italy and Portugal; could mechanically respond to David's conversation while entertaining twenty guests around the splendid London dinner table.

At first, she had been terrified of using the electrode outside the apartment, but now whenever David insisted that they go to dinner or a movie she would keep the transmitter with its taped-down button in her purse, sending out a steady two-volt stimulus. No one knew or cared, and as long as she could still see David, even dimly, he would get the two of them to the restaurants and cabs and theaters, he would keep her out of danger.

David seemed to be getting used to the fact that she was often preoccupied with something else, and he never voiced a suspicion that he knew what she was really doing. Once, they had been walking through an opening at the Whitney, while Elizabeth was secretly busy with a frantic and hilarious game of French lawn tennis at the country house. She had actually started to perspire from the vicarious activity. David thought she had a fever, and insisted on taking her home.

Through all of this, she knew how much it was disrupting her relationship with David, even though he didn't know the reason for her constant quiet distance. It saddened her a little when she thought about this. They had had so many plans for what their lives would be like if the operation worked, if her epilepsy went away; but there was no way to stop now.

She was learning, through Jenny, so much that was new about herself and her ability to respond to life, in ways she'd never felt or allowed herself to feel before.

Once in a while, she remembered David's earlier accusation that she was addicted to the electrode's effects, that she was . . . how did he put it? an "electronic junkie." But that wasn't so. This wasn't something sick, like drugs; she could stop it any time she wanted to. And she would, soon, when she had learned and felt all she needed to. It was entirely her decision, she told herself; she was in complete control of the whole thing.

Just a few days more, and she'd be satisfied.

Just a few days more.

Just a few.

". . . and then of course Roger, well, he had to go and cast this new boyfriend of his opposite me, as the male lead. Which is going to be an absolute disaster, because this guy is very cute, but he isn't just pleasantly, discreetly gay: He's going to make *me* look butch!"

Elizabeth finished the last of her shrimp and tried to concentrate on Mindy's stream of off-Broadway gossip. This lunch-and-shopping trip had finally been unavoidable, after her friend had called for the fourth time, and David had answered the phone. Anyway, she really did have to get some things for Christmas.

Christmas. It was hard for her to relate to everybody else's holiday orientation; for Elizabeth, most of the past few weeks had been midsummer.

". . . at the Improv last week, and he just totally *bombed*. I mean, sometimes he can be funnier than Richard Pryor, even, but other nights his pace is completely off and he has no rapport at all. He just can't seem to establish any consistency, which of course is the main . . ."

The Oyster Bar at the Plaza was full of people, all of them busily talking and laughing and planning. Elizabeth found herself wondering how they could seem so happy, when they all had to spend their days and nights in only one world, one time, one body. Before the operation, she had always resented the fact that her epilepsy kept her from having whole sets of experiences that most people accepted as commonplace. Now, looking at the random faces in the restaurant, she was aware that she, and she alone, held the key to a fantastic reality that none of them would ever know. The others were the limited ones now, and she the exhilarated discoverer of new sensation.

". . . some *soap opera*, for God's sake. It'd be great if she could honestly see it as just a good way to pay the rent, but she really seems to think this is her true path to stardom. They've got her pregnant, so she's convinced that means at least another year on the show, but personally I think they're going to have her commit suicide . . ."

The transmitter was right there beside Elizabeth, resting safely in her purse. She longed to slip her hand in there, maybe pretend to be looking for her lighter, and press the button just once. Jenny would probably be strolling in the garden now, with the crinkly lace brushing against her legs and the smell of honeysuckle everywhere . . . but Elizabeth had promised herself she wouldn't use the electrode this afternoon, not while she was with Mindy. Besides, she'd be back in the apartment in another hour or two, and by that time Phillip would be home.

". . . and speaking of television, Larry's going on "The $20,000 Pyramid" next week. He's been rehearsing enthusiastic leaps for days, in case he wins. Charlie Curtis even loaned him a Sony VTR so he could tape himself jumping around and get it just right for the camera. Of course, those game shows hate it when you come on and say you're an actor, so he put down his occupation as 'piano mover,' and they loved that . . ."

She and Phillip—Jenny and Phillip, rather—were dining at the French Embassy tomorrow night. Phillip was completing the arrangements to import a large shipment of wine from France, and he'd probably be making a trip there sometime soon. Nothing had been decided yet, but Elizabeth hoped that she—that Jenny— could go along.

That would be a wonderful way to see Paris for the first time, she thought: to see it when the Arc de Triomphe was still new and Sacré Coeur was the highest thing on the skyline. The Eiffel Tower wouldn't even have been planned yet, and Toulouse-Lautrec would be a child. Judging from the extent and quality of the art that already hung in the London house, they would probably visit some *ateliers* in Montmartre, might even purchase a Renoir or a Dégas from the artists themselves.

". . . was really beautifully done, a masterpiece in my opinion, but of course Clive Barnes took up half the review complaining about the creaky seats and the smells from the Spanish restaurant downstairs; which has the most fabulous *paella*, by the way, you've got to . . ."

She and Phillip had gone riding again when they were at the country house last week. Now that the epilepsy was no longer an issue, Elizabeth had thought that perhaps she and David should take some horses out in Central Park soon; but that couldn't begin to compare with the racing freedom of those pathless trips across the English countryside, and she had never mentioned the idea.

The country house, she'd learned, was equally as grand as the one in London, with an entrance rimmed in exquisite carving and engraved glass panels, and an imposing hall lined with Etruscan vases. The drawing room, where she'd first been playing the piano that day in the lab, was open and airy, with six huge windows opening toward the south. There was a greenhouse full of orchids, and a shrubbery maze with a cool fountain and a wading pool at the center, set in a fleur-de-lis of daffodils and roses.

Phillip had chased her through the maze one afternoon, and she could still remember clearly how it felt to laugh and shriek with Jenny's voice, running through the moist grass on her lithe, bare legs, and the feel of Phillip's hands around her waist as he had caught her and they tumbled down together, laughing, on the crushed cushion of yellow, fragrant flowers . . .

". . . anytime soon, do you think?"

"What? Oh, I'm sorry, Mindy, I was . . . my mind was kind of drifting for a second there. What did you say?"

Her friend cocked an eyebrow at her and smiled. "Wow, you really have been off in space or somewhere this afternoon. When we were in Saks, I practically had to lead you through there by the hand so you wouldn't get lost. Are you sure you're feeling O.K.?"

Elizabeth laughed apologetically. "I'm fine, really. Positively. I've just had a lot on my mind recently, but there's nothing wrong at all. Now, what were you saying?"

"I was just wondering if you had plans to get back to work in the near future. Richard Finley's got a new production planned for the Circle in the Square, and I happen to know that he still hasn't chosen a set designer. You've worked with him before, and I think you'd have a damned good shot at the job if you went after it. I can sneak you a copy of the script if you want to make some preliminary sketches to show him."

They were interrupted by the waiter, who cleared away the remains of their lunch and set down the coffee. Elizabeth focused her attention on the steaming cup, slowly stirring in the sugar and the cream as she tried to think of what to say.

"I don't know, Mindy . . . I'm really not sure if I'm ready to get back to work yet. Not right now."

The girl across the table regarded her quizzically. "But I thought you said everything was all right, that the operation was successful and that you'd completely recovered from it."

"Well, yes . . . everything is fine. No problems. I just don't feel like committing myself to any long-range project right away. There are a lot of things I have to . . . think through, first."

Mindy looked away for a moment, taking a sip of her own coffee. When she raised her eyes again they were full of sparkling boldness.

"If I didn't know you better, Elizabeth . . ."

"What do you mean by that?"

Mindy leaned over the table, smiling conspiratorially. "You never did tell me what that surgeon was *really* like, you know."

Elizabeth was momentarily confused. "Dr. Garrick? Why, he's . . . very nice, I suppose, and a very competent doctor . . . Mindy! You've got to be kidding!"

"Let's just say that if you were anybody else I know, acting the way you have been, I'd say you had all the symptoms of a well-known condition called love. And a pretty serious case of it, too."

Despite herself, Elizabeth could feel the flush rising to her face, and she tried to cover it with a laugh. "No comment," she said with a smile, her eyes fixed on the spot where the transmitter rested in her purse. "No comment, and it's time I got back home."

". . . il faut simplement changer, en effet élever, le goût de la bourgeoisie Anglaise. Dans le vingtième siècle, chaque homme du monde préfera le vin Français."

The incomprehensible words flowed smoothly from Phillip's sculpted lips. The white-bearded man at the head of the table, resplendent in his colorful medallions and red satin sash, listened attentively, nodding and smiling from time to time. Whatever Phillip was saying, it seemed to be pleasing him.

"Et chaque femme aussi, mon cher. N'oublies nous pas, s'il te plaît."

Elizabeth felt her mouth twisting into unfamiliar patterns as Jenny spoke the meaningless phrase. Elizabeth was comfortable with the rounder, more open vowels of high-school and college Spanish, the resounding syllables of Lorca and Cervantes; the tight, almost puckered shape of French was new to her, but Jenny seemed at home with it.

"D'être sûr, madame, il serait impossible pour un homme— même votre mari—d'oublier une femme comme vous."

The bearded man must have made a joke, but one that was complimentary to Jenny, because everyone was laughing politely, and Elizabeth felt her head bob and her lips curl into an expression of amused gratitude. Then Phillip was speaking again.

"Je vous en remercie, monsieur l'ambassadeur, mais j'ai peur que ma femme sera ruiné par votre charme Française. Mais, sérieusement, c'est probable que dans l'année prochaine nous pourrons vendre cinquante milles bouteilles de . . ."

"I'm about ready for bed, honey. Want anything while I'm up?"

She opened her half-closed eyes, hastily turning a page of the book that rested, unread, in her lap. She hadn't turned a page in fifteen or twenty minutes, she realized; had David noticed?

"No, thanks. I think I'll stick with this book for a while, though; it's hard to concentrate on it, but at least maybe it'll help me doze off soon."

". . . *de la région du sud. C'est un des plus délicats* . . ."

David looked at her worriedly, but there was no hint of suspicion in his face. "Well, I hope so. You've been staying up pretty late recently. Want a Valium?"

"Not right now. I'll get one later, if I'm still awake. Maybe it's Mindy's fault, corrupting me with her night-person habits. You know what they say about 'off-Broadway babies.' "

In her vision, David seemed to be hovering above the long dinner table, behind the ghostly image of a silver-haired dowager who sat across from her. She could see him smiling, though, and she was glad to see that her little stab at a joke had lightened the mood.

"How well I know. Did you have a nice time with her yesterday?"

An efficiently Gallic servant was ladling huge helpings of fresh fruit compote into silver bowls already half filled with cognac. As he moved, his arm seemed to slice smoothly through David's waist, and he happened to smile and say "*Voilà, madame*" as it occurred. Elizabeth was used to this three-dimensional intermingling of realities but sometimes, as now, the effect was still comical. She suppressed a laugh, forcing herself to focus only on David.

"Yes, it was very pleasant. I was glad you finally talked me into getting out."

". . . *dans la collection du Louvre, naturellement, il n'y a encore que* . . ."

"Good. Did she . . . did she mention anything about any spring productions in the works?"

Could Mindy have told David about the Finley play? That was a possibility, so it was better not to lie. "She did say that Richard Finley was doing something at the Circle in the Square. She's going to send a script over, and I thought I might try to work up a few sketches." Easy enough to pretend that there were difficulties with that, or to say later that she'd tried for the job and hadn't gotten it.

". . . *en tout cas, Paris n'a pas besoin d'une nouvelle musée immédiatement. Si ces jeunes 'impressionistes' gagnent l'acceptance de l'Académie—alors, on verra ce qu'on verra.*"

David looked genuinely happy, and he leaned down to kiss her goodnight. As he did so, Jenny lifted a spoonful of melon and brandy to her mouth, and the warmly liquid taste was pleasantly intermingled with the kiss. Elizabeth felt a surge of affection for David, remembering the desires he had stirred in her during their first few years together. She raised her hand to lightly touch his neck, and for a moment she considered joining him in bed, but then she realized that the dinner at the Embassy would soon be over. She wanted to hear the conversation that Jenny and Phillip would have in the carriage going home, so she could find out at least part of what all the discussions in French had been about. Maybe Phillip would talk about his upcoming trip to Paris, and whether she would be going with him or not. With a slightly poignant reluctance, she let her hand fall back to her lap and gently pulled her face away from David's.

"It'll be nice to see you busy with a play again," he said.

She smiled and nodded, pretending to agree. "I'm really looking forward to it. All I need is just a little more rest, and then some purposeful activity . . . and you and I can get back to where we should have started from all along."

He kissed her once again, lightly, and then turned away and walked into the bedroom alone.

". . . en France qu'en l'Angleterre."

Phillip had said something amusing, and everyone at the table was laughing again. Elizabeth shut the book, closed her eyes, and joined them.

So she wasn't going to France, after all. They had discussed it in the carriage back to Eaton Place, and Phillip said he'd only be gone for two or three weeks, all of which time would be taken up with business matters. Elizabeth was disappointed, even hurt, but Jenny didn't seem to mind. Apparently she'd made the trip before, and often.

Elizabeth stared at the glowing numbers on the digital clock radio beside the bed, and watched them turn in unison to read three o'clock. David was fast asleep on the pillow next to hers. He hadn't even heard her come into the room, more than an hour earlier.

She reached for a cigarette and found the pack on the nightstand empty. It had lasted her two days, though; one good thing about the time she spent in Jenny's world was that she never smoked while she was there, preferring to appreciate unhindered the clean, sweet-smelling air that Jenny breathed. But afterward, restless and unable to sleep, the habit came back in force.

Raising herself on one elbow, she opened the nightstand drawer, quietly, so as not to bother David. She groped around inside, feeling for the carton of Marlboros that she kept there; instead, her fingers came to rest on the smooth, cool surface of the transmitting unit.

Well, why not, she thought; if David couldn't tell she was using it when he was wide awake and even talking to her, it certainly wasn't going to disturb him in his sleep. It was better for her than a cigarette, and besides, maybe Jenny would be going to sleep herself. It might help Elizabeth drift off, too, to share the darkness and to feel the soft silk sheets on her body.

Carefully lifting the little box from the drawer, she lay back and turned the dial to its highest setting. She put it on the bed beside her, and her fingers found the oblong switch.

Jenny wasn't asleep yet; she was just now climbing the stairs to the master bedroom. Looking over the spiral banister, Elizabeth could see the entrance hall beneath her, and the drawing room beyond. Phillip stood there, talking to the butler, who was snuffing lights out one by one. The increasing dimness had a soothing effect, and Elizabeth could feel herself already growing drowsy. For a moment, her hand slipped from the transmitter, and the scene went black and silent, even the rustling of Jenny's long blue gown no longer audible. Sleepily, she moved her hand back to reestablish contact just as Jenny walked into the bedroom.

There was a cool breeze from the window and a smell of lilacs in the room. Elizabeth mused, dreamily, that the flowery aroma no longer called up images of her grandmother's musty house, but of youth and life and beauty; probably, she thought, the same way that her grandmother had perceived the scent.

Jenny stood before the long mahogany-framed mirror that faced the bed, while the upstairs maid undid the stays and ties that held her crinkly gown together. It fell away from her breasts, and Jenny looked with satisfaction on the reflection of her body in the soft gaslight. Elizabeth shared the pleasure, shared the pride; in this half-waking state, the conscious lines between their beings blurred, and Elizabeth was someone else entirely, not herself and not quite Jenny, but an abstract self between the two, some floating nexus of womanhood and warmth, serene and happy in the mirrored image of her unfolding beauty.

The maid left, carrying the gown, and Jenny/Elizabeth stood before the mirror undoing her thick, wheat-colored hair, wearing nothing but a thigh-length lacy camisole and powder-blue silk stockings gartered a few inches above the knee.

Her hair came tumbling in a softly buoyant rush to her bare shoulders, just as Phillip walked into the room. He stood there, silent in the semidarkness, looking at her breasts and thighs clearly outlined beneath the thin white fabric. Elizabeth felt Jenny, felt *herself*, turn slowly toward him. Without a word, she began to lift the hem of the brief chemise.

Her fingers pulled away from the transmitter as if it were a burning coal, and the scene went blank. David still breathed quietly beside her, while her own breath came in tight, sharp bursts. Her heart was pounding heavily, and her nipples pressed against the sheets. She was wide awake now, and achingly aware of the pulsing wetness that she sensed beneath her belly.

Nervously, she turned to look at David, but his face was crushed into his pillow, and he showed no sign of consciousness. She could feel the spreading moisture dampening her inner thighs, and the coursing blood that made her body one vast zone of sensitivity and anticipation.

It's only my imagination, she thought. Only a hallucination, only a fantasy. I can't get this involved in it, it can't be real.

She took a long, deep breath, and as she let it out the stirring air made her recall the breeze, its searching touch all light and cool and everywhere upon her body as the silken camisole moved slowly upward, past her hips and waist and toward her rising breasts, as Phillip watched and waited.

He's leaving soon, she thought. He's going off to France.

But it isn't real, she thought again, it isn't true, it's only in my mind.

Nude, she thought, nude in the flickering dimness before his hungry gaze, nude beside the open window and the nighttime summer wind, completely nude but for the pale blue stockings and the tight white garters.

It isn't real, I can't get this involved.

Her hand jabbed sharply down as if in anger, activating the transmitter.

The breeze, the silk, and Phillip all engulfed her in a mindless universe of sybaritic plenitude.

And then, at last, she slept.

The next few weeks were an agony of confusion for Elizabeth, a heady mixture of love and guilt, of ecstasy and bewilderment. Once broken, her self-imposed taboo on participating in the intimacies that passed between Jenny and Phillip could not be re-established. She had perceived Jenny's orgasmic pleasure as her own, and had known at once that she would not be able to resist returning to it in the future.

Phillip was a marvelous lover; Elizabeth's body responded to his as if she had been seeking this one man for years. In a way, she thought, perhaps she had. She was linked to him on some deep and unknown level, even if he proved to be no more than the product of her own hallucinating brain; and the possibility remained that this strange connection joining her mind and essence with those of Jenny might have a realistic existence of its own, might even have affected her subconscious all her life. Perhaps the bond had always been there, had been born with her and waiting all these years for the sudden boost of the electrode to bring it into conscious focus.

Whatever the truth, the relationship was now complete; and it seemed as natural as anything she'd ever felt or done before.

Her emotions about this were complex, and hard for her to pin down or to clarify. David still knew nothing of where she went and what she did almost every night now, as she lay beside him in their bed. The journal that she kept for Dr. Garrick was bowdlerized as well, so that only she was aware of her nightly rendezvous with Phillip, of the slow, delicious pleasure that she found beneath the flowing canopy and between the silken sheets of another world that no one else could see or hear.

Nor did Jenny and Phillip, so far as she could tell, suspect the regular intrusions that she made into their private moments. From time to time, after Elizabeth had spent an hour or more of passionate lovemaking in the spacious London bedroom, she would be depressed to think that no one ever knew she'd been a part of it. Phillip's loving words and soft caresses were not meant for her at all, but for another woman, a woman whose lean and lovely body Elizabeth was secretly, and maybe wrongfully, inhabiting.

Elizabeth was exercising privileges extended heretofore only to the mythic gods and goddesses of Greece and Rome. She had hoped to use that unique opportunity with wisdom, in the cause of reason and of scientific knowledge; but her desires had proved too strong to spurn the pleasure she had found there and had stolen for herself.

With that pleasure came a strange, sad jealousy: Elizabeth resented the slender body that her lover held, even as she felt his touch. When she saw him looking straight and deep into her eyes, she knew the eyes he spoke to weren't her own, knew that the moist warm flesh with which she answered him belonged to someone else.

Often, Elizabeth would feel a sudden urge to touch him in some particular and personal way, to laugh her own laugh or to speak her own true thoughts and feelings; but the responses all were Jenny's, and the words too.

Elizabeth renewed, and doubled, her previous efforts at direction of the other woman's movements. Once in a while, when she was concentrating every portion of her being on the task, it would seem to be within her grasp; but then her brief half hold would end, at most, with some slight tremor, an unwilled quivering of Jenny's hand or a sudden stiffening of random muscles. Nothing more.

Her daily schedule was a shambles now. She seldom woke before two or three in the afternoon, and the hours that she somehow had to pass before midnight were gotten through mechanically, by rote and ritual.

Christmas passed, and the party David had wanted her to plan was left undone and undiscussed. New Year's Eve was spent with Mindy and her latest boyfriend: a raucous, drunken evening for everyone else, and an ordeal for Elizabeth.

She and David hardly spoke now. His early sympathy for her recovery, and his attempts to "draw her out of her shell," had lapsed into a polite but chilly general silence. As he said, it was her life; he could only do so much to help her live it.

He had no way of knowing that her problem lay, instead, in the hows and whys and ifs of living someone else's life, and loving that same someone's husband.

Phillip went to France in mid-January. It was snowing heavily outside the Sixty-fifth Street window on the day he left, but Elizabeth was sweating in the August sun that beat down through the high glassed roof of London's Victoria Station.

It was sad to watch the puffing train pull out, knowing that she might have been on it with him. After it had gone, the din and babble of the station were too much to take, so she switched off the transmitter and made a light lunch of pears and cottage cheese. A fruit seller at the train station had made her hungry for a ripe, fresh pear, and she stared glumly at the Libby's can in the kitchen before she opened it.

For the next few days, Elizabeth would check in on Jenny once or twice every afternoon, just to reassure herself that the house and everything was still there, and to bask in the memories of Phillip that it evoked. That soon began to pall, though: Jenny, alone, had gone back to her reading and her shell arranging and her quiet tea times in the garden.

Elizabeth began to regret not having followed through with the project Mindy had tried to arrange for her. Richard Finley's script still lay, unread, on the bookshelf, but the play itself was in the final stages of rehearsal and would open in a week or so. The sets had been designed by someone else, someone whose work Elizabeth knew was not as good as hers.

Just to keep in practice, she started sketching again. Most of the scenes she drew were interiors of the houses in London and Sussex, reduced in scale to fit as imaginary stage sets; but David didn't know that. He was simply pleased to see her active again, and back on a normal sleeping schedule.

They dined with friends two or three times, and Elizabeth was, as far as anyone could tell, "finally back to normal." They were all aware of the delicate and dangerous surgery she had gone through in November, and they attributed her odd, reclusive behavior of the last month or so to the aftereffects of the operation. None of them knew about the electrodes or the experiments, and they all thought it somehow in bad taste to ask about her time in the hospital; after all, brain surgery for epilepsy wasn't quite the same as the appendectomies and hysterectomies and abortions that made for standard gossip.

During the last week in January, David's plans for the West Side project were given final approval, and they celebrated by taking a long weekend at a ski resort upstate. Elizabeth, of course, had never skied; but a quick phone call to Dr. Garrick, now back from California, assured her that she could safely try the beginner's slopes as long as she kept the transmitter strapped to her belt in case of emergencies. David was overjoyed at this opportunity to finally teach her his favorite sport.

She stuck to the easy hills, as ordered, but even so she could readily appreciate why David had enjoyed it so before they'd met: the vistas of fresh powder covering the mountains, the icy wind that somehow seemed to warm her face instead of freeze it, the absolutely smooth, unbroken flow of silent movement down the white hillside . . . they hadn't had this much fun together in years, and she felt a pang of guilt that he had so long forsaken such an exhilarating activity, even though she'd never asked him to.

She was thrilled and proud when he spent one afternoon expertly maneuvering the slalom course while she watched him from the deck of the hotel below. Sipping hot rum in the lounge that night, laughing and talking with the other skiers, she felt as if they had truly found a new beginning to their lives together. She huddled cozily in his arms before the crackling fire and was sure that everything was going to be all right, after all.

Later, in their room, he slowly stripped her of her tight ski pants and pulled her down to straddle him as he lay back on a thick fur rug before their own fireplace. As she rode his familiar body, his hands reached up to lift the bulky sweater she still wore. He pushed the knitted wool above her naked breasts and she shut her eyes, and gasped, and reached her climax. Thinking, guiltily, of Phillip.

Back in the city, David's work, now that the project was accepted, took more of his time than ever. Elizabeth was left with no one to talk to and nothing purposeful to do. Mindy was totally involved with her own new play, which, despite her earlier concern over the leading man's apparent sexual preferences, had gotten surprisingly good reviews. It was rumored to be moving uptown soon.

As February started, Elizabeth once again began to spend her afternoons with Jenny, sitting in the garden looking at the flowers of late summer . . . and wondering, as she stared out through this other woman's eyes, at this other woman's world and home, what would happen to them all when Phillip finally returned from France.

Elizabeth had just finished lunch when Jenny left the house. She turned on the transmitter as the carriage was making its way into Regent Street, and was surprised to see its gray silk-lined interior instead of Jenny's boudoir or the garden. There had been no trips outside the house since Phillip left, and it seemed odd that Jenny was going shopping alone, without one of the maids along to help her with packages and things. Elizabeth, interested, turned the transmitter up to four volts as Jenny told the driver not to wait, but to meet her back on Regent Street three hours later.

Walking into the emporium she had visited before, Elizabeth expected Jenny to go upstairs for a lengthy fitting; three hours seemed a long time to spend in aimless browsing. To her surprise, she found herself walking straight through the store and then out of it again by one of the side doors. The traffic was louder back there, and none of the shops was fashionable; Jenny looked out of place, and several passersby regarded her curiously.

Suddenly, she hailed a hansom cab. The driver seemed taken aback by the sight of a Fine Lady stopping a cab by herself; and when Elizabeth heard herself, through Jenny's mouth, give the man an address on Wardour Street, he grunted disapprovingly and whipped the horses into motion with a vicious start.

The long ride went in silence. Jenny sat well back in the cab, staring straight ahead. Elizabeth caught only glimpses of the street scenes that they passed, but she soon began to understand the reaction of the hansom driver. Wagons loaded with beer kegs and fish lumbered past them, lurching in and out of mud-filled potholes; street vendors shouted raucously from every corner, and there was a growing stench of rotten vegetables and stale human-smells. There must have been some mistake; why didn't Jenny look out the window and realize . . .

The cab was drawing to a halt. Jenny paid the driver, who looked at her up and down in a way clearly out of keeping with their respective social stations. Elizabeth knew the look too well from New York streets, but had not expected to confront it here.

Jenny's face remained a mask of calm indifference and repose as she stepped down into the street.

A foul-odored slime ran through the gutters, and from across the street a crowd of sooty urchins shouted cockney taunts at her. An old woman lay curled up in an alleyway, while a toothless man, at least as old as she, rifled through her ragged pouch. He looked up suspiciously, but Jenny ignored him and rapped the wooden knocker of a door in front of her. Elizabeth turned the voltage on the transmitter down to one, unable to bear the assault on her nostrils any longer. Then she could sense the door being opened, and she fought back a gagging reflex as she increased the power once again.

A young black girl had opened the door a crack, then wider as she saw Jenny on the step. The black girl smiled and turned away, shouting something in a thick West Indies accent. Then the girl was pushed back from the door by an enormous white woman in her late fifties, her thick arms and neck smothered in gaudy jewelry. Her gray hair was piled into an elaborate coiffure, and she wore a bright green Chinese robe. The woman grasped Jenny by the wrists with a grin, pulling her inside the doorway and embracing her in a massive hug. The lingering street odor was replaced by a cloying sweet perfume.

"'ere, Charlotte, look who's come to visit Auntie Maggie! And a fine figger of a lady she is, too, i'n't she! Blue sateen an' pearls it is fer our darlin' little Jennifer!"

The three of them were standing in a tiny foyer, closed off by thick red imitation-velvet curtains. It seemed to be a private side space of some sort, not a main entrance. From the other side of the curtain, Elizabeth heard murmured voices, broken now and then by girlish laughter. Abruptly, the curtains parted and a young woman about Jenny's age burst through. She had long, dark hair and was wearing a dress whose already low-cut bodice was partially undone. Elizabeth could see one of her nipples, covered with bright rouge. The girl looked back at Jenny interestedly, then turned her attention to the older woman.

"It's Lord Childress, Aunt Maggie; he wants another bottle o' champagne, an' I haven't got the key."

Jenny and the woman called Aunt Maggie exchanged a quick glance, and Elizabeth could feel Jenny nod almost imperceptibly, then turn her face carefully away from the partially open curtains.

Before she did, Elizabeth briefly saw a large sitting room, garishly decorated and full of plumes and mirrors. Two elegantly dressed men sat on an ornate sofa, wine glasses in their hands. One of the men had been in Jenny and Phillip's party at Ascot six weeks ago.

"Aunt Maggie" quickly handed the dark-haired girl a key ring, then motioned her back into the sitting room, pulling the curtains fully shut again when the girl had left. The woman grinned broadly at Jenny. "*Never tell a secret, never tell a lie, darlin'.*"

Jenny laughed and hugged the fat woman again. "*Is Charlie here?*"

"*In his suite, darlin'. You can take the side stairs; an' ring down to Charlotte before you leave, so's your Auntie Maggie can kiss you goodbye till the next time, you hear?*"

Jenny nodded, smiling. The woman blew her a kiss and disappeared through the curtains. Jenny turned to a small door and walked through to a steep, dark flight of stairs. She was obviously familiar with the surroundings. At the head of the stairs, there were two more doors. Through a pane of semifrosted glass, Elizabeth could see a hallway behind one of the doors; a man walked past with a young girl on his arm, and Jenny quickly stepped through the other door.

It led into a small alcove; a large closet, actually, with several well-made men's topcoats hanging on the walls. Jenny walked through and into another, larger room that extended beyond. It was a tastefully appointed sitting room, at the other side of which Elizabeth could see an open door leading to a large bedroom. The furnishings were expensive, though nothing to compare with the mansion in Belgravia. There was none of the fussy clutter that marked most Victorian living spaces; this apartment was neat, elegantly spare, and unmistakably masculine.

There was a large leather armchair in the center of the room, and in it, lightly dozing with a magazine in his lap, sat a husky, immaculately groomed man of thirty-five or so. His black-stockinged feet were propped on a leather ottoman made in the shape of a rhinoceros, and he wore fitted gray trousers with a ruffled silk shirt open halfway down his chest.

Jenny moved straight toward the man. He had not stirred when she came into the room, and Elizabeth surveyed his sleeping form through Jenny's eyes as she approached him. He was clean-shaven, and quite handsome, in a slick, Italianate fashion. *Too* handsome, in fact; Elizabeth had never been attracted to the smooth, cock-sure type he represented.

Elizabeth wanted to leave the room at once, wanted to forget this afternoon and be back in the garden in Belgravia, sipping tea and waiting peacefully to see if the post would bring a letter from the Continent. Instead, she felt herself sit on the chair arm beside this stranger, close enough to smell the almost syrupy sweetness of his shaving lotion. Jenny moved her hand out to touch his face, and his dark brown eyes came open.

"*Well, well,*" he said. "*If it isn't Lady Jennifer herself.*" He smiled, revealing a row of perfect, even teeth; but Elizabeth sensed something vicious underneath the smile, something bright and cold behind those thick-lashed, sensuous eyes. She wished that he had stayed asleep.

"*How long has it been now . . . two months? Three? Surely our Mr. Curran hasn't been all that satiating, has he?*" The man's hand moved up around her waist, lightly and familiarly caressing her belly. Elizabeth's instinct was to recoil, but Jenny sat relaxed, accommodating, her own hand stroking the man's smooth cheek.

"*Of course not,*" Jenny said. "*I just couldn't get away, that's all. I had to wait for him to leave again—he's gone to France this time—and then I had to wait another week, so no one would suspect. But I've missed you all the while.*"

"*All the while? That's quite a while.*" The coldness in his eyes was unmistakable now, though his smile had not diminished. "*I'd almost thought you had forgotten all about me.*"

"*Never, Charlie. You know how I feel . . . how you make me feel. And I know how lucky I've been, because of you.*"

"*Bloody right, girl!*" His eyes were flashing now, full of anger, full of power, full of something strange and frightening. Get up now, thought Elizabeth, get back to the carriage and back home; but Jenny stayed where she was, unmoving, silent, as the man's cold eyes impaled her. "*You owe everything you have to me, and don't forget it! It was me who picked you off these rotten streets eleven years ago; you no more than thirteen at the time, and a riper one I never saw. Aunt Maggie wanted to put you downstairs right away, but it was me who told her to hold off—me who had the bright idea of fancying you up to be a lady, of sending you to school in Switzerland all those years, and making up that silly tale about you being orphaned, losing your inheritance and everything.*"

Do you know how much cash it took to make that story stick, to get you introduced into society, to set you up to meet a man like Phillip Curran? You were an investment for the future, luv, and I knew it from the start. You had the look, and you always had the head for it. But it was me, Charlie Ferrara, who found that out, and me who saw it through."

Elizabeth fought back her own repulsion as Jenny leaned forward and kissed the man, full on the mouth. *"You're the only one that saw those things back then,"* said Jenny. *"Everybody treats me like a lady now, but you're the one that saw it first, and set it up so I could put it all together. I loved you for that, Charlie; and you've always been as much a part of my plans as I've been part of yours. Everything I've done has been for us."*

"Well, how, then? You're the one that's sitting there on all the property. The little money you've been bringing back these past four years wouldn't pay a tenth of what Maggie and I laid out on you. Not a tenth!"

"Have you forgotten what we talked about, that week when I got married? The plan we had?"

He waved his hand impatiently, dismissing her. *"Talk, Jenny. Talk and more talk, that's all."*

She got up from the chair, reaching for her satin purse. *"More than that, Charlie. I'm as tired of talk as you are; tired of sneaking off down here to see you every month or two. I brought you something this time, Charlie. Something to show you."* She opened the purse and dumped the contents in his lap. *"Something for Phillip, when he gets back from France. I thought you'd like to see it."*

He stared in silence for several moments, his lips pursed carefully together. Then his mouth broke into an open grin, and he grabbed at Jenny's thigh. She laughed throatily, pulling up her skirt.

Elizabeth jabbed at the transmitter, shutting off the sights and feels. Then she began to shiver uncontrollably, because there was no way she could cancel out the memory of that final image, of the erection rising in the man's gray trousers, and beside it, lying in his lap, an exquisite and ladylike pearl and silver derringer pistol.

PART FOUR

Elizabeth sat on a wooden folding chair in the apartment building's musty basement laundry room, watching the constant rise and tumble of the clothes in the spinning drier. None of the other young women in the nearby seats, neighbors whom she knew only by sight, disturbed her seeming reverie. Most of them stared as if transfixed at their own washers or driers, absorbed in problems of their own. They used the cyclical display of the cleaning machines as a visual background to meditation, much as men and women elsewhere, or in other times, would stare thoughtfully into the lifelike undulations of an open fire. One or two read paperbacks or magazines, but no one spoke. The only sound that echoed from the fluorescently illuminated concrete walls was the steady, thrumping rhythm of the machines.

Elizabeth was still half in a state of disbelief over the scene that she had witnessed, had participated in, two days before. The hansom ride into the slums of London; the garish brothel and its fat, perfumed, and painted keeper; the dark and unctuous man in the second-floor room . . . and most of all, the gun, and Jenny's horrifying promise.

Several minutes after her initial shock at that, Elizabeth had reactivated the transmitter, hoping against hope that perhaps the whole thing had never really taken place, that she had only imagined it. Instead, she had found herself in the midst of an even more incredible scene, with Jenny naked and spread-eagled on Charlie's bed, and the dark-haired girl she'd seen downstairs locked in a passionate embrace with *both* of them: hands everywhere, and tongues, and legs, and bodies intermingled without regard to gender or to purpose. Elizabeth had shut the image off at once, gagging in revulsion at the memory of where her mouth—Jenny's mouth—had been placed.

It was all too much to absorb immediately. Elizabeth had grown accustomed to the calm, idyllic patterns of the other life she'd found through the electrode, had accepted them as a tranquil yet exciting alternative to the dilemmas of her own existence.

Even her curiosity about the visions' source, or their objective reality, had almost ceased as her love for Phillip deepened. But now, her secret haven had been invaded and defiled by incomprehensible and ugly forces, threatening the violent destruction of the one thing that had come to mean the most to her in either world.

The whirling drier stopped. The clothes were probably dry by now, but Elizabeth inserted another quarter, unwilling yet to leave the soothing, senseless image of the tumbling sheets and garments. They began their dance again, like tiny clouds folding in and through themselves.

It seemed beyond the realm of possibility that Jenny could actually prefer the slickly serpentine charm of the Ferrara man, and the orgiastic revels in which she joined him, to the intelligent masculinity and real affection that Phillip offered. Elizabeth closed her eyes, trying to imagine what it must have been like for Jenny as a child.

The man had said he'd found her in the streets when she was twelve or thirteen. She must have been abandoned by her parents, or maybe orphaned; but not by a wealthy family, as they had apparently pretended when Jenny was sent away to school. One brief glimpse of the Soho of that time had been enough to horrify Elizabeth. How might it have affected a young child, growing up either in that section of the city or in the toiling poverty of peasant life? The English countryside meant more than mansions and gardens like the estate that the Currans owned. Jenny would have known hunger, *real* hunger, and cruelty as well. Elizabeth winced at the thought of a sensitive young girl wandering through those awful streets, her belly empty and her body covered with bruises from her father's leather strop. Jenny's home life may have made any other option seem an improvement.

Nineteenth-century London, Elizabeth knew, would have offered quite distinct alternatives to a desperate young girl. For all the cloying morality of Victorian society, it possessed an underside as dark or darker than that of present-day New York. The nighttime streets and alleyways of every slum were filled with literally thousands of milling girls, many of them not much older than Jenny would have been: small-town girls who had been "ruined," some with illegitimate children, some whose husbands or families had been murdered by smallpox or one of the other deadly, incurable scourges of the age. Limited by lack of education or of "breeding," they could only keep alive by bartering their bodies: either to satisfy the repressed sexuality of the middle- and upper-class "gentlemen," or to labor like flesh-and-blood machines in the burgeoning factories of the new Industrial Age. Given the choice, sexual prostitution was probably less wearing, even less degrading.

Jenny would certainly have been, as Charlie put it, "a ripe one." Even clothed in rags, even caked with mud and bloody whipping sores, the transcendent beauty that Elizabeth had seen reflected in so many mirrors would have stood out like a peacock in a flock of geese. Her soft, uncut blond hair would have hung below her waist, projecting radiance even if unwashed for weeks. Her firming breasts would have strained enticingly against the bodice of an outgrown child's smock, her supple calves and thighs clearly visible beneath a cheap, thin skirt that rose immodestly above her ankles. The sexual hypocrisy of Victorian men would have no longer been a secret to her; perhaps her father had abused her, or an "uncle," or a passing stranger in the gaslit evening. Young girls were the favorite prey of the righteous Victorian male, for much the same reason that he insisted on a rigorous double standard for the women of his own family and social class: That way, his own incompetence and fears in bed were left unchallenged. Child prostitution, male and female, was a common thing in the age of moral perfection. Yes, Jenny would have been a very ripe one.

She would have surely known what lay in wait for her. Elizabeth now realized that the bright alertness she had noticed in Jenny's eyes must have come from her knowledge of the streets. The same look could now be found on any Harlem stoop: cunning, ageless eyes looking out of children's faces. How must she have reacted to her maturing figure? To the first blood flow from between her thighs, stopped up with dirty rags? Elizabeth shuddered, recalling the traumatic coincidences of her own unwelcome puberty. Had Jenny, too, met womanhood with fear and bitterness? Had she wept at what it held in store for her? Had she lain awake at night in some crumbling London tenement, trying to press her growing breasts back into her chest . . . trying to hold on, impossibly, to even the most miserable of childhoods?

In that context, in that setting, Charlie must have seemed to be a blessing. Slickly smooth in a world of stinking crudity, gently patronizing in a universe of violence and bruising exploitation . . . his game was not a new one, but with Jenny at thirteen it must have been incredibly effective. The smallest pleasure, or the simplest kindness, would have earned her overwhelming gratitude: a warm bath, bright new clothes, a fresh-cooked meal . . . and then, when "Aunt Maggie" had wanted to put Jenny immediately to work, Charlie had convinced her not to. Elizabeth could imagine their arguments over Jenny's fate, and their slowly developing plan to make of her an even more worthwhile "commodity" over the years: the diction classes, the years of schooling on the Continent, the carefully constructed cover story of her being orphaned and shut off from her inheritance, the subtly orchestrated introductions to society, to bachelor gentlemen . . . to Phillip.

In order to assure an eventual return on that investment, it would have first been necessary to establish a powerful degree of control over Jenny, so that there would be no chance of her later skipping out on her part of the unbalanced "bargain." Cruelty could not have been the key; her childhood experience would have diminished the effectiveness of beatings or enforced starvation. No, she would have been enslaved through a carefully planned apparent benevolence, a sick parody of familial love that would elicit lifelong devotion to her benefactors; and the final step, gradually applied as the girl matured, would have been her introduction to orgiastic sexuality, with Charlie and with the women working in the house. Teach her the many patterns of sensuality and physical fulfillment, addict her to the drug of absolute orgasmic freedom, and then send her out into a world in which propriety and chastity were rigidly enforced for young ladies of her supposed social station, a world in which hashish and opium were more available, and more publicly acceptable, than feminine sexual pleasure. She would have been forced to return again and again to the people who had raised her, not out of threats or punishment, but from devotion and desire.

How old would she have been when the lessons started? Fourteen? Fifteen? Secreted in a plush back room of the house in Soho, fed and bathed and pampered, far from the eager eyes of the customers who would have paid a small fortune for the privilege of having her, she would have been attended by a constant stream of knowing hands and mouths, would have been caressed and kissed and brought to aching ecstasy a thousand times and more while her mentor watched and taught and then joined in. After that, the prim young girls at school in Switzerland, the fancy-dress balls, and the delicate, swooning young men of high society would have been a disappointing joke to her.

No wonder, then, that even Phillip offered less than total satisfaction; Phillip, whom Elizabeth had thought to be the height of sensuality, would have seemed, to Jenny, not too far beyond the simpering and impotent romantics idealized by the era.

But could Jenny's cravings really be so strong that they could lead her to an act of murder? Elizabeth had come to recognize her own desires through Jenny's body, had learned and felt more in the past two months than she had ever dreamed she might . . . but still she found it difficult to imagine an extension of those pleasures and those needs to the extent that one would kill to satisfy them.

If only she could perceive Jenny's thoughts and emotions, rather than just her physical sensations, then she could know the full truth, could understand what had led her to this point . . . but understanding wouldn't help now, wouldn't change a thing.

The drier stopped again. Elizabeth took out the warm, fresh-smelling clothes and neatly folded them. The other women were still absorbed in their own machines as Elizabeth stepped into the elevator.

Back in the apartment, she put the clothes and sheets away, then sliced a plate of cheese and apples. The transmitter sat on the table as she ate her lunch. Elizabeth was acutely aware of the silver electrodes in her skull, and now their presence seemed less a blessing than a menace. The pathways they had opened, whether only in her mind or in the very stuff of time itself, had turned in strange and undesired directions, almost obliterating the pleasure they had led her to at first . . . but still, she couldn't keep away. Her life had been divided into two, and there was no escaping or ignoring it.

She pushed the unfinished fruit and cheese away and reached for the transmitter.

Jenny was sitting in the garden again, as calm as she had ever been. Elizabeth could almost believe that the episode in Soho had never happened, that this was just another day like all the others, full of endless peace and sunlight. A servant brought a tray of tea and scones, and Jenny smiled, nodding her thanks; there was no outward sign of upset or remorse over what had happened, and the plans Elizabeth now knew she'd made. She just sat there in the garden shade, placid and composed, waiting.

Waiting for Phillip to return.

He came back to London on the seventeenth of February, according to the New York calendar. Elizabeth was at a cocktail party with David, her transmitter taped down at a steady two volts, when Phillip arrived in the carriage from Victoria station. He was laden with gifts for Jenny: fine Belgian lace, huge bottles of the latest French perfumes, an exquisite collection of crystal figurines. Jenny embraced him warmly, exclaiming over all the presents he had brought and telling him repeatedly how much she'd missed him. There was nothing in her words or actions to betray the hypocrisy of her performance.

The cocktail party was being given by the president of David's architectural firm, in his Fifth Avenue penthouse suite. Elizabeth knew almost no one there, except for two or three of David's office associates and their wives. It was an important gathering, partially in honor of David's work on the West Side housing and office complex, and he had been solicitous in his concern over whether Elizabeth felt up to going; she knew, though, that his worry over her condition was largely rooted in anxiety over whether she would seem "alive" enough to make a good impression. She couldn't really blame him for that, and she had no desire to embarrass David in front of his colleagues and superiors; but still, she couldn't resist taking the transmitter along, just in case. She would have preferred to be alone herself when Phillip returned, but there was nothing she could do to change it.

Fortunately, she wasn't being called on to converse at length. Early on, she'd attached herself to Marcia Hastings, one of the young wives who knew about her operation and her supposed slow recovery. Marcia was kindly doing her best to keep the pressure off Elizabeth, handling most of the conversations that came their way, so Elizabeth was free to focus most of her attention on what was happening with Jenny.

Suddenly Marcia excused herself to go the ladies' room, and Elizabeth wandered over to the massive window overlooking Central Park, not wanting to seem like an invalid who had to follow Marcia everywhere. She struck a pose of rapt attention on the park and the surrounding buildings; they made a strange backdrop to her other vision, the scene inside the London house. The odd effect was heightened by the different focal lengths of what she saw, an effect she'd noticed before but never quite so strongly: If she concentrated mainly on the distant trees and skyline, the close-up views of Phillip and the presents and the house through Jenny's eyes seemed incredibly large, like actors' faces seen from the front row of a movie theater; while if she focused her attention on the London scene, the buildings and the park became a blurry, superimposed miniature. Even now, these minor aspects of her dual perceptions continued to fascinate her.

Jenny had just opened the last of the gaily wrapped packages. In it was a sheer blue negligee, obviously risqué for England at the time. Phillip was smiling slyly as she opened it, and they locked eyes as she pressed the fine-spun silk against her body.

"You may've got the wrong size, darling. Why don't you come upstairs and tell me if it fits."

"Hi there, need a refill?"

Elizabeth turned away from the window with a start, her eyes confusedly trying to refocus on the crowded living room. There was a man standing beside her, someone she didn't know. David hadn't introduced him earlier, and she didn't think it was anyone from his office. She glanced down at her almost-empty glass, seeing Jenny's booted feet move up the stairs.

"No, no thank you. I'd really rather nurse this one for a while."

"You seem like an observer, too."

"What?" Jenny was in the bedroom now, taking off her dress. Elizabeth tried to stop a blush from rising to her cheeks as she faced this stranger and simultaneously felt her breasts spring loose from the binding cloth.

"You know; stay relatively sober, just sit back and watch everybody else get silly. These parties can be really funny movies sometimes, as long as you don't involve yourself in the acting. I noticed you earlier, with Marcia Hastings; you seemed to be content with letting her do most of the talking."

"Yes, well—I haven't been too social lately, I'm afraid. I've had a lot on my mind." Jenny was naked now, slipping the smooth new gown over her head and shoulders. Elizabeth felt the slinky, transparent fabric slide down her body, and her nipples became erect and sensitive in unison with Jenny's. She glanced quickly into the eyes of the tall young man who was speaking to her, but he didn't seem to notice any change in her appearance or expression.

"To talk about or not to talk about?"

"Not to, if you don't mind."

"Fine. Then I can tell you all my problems, instead. Beginning with the fact that my name is—really and truly—Billy Graham, and ending with the fact that I don't know yours."

Elizabeth smiled in spite of herself. "Is your name actually Billy Graham?"

"So my mother told me. Billy or Bill. I'd be glad to save you from all the sin around here, if you'll tell me who you are."

"Elizabeth. Elizabeth Austin." Phillip had come into the room now, and Jenny was pirouetting slowly in front of the open window, modeling the filmy negligee. The sunlight shone straight through it, illuminating and outlining her slender body as clearly as if she had been completely nude. Elizabeth felt an urge to cover herself with her hands, and had to forcefully remind herself that no one at the party was seeing her that way.

The young man gestured with his hand, indicating the crowd of people in the sunken living room beneath them. "Does one of these belong to you?"

"Yes, I'm here with my husband, David." She turned her head to try to locate him, but wherever she looked, all she could see was Phillip, smiling and unbuttoning his waistcoat. Flustered, she forced herself to keep on talking. "He's with Rampling, Rampling and Hodge. The host's firm. He's the principal designer on their new West Side project."

"Oh, then we'll be working together soon. Bob Rampling's hired me to collaborate with your husband on the landscaping of the mall in that complex."

"How nice." Phillip was naked to the waist now. Jenny had stopped her coquettish spinning, and was leaning with both hands behind her on the windowsill, her back arched and her head atilt. The position stretched the thin silk taut against her breasts and thighs and belly. As Phillip walked slowly toward her, his face and form seemed to merge into the body of the young man who was still innocently chatting away. The effect was highly disconcerting, and Elizabeth was getting a little nervous. She thought she should turn off the transmitter, and yet she wanted to leave it on; this was the first time she had been with Phillip in weeks, and her underpants were growing damp with anticipation. Besides, her purse, with the transmitter in it, was in the cloakroom, sending out its stimulus from the other end of the apartment; in order to get to it, she would first have to cross the crowded living room and deal with new encounters on the way. Best to just stay where she was, and try to remain cool.

"Yes, I'm looking forward to it. It's a beautiful design, and I'm sure we'll be able to work together well. What about yourself? Do you work?"

Phillip was standing directly in front of her, and his image had now completely intersected with Bill Graham's, blending fully in three dimensions so that Elizabeth could hardly tell the two apart. She wanted to back away, to separate them, but she couldn't. Phillip's hands were reaching out now, caressing Jenny's breasts; then he bent forward, kissing her rigid nipples through the delicate fabric of the gown. Elizabeth turned away toward the window, her breathing deeper and her pulse accelerating. Somehow, she managed to speak. "No. I'm not working now. I'm a theatrical set designer, but I've taken some time off recently."

"Oh, really? Do you know Craig Fischer?"

Phillip was pulling her gown off now, slowly, kissing and lightly licking each new area of flesh that was exposed as the silk came away from her body. He was almost kneeling before her, his lips moving with increasing passion down her exposed belly. "Yes. Yes, I . . . know him very well."

The gown was down around her ankles now, and Phillip's face was pressed with loving eagerness between her thighs. She could feel her hands, Jenny's hands, stroking his thick dark hair and grasping at the muscles of his naked shoulders, as his own hands moved up behind her, caressing the backs of her thighs and cupping her softly rounded buttocks. His tongue moved expertly inside the moistness of her cleft, and she could feel the coursing blood that concentrated there, heightening her sensitivity to an excruciating degree.

"We went to school together. Have you see his sets for *Halfway Through the Storm?*"

"Yes. They . . . were magnificent. I was very happy for him."

Phillip was standing again, nude himself now, and was leading her to a velvet-covered stool in front of the dressing-room mirrors. He and Jenny both sat down, she on his lap, facing him. He guided himself into her, and Jenny began moving slowly up and down, then closed her eyes. As she did so, the dual vision ceased, and Elizabeth could only see the window and the party and the young man talking to her; but she still felt, with increasing intensity, the sensation of moving rhythmically on the velvet stool, her legs spread wide and clasped tightly around Phillip's thighs, and his full, firm penis pumping inside her. She bit her lip and closed her own eyes, hoping that she wouldn't inadvertently cry out with pleasure.

"Yes, I know he's worked a long time for . . . Mrs. Austin? Are you all right?"

Jenny and Phillip were both moving faster and harder now, she raising herself higher with every stroke, he moving his body forward to meet her each time she moved back down. Elizabeth kept her eyes shut tightly, and she was biting her lip so hard that she was afraid she might be drawing blood. Then Jenny opened her own eyes and looked into the mirror. As the climax came, Elizabeth was watching herself watch Jenny watch herself watch both of them, watch all of them together, all naked and complete and full, linked in an endless reflective chain of perfect ecstasy.

Elizabeth dropped her glass, and it shattered loudly on the floor.

"Mrs. Austin . . . Mrs. Austin!"

She opened her eyes again, exhausted. Most of the conversation in the room had stopped, and everywhere she looked people were either staring at her or carefully averting their gaze. The young man she'd been talking to was picking up the shards of glass from around her feet, and David was rushing over to where she stood.

"Elizabeth?" What's the matter?"

"Nothing, David. I just . . . had a dizzy spell for a moment, that's all. I'm fine now."

"Was it a seizure coming on? Do you need the transmitter?"

"No, it was nothing like that. I'm fine, really I am."

The party chatter in the room had started up again, and no one seemed to be paying any attention to them now. Elizabeth wondered how many of the muted conversations were about her, though, and what they might be saying. They'd have a lot more to talk about if they knew what she'd actually been feeling for the past few minutes; was experiencing still, in fact. Jenny sat slumped on Phillip's lap, her head on his shoulder and his gradually subsiding penis still inside her. Elizabeth felt a renewed burst of excitement, strangely titillated by the sensation of being nude in Phillip's arms while standing in a crowded room, no one suspecting anything of what was going on. The other wives might have their secret dalliances and affairs, but she was certain that none of them had ever had a session with their lovers in the middle of a cocktail party at Bob Rampling's penthouse. The deliciously naughty humor of the situation caused Elizabeth to smile, forgetting for a moment the other problems that she somehow had to deal with.

"Well, I'm taking you home anyway. I don't want you taking any chances with your health."

"You mean chances that I might start flipping out and embarrass you in front of your boss and his friends?"

David flushed and turned away. There was just enough truth in her statement to catch him off guard, but it had been a cheap dig. Of course that would be embarrassing, for her even more than for him, and she also knew that it wasn't his only concern.

She said their goodbyes to everyone, while David collected their things from the cloakroom. They made the long ride down the elevator in silence. Elizabeth's enjoyment of and amusement at the love-making episode was beginning to wear off, and was replaced by sadness at the knowledge that, for Jenny, it had been nothing but hypocrisy.

A bitterly cold wind was blowing down the avenue as they waited for a cab. The chill was deepened by a simultaneous sharp breeze through the open window of the bedroom in London. Jenny got up to close the window and get dressed again, and Elizabeth could see the gathering grayness of approaching autumn in the sky above the garden. She shivered, clutching her arms tightly around her waist, and began to feel as though she might never sense the warmth of summer again.

Once outside the cab, she slipped her hand into her purse and removed the tape from the transmitter button. Phillip had already dressed and gone downstairs, and Jenny was rearranging herself in front of the long mirror. Elizabeth could imagine what must be going on inside Jenny's mind, and she was horrified and sickened by the unblinking calm with which the young woman readjusted her blond ringlets and sprayed herself with the perfume that Phillip had brought from Paris.

Jenny couldn't be allowed to carry out her plan. *Something* had to be done to stop her, and soon, no matter how difficult it might be. Elizabeth recalled the times before when she had tried to gain access to Jenny's mind, with no success, and the occasions when she'd made an effort to take control of her physical actions, simply out of curiosity or a desire to relate to Phillip in her own ways instead of relying just on Jenny's actions. She'd never been able to pull it off, but there had been times when she had felt that she was close, and when Jenny herself had seemed to notice something peculiar happening to her. She had, at least, been able once or twice to slightly interfere with Jenny's bodily control, to cause a sudden mild spasm or a stubborn muscular stiffening; or so it seemed. It was impossible to know for sure. Maybe she had only imagined that she'd been able to exert her influence, however small, over the woman in the past; maybe those minor spasms had been mere coincidence, and unrelated to her efforts.

Still, the possibility was there; the effect of the transmitter might well be more than just a one-way perceptual flow. A rigorous and concentrated schedule of practice might enable her to seize complete control over Jenny's activities. There was more than enough reason for that now, and Elizabeth felt driven by a desperate sense of urgency. It was no longer enough simply to perceive; she had to act, had to focus all her strength on literally *becoming* Jenny—even if that meant that the results could possibly be permanent, and that she might never be able to return to her own life.

If only there were time enough. If only there were time.

> . . . *Present fears*
> *Are less than horrible imaginings.*
> *My thought, whose murder yet is but fantastical,*
> *Shakes so my single state of man that function*
> *Is smothered in surmise and nothing is*
> *But what is not.*

It was only shortly after midnight, but David was already asleep. The follow-through work on his design for the West Side complex was occupying more and more of his time now. Elizabeth lay quietly in the bed beside him, the transmitter discreetly placed in the nightstand drawer and set for a full four volts.

The Drury Lane theater was crowded, and Jenny sat with her crinolines squeezed into a sixth-row center seat between Phillip and one of his visiting Dutch clients. The Dutchman spoke almost no English, but he seemed to be appreciating the ornate interior of the theater itself, and the lavish costumes and special effects that would have overpowered a lesser plot.

They were watching *Macbeth*, with Charles Kean in the title role. Elizabeth noted the details of the production with a sharp professional interest. The onstage presence of Charles, rather than his father, Edmund Kean, definitely placed them in the latter half of the century, probably the sixties or even early seventies.

This was, she realized, one of the least important periods for English drama: There were few actors or actresses of major stature, and even fewer original plays, most of them little more than florid melodrama. Elizabeth regretted that, as long as she had the opportunity to observe, firsthand, part of the history of theater, she would have much preferred some other—almost any other— age. As it was, even Shakespeare was being overburdened with unnecessary physical pyrotechnics. The witches' scene in the first act had bordered on the absurd, something more fitting to a Ken Russel movie than to the play's appropriate simplicity and starkness.

No one else in the richly dressed audience seemed to share her views, though; the overdone sets and effects seemed to be receiving more applause than the actors or the play itself. This was a time for pomp and pageantry, for the English to affirm their world supremacy through garishly pretentious public rituals; but it was hard to hate, or even to disdain, knowing how thoroughly that cocky power would someday be lost.

> *. . . To beguile the time,*
> *Look like the time; bear welcome in your eye,*
> *Your hand, your tongue; look like the innocent flower,*
> *But be the serpent under't.*

A sudden chill ran down her spine, lying there in bed. What did it matter that the British Empire would decay—had long since decayed already, from her standpoint in the present? What difference did it make that, seen in one light, the people in her visions were all dead, all decades underneath the ground; assuming, even, that they had ever actually existed in the first place? What mattered now was Phillip's life, and Phillip's love.

> *. . . that but this blow*
> *Might be the be-all and the end-all here,*
> *But here, upon this bank and shoal of time,*
> *We'd jump the life to come . . .*

Another shiver went through Elizabeth, listening to the familiar lines in this new context. Jenny sat calm and quiet in the theater, her breathing easy and her pulse quite normal. Not so much as a droplet of perspiration dampened her brow or palms as she coolly watched this ultimate drama of betrayal and death unfold, with her husband and intended victim at her side. Elizabeth felt a surge of despair at ever being able to fully understand a mind that could be this devoid of guilt or fear or even indecision.

Clearly, empathy and comprehension were hopeless, useless. Control was all that mattered. But where to start? And how? Elizabeth turned the transmitter down to one volt and lit a cigarette in the darkness, thinking.

On the previous occasions when she'd tried to exert her own influence over Jenny's thoughts or actions, she had approached the problem with an all-fronts effort. Maybe it would be better if she started on a smaller scale, focusing all her mental energy on one isolated part of Jenny's body, like an eyebrow or a hand. She should decide in advance on a specific movement, or blockage of movement, something that she could know for sure had been her own doing, and not just a coincidental simultaneous action of Jenny's. Try to make her bite her tongue, perhaps, or keep her eyes from blinking until they teared . . . yes, something like that, something that would also be apparent and hopefully even worrisome or confusing to Jenny. Something with her hands, those pale, slim, lovely hands that remained so preternaturally dry and still. Make her clench one hand into a tightened fist, say; that might even make her wonder if she weren't being more affected by the play than she had thought.

Elizabeth put out the cigarette and turned the transmitter all the way back up. The first act had ended, and the second was beginning immediately, with no intermission. There would probably be no break until between the third and fourth acts, so she should have forty or forty-five minutes to experiment without interruption.

Jenny sat as quietly as ever, her left hand crossed casually in her lap over her right, in which she loosely held a program. Elizabeth would concentrate on that right hand, she decided. The first step would be to feel it, sense it totally, almost as an entity apart from and greater than herself or the rest of Jenny's body.

Elizabeth forced herself to ignore the play that passed before her eyes and sounded in her brain, to forget that Phillip was in the seat beside her. There must be nothing in the world but that one right hand. Elizabeth could feel the gentle touch of lace at its wrist, and she began to identify the points of contact one by one: three tiny folds in a row touched the back of the wrist, the middle fold with still infinitesimal, but slightly more, pressure than the others. At the sides, the lacy cuff fanned out a bit, and nothing could be felt. Beneath that, on the underside of the wrist, the lace was delicately crushed against the fabric of the gown that Jenny wore, and registered as an unbroken tiny line of crinkliness.

Elizabeth focused for a moment on that line of demarcation, between lace and velvet. It was easy to define the feels and to maximize her awareness of them for a moment or two, but then they seemed almost to fade away, to merge into a single, indefinable slight pressure. It was as if her brain refused to spend more time than necessary on such a trivial perception, or as if some movement would be necessary to restimulate new touch receptors. Elizabeth was reminded of the first time she had ever hesitantly placed her hand on a boy's upper thigh, or the first few times a

date had done the same to her breasts: Caressing motions naturally followed, not out of desire so much as sheer necessity, a constant movement being needed to maintain the electricity of initial
contact. Immobility, a simple point-to-point juxtaposition, even of
such highly tactile areas as thighs and hands and breasts, seemed
to deaden sensation; the brain demanded change, demanded
newness, motion.

With a start, Elizabeth felt a warm rush of renewed sensitivity
at Jenny's wrist, a fresh torrent of velvet/lace sensory input. Jenny
had shifted her hand slightly in her lap, just as Elizabeth had
been thinking of the need for that. Was it coincidental, or had
Elizabeth's thoughts caused that minute action? It was impossible
to tell; she would have to keep on working toward the clenched-
fist response.

She shifted her attention from the wrist to the hand itself. No
lace there, only velvet, lightly touched, beneath the base and the
palm, and then the smooth paper of the program loosely held between the thumb and the side of the forefinger. Rings on the second and third fingers: Elizabeth knew from memory that they
were a large star sapphire and a perfect emerald, each set in a
diamond cluster, but now she concentrated only on the feel of
the encircling gold itself, the cool but somehow gentle metal
touch. Each of the fingers was curled *just so*, their tips resting
gently on Jenny's left leg through the expanse of velvet. There
was still no hint of dampness, no nervous drumming or even apparent tension in the muscles. This was the hand of a relaxed
composed young woman; Elizabeth now brought her will to bear
on shattering that composure, or at least its expression through
the response of this one hand.

How to do that? Where to pull the strings, where to press the
buttons? Elizabeth strained with all the mental force that she
could muster, but still the hand remained serene and motionless
in Jenny's lap. She stopped trying and just rested for a minute or
two, frustrated by her failure so far. How could she possibly stop
the action of a determined murderess if she couldn't even make
her move her fingers? The whole thing began to seem hopeless,
and Elizabeth felt on the verge of crying.

No. Breaking down wouldn't serve any purpose, and it was too
early to give up. Besides, maybe she *had* caused Jenny to shift the
position of her hand earlier; if so, it was just a matter of figuring

out how she had done that, where in the other woman's brain she had taken hold.

Where in the *brain!* Of course; that was the problem. She had been trying to focus her struggles on Jenny's hand itself, on the muscles and bones and tendons inside her wrist; but the crucial points of control had nothing to do with those tissues at the end of Jenny's arm; they were all located inside her skull, in the same organ where the point of perceptual contact had somehow been established between the two of them. Somewhere in that brain was an imaginary *homunculus,* a tiny mental copy of Jenny's whole body structure, whose planned or spontaneous thought movements were mirrored by actual external physical reactions. The hand moved only when the brain moved. The visible, effective movement was nothing more than a reflex response to something far more basic, and totally internal. All that was obvious, first-year biology stuff; but knowing it and feeling it were two different matters. Elizabeth had been concentrating on those relatively distant nerve endings; what she really had to do was feel her way around *inside,* here in Jenny's motor cortex, inside the neurons and glial cells and synapses of her brain.

Elizabeth shifted to a more comfortable position in the bed. All along, ever since the electrode had first been activated, she had used Jenny's body merely as a conduit through which to perceive external events and sensations; now she would have to bypass that body's receptors and somehow feel her way into a far deeper level of reality. She felt like a paralyzed accident victim, blindly groping to re-establish a vast network of internal connections that had always been taken for granted and never really *known.*

Visualizing the anatomical or cellular structure of Jenny's brain wouldn't be of any help, she thought; in the first place, she didn't know that much about the subject, and besides, there was no sensation of differentiation among brain areas even in her own actions and perceptions. What was required of her was obviously going to have to be something almost approaching a mystical level, a metaphysical yet concrete search for the ultimate sensory essences within someone else's self.

. . . But let the frame of things disjoint, both the worlds suffer,
Ere we will eat our meal in fear and sleep
In the affliction of these terrible dreams
That shake us nightly . . .

The actors' voices were coming through again, and Elizabeth renewed her efforts to dim out the sensations that streamed through Jenny's open eyes and ears. She tried to picture herself at the center of a totally abstracted, freely floating, and bodiless awareness that was defined as "Jenny Curran," only through the filtered perceptions of other, outside awarenesses, her own among them. Recalling bits and pieces of her scattered reading on Zen Buddhism and Transcendental Meditation and the like, she began constructing a multisensory metaphorical image: herself as a "black hole" at the far edge of the galaxy, a voracious point of pure gravity, an infinite mass of infinitesimal size . . . searching for a star on which to feed, a brilliant point of light that she would devour on contact. She made herself relax, as if she truly had eternity in which to find the hidden star.

The blackness swept around her as she conducted her drifting, undirected quest. From time to time, there would seem to be a brief flash of sensation: Once, she thought she felt the blood pumping through Jenny's network of veins, as if she had established a momentary link with some deep level of the autonomic nervous system; then, a few minutes later, there was a fleeting image of snow-covered mountains, perhaps a memory of Jenny's; too dim and brief to be sure of, though.

Suddenly, an amorphous wave of sound was bursting all around her, and at first she thought she might be near her goal; but then she realized that the play was breaking between the third and fourth acts, and the sound was only the audience's applause. She could feel herself move up through the levels of Jenny's mind, finally breaking clear into the conscious perceptions with which she had become familiar. She turned off the transmitter and lay quietly in the darkness, not wanting to be distracted by Jenny's movement and conversation during the intermission. She waited fifteen minutes, breathing silently and resisting the urge to light a cigarette, and then she reactivated the stimulus.

> . . . Rebellious dead rise never till the Wood
> Of Birnam rise, and our high-placed Macbeth
> Shall live the lease of nature, pay his breath
> To time and mortal custom . . .

The play was on again, and Jenny was once more motionless in her seat. This time, Elizabeth found it easier to block out the primary visual and auditory input, and return to that other level of internalized awareness. Her imaginary perceptual metaphor for the feeling was altered now, without destroying the sensation of depth: No longer was she in space, searching for a single star, but rather she saw herself as a wisp of gas moving through the darkly tangled cypresses that grew out of a marshy blackness . . . here and there, beneath her, she passed over phosphorescent liquid pools. Some of the pools were wide and obviously bottomless, while others were mere spots of watery light. Somehow, she knew that one of them . . . eventually . . . would draw her down . . . into its shining wetness . . . would . . .

Nerves. Tendons. Muscles. Blood. Bone. Shoulder. Arm. Wrist. Hand. Hand. Hand. Hand.

Jenny's hand, the one that had held the program, was now jerking wildly, its fingers pulled into a rigid claw, desperately clutching at the fabric of her gown. Her eyes were wide with terrified confusion, and her other hand was firmly clasped around the wrist of her quivering right arm, trying without success to keep it still in her lap. Phillip had noticed the spasm immediately, and had his arm around her, asking what the trouble was; but as Elizabeth returned to conscious awareness of what was happening, her concentration broke, and Jenny's hand began to slow its violent trembling.

Elizabeth turned off the transmitter and found herself drenched in sweat, the sheets damp and sticky beneath her. The link had been established. What had happened could hardly be considered a conscious or useful direction of Jenny's mind or body; but at least Jenny's own dominion over one part of her anatomy had been temporarily interrupted.

Elizabeth had proved, to her satisfaction, that she could at least have *some* effect on Jenny's actions. Now it was only a matter of focusing that control, and then expanding it, until her will had completely taken the place of Jenny's.

But what then? How much of each of them, as individuals, would remain? If she were able to wrest complete control from the woman in the past, would she remain there permanently? If so, then her own body, the shell that she had always thought of as her *self*, might lapse into a seeming coma, might even die . . . Elizabeth wondered if she could handle that, if she was genuinely prepared to live out the rest of her life in Jenny's time, in Jenny's body.

Setting the transmitter back in its drawer, she opened the bottle of tranquilizers that she kept there, and took two Valiums. She was curious to know what Jenny might tell Phillip about her brief spasm; but she couldn't bring herself to go back again, not just yet. Even more, she had no wish to sit there in that theater and watch *Macbeth* grind on to its inevitable, bloody conclusion. She only wanted to sleep, as deeply and as long as possible.

There were eighteen people around the table, which was covered with splendid bouquets of flowers and preserved fruits in Dresden baskets. The dinner had begun with turbots of lobster and Dutch sauces, portions of red mullet with cardinal sauce, trays of fresh cucumber followed by elaborate cruet stands, and an oyster paté. The entrees had included a *suprême de volaille aux truffes*, a sweetbread *au jus*, and lamb cutlets with asparagus, peas, and a *fricandeau a l'oseille*. Venison had followed, with side dishes of salad and beetroot. The second course had begun with duckling, more peas and asparagus, and plover's eggs in aspic jelly. Sherry Madeira and champagne had been flowing copiously throughout the meal, and the servants were just now bringing in the desserts: a *macédoine* of fruit, *meranges à la crème*, a pineapple-orange-and-melon salad, a chocolate cream, scones with butter and cheese, and both cherry and lemon ices.

Elizabeth had noticed little of the meal. The tastes and textures of the food and wine had served only as a subtle, pleasant background to her attempted reopening of the reverse line of contact and control of Jenny. It seemed more difficult tonight, probably because Jenny wasn't simply sitting still and staring at a stage, but was busily involved in conversation and the acts of eating and ordering the servants about. Still, Elizabeth had been concentrating for over an hour, again using the imagery of a darkened forest dotted with inviting pools of light. She had managed to shut out most of the conversation around her or that Jenny was engaged in. Only bits and pieces crept through now and then, and most of those were meaningless anyway, so they had little distracting effect.

"... *that Lord Overstone's protest was utterly absurd. Limited liability will have no effect whatever on our sense of public responsibility; rather, as Robert Love put it, the principle is simply the freedom of contract, and the right of unlimited association. This nonsense about the deterioration of commercial morality is ...*"

Elizabeth had somewhat changed her tactic tonight: She was no longer attempting to limit her hoped-for effects to only one part of Jenny's body, but was vaguely aiming toward a more generalized incursion. If she could find a pathway like she had the night before, in the theater, she planned to avoid pouring all her efforts into a focus on one hand. Instead she would try to keep the new awareness firmly centered, hopefully establishing a foothold in the upper regions of Jenny's mind. Perhaps she could even learn to home in on her thoughts.

"*. . . of course, the cattle-movement question is an entirely different matter. Gladstone was perfectly correct in rejecting the insurance proposal. If the Exchequer were to guarantee . . .*"

The pools seemed brighter now, and closer together, as if she were approaching something like their source. She had no idea what physiological reality, if any, this imagery reflected; she had no desire to know. It was enough that her crude symbolism seemed to work for her somehow. Any attempt to explain it rationally might well negate her efforts.

Yes, the pools were definitely increasing, and the areas of shimmering light were now greater than the surrounding darkness . . . they were spilling into and out of each other with a sinuous, regular flow, overlapping and combining and coalescing like spilled mercury, like a whirlpool of liquid quartz that was drawing her with inexorably increasing swiftness toward its endless center, like . . . Suddenly, Elizabeth's head seemed to implode with a crushing, incandescent suction, and . . .

Elizabeth was pulled sharply and suddenly alert, partially by a sensation of abrupt and uncontrolled movement, partially by her perception of Jenny's overwhelming fear. Elizabeth's mind leaped back to the scene at the dinner table, and she was immediately filled with a chilling sense of familiarity: Jenny's mouth and eyes were open wide, and her entire body was being wracked by a rapid series of turbulent convulsions. Her head jerked back between her shoulders, and her limbs were flailing in frenzied spasms. As Elizabeth relaxed her mental grip, the fit abated. Then she could see the astonished faces of the guests at the table, regarding her with horror and concern. A large carafe of wine lay smashed on the floor beside her, where she had apparently knocked it off the table as the convulsions began. Two servants came running to pour salt on the red stain that was spreading across the patterned carpet, as Phillip reached her side and gently moved her away from the table. Jenny shook her head slowly back and forth, staring at her limp hands in bewilderment. She tried to regain her composure, and began murmuring apologies to the silent guests. Phillip shushed her and asked one of the men to call for a physician, then helped her to her feet and led her toward the stairs.

Elizabeth shut off the transmitter, shaken and confused herself. She remembered finding what had seemed to be an entrance to the core of Jenny's mind . . . then, without warning, Jenny had suffered something very like an epileptic seizure. The implications were perplexing, frightening . . . she felt a rising nausea in her throat, and lit a cigarette to try to quell it.

It couldn't be, of course. Or could it? Could her own affliction, her own long and painful history of seizures, have been the result of . . . something like this? Someone, like herself, struggling for control of *her* mind? The concept was revolting, reminiscent of the barbaric, medieval notions of epilepsy as "possession." But had they been, at least in part, correct?

If so, then who—or what—had she, as a girl, been "host" to? Had they looked through her own eyes, secretly shared her life, participated in her most intimate moments . . . just as she had done with Jenny? But she had only been able to do that through the electrode in her brain and the transmitter to which it was linked; both of those were new developments, the result of a technology that had not existed when she was a child.

An icy shiver ran down her spine as she contemplated the possibilities: If she and Jenny could somehow coexist, a hundred or more years apart, then it was no less logical to assume that there were still other concurrent levels of time—including, perhaps, the distant future. If that was so, then time itself, and human individuality, might have no concrete meaning. She, the person called Elizabeth, might only be some midpoint link in an eternal chain of interconnected mind/body/selves, extending endlessly into both the past and future, and yet somehow, on some supra-universal plane, existing simultaneously.

Was she, then, or was Jenny, or was *anyone*, themselves at all? Or was everyone on earth, dead and living and yet to be born, just a different temporary vessel, whose purpose was to partially contain the multiple manifestations of some enormous, hydra-headed "self"?

Her head ached with worry, with effort, with memories of the vicariously experienced seizure, and with the magnitude of the unanswerable question. Hating herself for it, she reached again for the bottle of Valium. She felt incredibly alone—and yet at the center of an ominous and unseen crowd.

The night sky was magnificently clear, clear in a way that Elizabeth could only relate to her childhood memories of the star-filled skies above Virginia. From the hilltop where she lay, there was only a low, circular silhouette of oaks and alders framing the inverted, jewel-studded bowl of velvet blackness. Phillip sat behind her on the linen cloth they'd spread upon the grass, his arms around her waist. His fingertips were tracing delicate caressing patterns on the bare flesh of her arms. She was lying with her back against his chest and her head propped on his shoulder. She could feel his face pressed gently against her hair, and the distinctive smell of his brandy and tobacco was a subtle, comforting presence in the air she breathed. There were a dozen other couples at ease on other linen spreads around them. Two servants were quietly passing through the gathering with silver trays of fruit and cheese and wine. Everyone was looking up into the moonless sky, staring in thoughtful silence at the vast array of tiny, distant suns.

Suddenly, a new star seemed to rise into the sky, arcing upward in a gentle parabola from the direction of the darkened house behind them. It shot up in a valiant, glowing struggle against the pull of gravity, but soon its rate of climb began to slow, and its proud ascent seemed hopeless. Then, just as the bold intruder was about to plunge, defeated, back to earth, it burst into a thousand other stars, all fiery red, and that cluster in its turn exploded to become ten thousand more, a glorious profusion of burning violet and white.

The guests cheered and applauded the display, but Phillip's arms stayed where they were, clutching her tight and warm against his body. Jenny closed her eyes, and for several moments Elizabeth could see an afterimage of the dazzling sight that had, however briefly, rivaled and surpassed the brilliance of the naked universe itself.

They and the others had been at the country house for three days now. Phillip had, out of concern for her, at first suggested that they come alone; but Jenny had protested being treated like an invalid, and demanded that a weekend party be invited to accompany them. The slowly growing chill had broken temporarily, and it seemed likely to be the last such opportunity of the season.

The physician they had called that night at dinner had prescribed bromide to ward off further seizures, and Jenny now took daily drafts of the bitter liquid. Elizabeth knew, from having read extensively about the history of her own condition, that bromide had begun to be used against epilepsy in the 1850s. It was thought to be an anti-aphrodisiac, and certain theories of the time had held that epilepsy was the outcome of excessive sexual indulgence. Elizabeth had to smile at that; perhaps, in this case, they might not have been too far off the mark. The medicine's anticonvulsant properties were limited, however, and shortly after the turn of the century it would be rendered obsolete with the discovery of phenobarbitone. Elizabeth also knew that one of the major side effects of bromide was drowsiness, caused by its retarding many of the major functions of the brain. This filled her with new confidence and hope: If Jenny's thinking, and her will, were slightly dulled, it might prove easier for Elizabeth to impose her own resolve. Her early, blundered efforts to take control of Jenny's mind, and the unforeseen seizure that had resulted from the last attempt, might end up helping her more than she had thought.

Another flaming starburst was breaking above them now, this one even more spectacular than the last. The weekend had been filled with diversions both elaborate and simple, all planned and executed mainly for her benefit. There had been an afternoon of tennis, played on the lawn with broad, elongated rackets. As they played, everyone wore hats and studiously tried not to perspire. On Saturday, Phillip had arranged for a photographer to come and demonstrate his skill with the latest of the wet-plate processes, an improvement over the old daguerreotypes, though without the delicate silvery highlights of the earlier method. The wet-plate system was high-speed photography, with a sitting time of only several seconds. Still, Elizabeth had found it strange to join those stiff, intensely formal groupings, their smiles and laughter willingly surrendered for the duration of the exposure time. Being photographed was an act almost official in its purpose: God forbid their portraits should look frivolous. Already, though, this attitude to the newest art was beginning the changes that would affect it and, through reflection, the lives that it recorded. As she and Phillip stood waiting for the powder flash, Elizabeth thought of Charles Dodgson, later to be known as Lewis Carroll. At this very moment, he might be somewhere in the nearby countryside droning out his tales of Alice's adventures to calm and soothe some soft blonde child as she shed her clothes before the waiting camera eye behind which Dodgson peered excitedly. For her own part, Elizabeth wondered what would become of the photographs made that weekend. Would they still exist in the 1970s, faded curios of dead people in a dead time? And had the camera captured nothing more than Jenny's features, or was Elizabeth herself somehow visible to anyone who might look long enough and deep enough into the image on the coated glass?

When the photographs were done, they'd all gone boating. Phillip took his jacket off as he rowed the two of them around the little Serpentine at the bottom of the hill on which the house stood, and Elizabeth had watched with pleasure the flexing of his powerful but slender arms. Jenny's inner strength was weakened by the bromide and the sun, and at one point Elizabeth had managed to make her reach out and pluck a lily from a floating pad. It was the most complete, and complex, action she had yet controlled. Jenny, dazed, stared blankly at the flower in her lap, knowing that she hadn't wanted it herself. Elizabeth let herself lie back against the silken cushions in the boat, exhausted by the sudden mental effort but exhilarated by her unexpected triumph. The flower was *hers*, not Jenny's; and somehow, that had made the day hers, too.

The fireworks were over now, capped by one incredible display in which the profile of a beautiful young woman, obviously meant to be Jenny, was limned in blazing gold against the backdrop of the heavens. Phillip squeezed her tightly, and a string quartet began a piece by Mozart. The servants came around the lawn again, with steaming silver pots of coffee brandy.

Yes, Elizabeth thought. Yes, she could spend her life here if it came to that. It was well worth all the risks.

Mindy was half sitting, half reclining on Elizabeth's sofa, sipping a margarita. Her bright orange dress and the numerous multicolored bracelets, necklaces, and rings that she was wearing today stood out in brilliant contrast against the muted blues and grays of the living room.

David was in Buffalo for two days, consulting with a contractor. Mindy had dropped by for lunch to keep Elizabeth company, and the afternoon had easily extended into cocktails. The high-speed flow of random New York trivia had been a pleasant break at first, but now Elizabeth's mind was drifting back to her own more serious concerns. If she did manage to take full control of Jenny's mind, and if the switch was, as she suspected, permanent, this might be the last time she would ever see her friend. She suddenly felt a desperate need to talk, to *really* talk.

". . . so after all those weeks of hinting around the subject, they finally agreed that trying a threesome might help their marriage. But it was only *then* that they realized Eileen had meant an extra guy, and Robert thought she'd agreed to an extra girl. So they got one of each, and of course that's just a whole different thing entirely, but it seemed to work out pretty well anyway, because . . ."

"Mindy? Do you mind if I ask you a question?"

"What? Do you mean have *I* ever? Well, of course, silly, but which combination did you want to ask about?"

"No, no, it wasn't that. I'm sorry to interrupt, but—I've just been thinking about some things lately, and I wondered if we could talk about them."

"Of course we can, you know that. My God, here I've just been rambling on with all this trash, and I haven't even noticed how worried you look. Come on, what's the matter?"

"Nothing's the matter, really, I've just—I've just been wondering about some weird things, and you're the only person I can talk to about it without feeling ridiculous."

"What kind of weird things?"

"Oh, things like—like what happens to people after they die, and whether the way we perceive time is real or not, and—things like that."

Mindy shifted her position on the sofa, wriggling and hunching her shoulders forward a little, like a twelve-year-old at a pajama party when the conversation has started to take a deliciously dirty turn.

"Like reincarnation, you mean?"

"Maybe. That, or something—kind of like that. I don't really know."

Mindy smiled knowingly, her head nodding slowly up and down. "I knew it, Elizabeth. I always knew that sooner or later you'd start getting in touch with the mystical forces that guide our lives. You've always acted so cool and rational, but you're a Gemini, and eventually that side of your nature had to express itself."

Mindy's sudden air of superior knowledge was misplaced, and mildly irritating, but Elizabeth held her annoyance in check. "No, I'm not talking about astrology, Mindy. I'm talking about real things, serious things."

"But that's exactly what I'm telling you, Elizabeth. These things are *all* serious. I just hardly know where to start: There are the secrets of the Great Pyramid, of course, and all the *marvelous* works of Edgar Cayce, and . . ."

"But has anybody ever really studied all this? I mean like scientists in a laboratory, or something."

Mindy took another sip of her margarita and glanced briefly away. "Honestly, Elizabeth, you just can't approach the ancient mysteries with that kind of attitude. If you could *prove* them, they wouldn't be ancient mysteries, now would they? So the only thing you can do is just trust your own judgment and learn to accept the hidden knowledge that's been passed down for centuries and centuries and centuries. It's the *feeling* that counts."

But that, thought Elizabeth, is precisely the problem. I know the feeling all too well, and I want to know something more than that.

"The best thing to do," Mindy was saying, "is to get in touch with your inner spirit." Her tone became conspiratorial. "Have you been experiencing the flow of the eternal chain of being? Is that what you're trying to tell me?"

For a moment, Elizabeth was tempted. For all her illogic and naïveté, Mindy was using certain phrases that almost seemed to fit what Elizabeth had been going through. And yet this was different, it wasn't just chic party chatter. "I . . . don't think so, no . . . I've just been curious, that's all."

"Well, if you'd like to make contact with your past lives, I can introduce you to the most *amazing* young man. He knows more about the cycles of birth and rebirth than absolutely *anyone* in New York, and he charges practically nothing at all for a psychic reading. Through him, I've discovered that I was once a hand-maiden to Cleopatra, and the wife of one of the Medicis—I forget which one, but an important one—and then I was a cousin to Marie Antoinette, and after that I was one of Aaron Burr's mistresses . . . it's just fascinating, he knows *everything* about the history of your personal karma. And he's *so* mellow. Would you like me to give you his number?" Mindy smiled coyly. "He also gives training in some very wicked Tibetan exercises, and, well . . . if David's going to be so busy on this new project of his . . ."

"I don't think so. Thanks anyway, Mindy. It was just idle curiosity, nothing important. So tell me, what finally happened with Eileen and Robert?"

The apartment seemed unbearably quiet after Mindy left. Elizabeth started to mix herself another drink, then thought better of it. Her head should be as clear as possible. She compromised with a glass of wine, which she sipped while staring at the evening news on television with the sound off. Every minute or so John Chancellor's somber face was interrupted by a film clip. The color always seemed to be a little off in the film segments: The faces on the shouting mob in front of the Roman Colosseum were redder than they should have been, and the closeup of the pounding fist of a senator who was angry at someone or something was slightly yellow, and the flames that rose from the pieces of a shattered 747 were tinged distinctly purple. As someone whose profession centered on the use of visual effects, Elizabeth idly wondered if the networks would ever be able to standardize their remote equipment well enough to solve the problem. As herself, she no longer really cared. If everything went as planned, she would never see another television set. She finished her wine, and went into the bedroom to get the transmitter.

Jenny was lying down, half dozing, in the main bedroom of the country house. The effects of the bromide must be increasing, Elizabeth thought; Jenny almost never napped during the afternoon, but now she'd started taking to her bed for an hour or more almost every day.

The pathway to her mind was more familiar now, although Elizabeth still could not explain or understand it. The imaginary pools of light sped underneath her disembodied self, and the final, crucial reservoir that led directly to her goal offered no resistance at all this time. The ebb and flow of Jenny's deepest mind lapped weakly at the edges of her consciousness, and she absorbed them easily.

. . . *standing in the wind, with seven coaches pulled by fourteen horses, black, all of them black, waiting in a row beside the ocean at the bottom of the mountain . . .*

Jenny was dreaming, Elizabeth realized with a start. For all the times she'd tuned in to her sleeping brain, she'd never felt the other woman dream before. Her sleep had always been perceived as blank, as empty; now, even Jenny's dreams were not her own.

. . . as the ocean rises, and the horses stand in place, drowning without a sound or struggle, and the water coming up the mountain now, cold on her naked feet, her white dress beginning to billow in the rising tide . . .

Elizabeth felt herself shiver, not knowing whether it was her own body, or Jenny's, or only her own mind that was actually shuddering. She didn't like this dream, and she didn't like the idea of being in any of Jenny's dreams anyway. Time to end it. Time to practice.

She concentrated on opening her eyes, and soon felt Jenny's heavy lids responding slowly, against their will, but responding nonetheless. For a moment, Jenny herself was locked into the kind of dual sensory perception that Elizabeth had grown so used to, and Elizabeth could feel her drifting confusion: half seeing the dark water from the dream, and also seeing the interior of the room that her unfocused, involuntarily opened eyes were staring at. Elizabeth could feel her try to come awake, try to bring herself back to normality, but the bromide and Elizabeth's firm control both held her down.

Jenny's body felt like an inanimate covering, like some heavy costume that Elizabeth had put on. She pulled the hands up before her eyes, working their fingers like a pianist limbering up before a concert. She could feel Jenny there with her, confused and helpless in a haze of bromide and half sleep, watching her own hands flex and stretch against her wishes.

Slowly, carefully, Elizabeth forced her up into a sitting posture, then swung her legs out over the side of the bed. As her bare feet touched the floor, Jenny tried to pull them back into the bed, but Elizabeth didn't let her. She was standing now, still unaware of what was going on or why, but knowing that she'd lost control of her own movements. Elizabeth moved one leg out in the beginnings of a step, but the balance was wrong, and Jenny stumbled, bruising her arm against the high wooden bedpost. Elizabeth felt the pain, too, but ignored it, and focused all her efforts on getting her to stand again. She pulled herself upright, this time forcing herself to stay aware of her center of gravity and the positions of her feet and legs. One halting step came, then another. Jenny was walking.

Elizabeth was walking.

The steps became more natural, smoother. The balance was automatic now, and she could look around the room as she paced its length. She could look anywhere she chose, she could move her eyes and move her head at will. This was her here, not Jenny Curran. This was Elizabeth walking around the bedroom of the country house in England, walking and moving her whole body with more assurance every second, fixing her vision on any object that might hold her interest, moving her own hands across tabletops and up and down the fabric of the nightgown. Jenny was somewhere else entirely, somewhere in the background, quiet and ineffectual.

She moved to the dressing table, picking up small objects and setting them down again without dropping a single one. On impulse she dipped her finger into a tin of rouge, then smeared a trail of it across the waist-high makeup mirror on the table. She stood there for a moment, looking at the bright red line she'd drawn. Then she put her finger back into the rouge, and reached out to the mirror a second time, moving her hand across it in a careful pattern, watching the characters appear:

$$E \ldots L \ldots I \ldots Z \ldots A \ldots B$$

Her hand began to shake a little, and she could almost hear the silent screams of terrified bewilderment that Jenny was trying to force into her mouth. She swallowed hard, and almost choked as the swallow and the straining vocal cords collided in their opposing purposes. Jenny was fully awake now, and her consternation had almost overcome the bromide's effects. Elizabeth was fighting to keep what she had gained, but it was no longer easy. She grasped the edges of the mirror and slid down onto the stool before the dressing table. As she did, the reflected image moved to show her face.

Jenny's eyes went wide with boundless fright, recognizing that somehow they were no longer hers with which to see. Her mouth flew open in a gagging scream, and stretched into a shapeless grimace as Elizabeth tried to stop it. Then neither of them could maintain control, and as they both looked at the mirror, through the blood-red letters that Elizabeth had written, both their defenses crumbled and the seizure took full hold.

ELIZAB . . .

The letters seemed to swirl in a crimson blur around her head. It took her several moments to remember where the letters were, and how they'd gotten there; by that time she could see her hand wiping them away into oblivion. No. Not her hand. Jenny's hand, now. Jenny's hand again.

She swam up quickly through the long-familiar daze that always followed a major seizure.

Jenny was standing up now. There was nothing left to indicate that the thick red smears on the mirror had once been letters, distinct and well-defined. But they *had* been: Elizabeth had made them herself, she had written most of her own name right there on that silvered glass, that mirror that had probably been shattered or discarded before the twentieth century began. Nothing could wipe that away. Let Jenny live her life again, for now; Elizabeth was secure in the certain knowledge that she held the key to its permanent control.

Jenny washed her face, splashing the cold water on with vigorous slaps, as if to punish and admonish whatever unseen inner demon had taken hold of her before. The water felt good, and Elizabeth relaxed as Jenny slipped a fresh dress on, replacing the nightgown that was stained with rouge and sweat from their earlier struggle.

Sometimes it was nice to relinquish all the physical responsibilities of living, Elizabeth thought, to just lie back and let another mind take you through the boring, necessary motions, let it do the worrying and working, let it make all the decisions and responses. If things had worked out differently, if Jenny had been who she'd seemed to be at the beginning, if she'd been content to live her life in peaceful lovingness with Phillip . . . but that was a senseless, depressing thought. There were other things to cope with now, and Elizabeth would do what must be done.

The dull clip-clop of the horse's hooves and the constant rumble of the wheels against the road were muted by the thick silk padding that covered the coach's interior. The maples and the elms that lined the packed-dirt highway were beginning now to hint at the extravagance of colors they would soon display, and the thin gray clouds that blocked the setting sun were moving north to south, announcing the final termination of this Indian summer. On the horizon, a flock of sheep were huddling close together like a single, woolly beast, in practice for the even colder nights to come.

Jenny pulled her quilted wrap more tightly about her shoulders. Phillip saw the movement, and pulled her to his side, his arm firm and protective around her slender body. Jenny smiled and moved against him, closer still, her head tilted to his chest. Elizabeth watched the dimly passing images of trees and fields fade out entirely as Jenny let her eyes fall slowly shut.

It was so easy to forget that this drowsy, quiet young woman had planned what she had planned. If this was only a hallucination, as Dr. Garrick had believed, then perhaps Elizabeth could change the course of its events by means less drastic; but she knew that wasn't possible. Things had progressed too far, and she must proceed on the assumption that she was dealing with reality, however strange or inexplicable. Her only hope was to achieve an absolute, and permanent, control over Jenny Curran's brain and body.

Jenny was still now, dozing under the effects of the bromide. Elizabeth relaxed within the rocking movement of the coach, and could feel the soothing brush of Phillip's cashmere coat against her cheek. This evening was the first time he had worn the coat, and she loved the look and feel of it on him; with winter coming, she thought, he would wear it often . . .

Winter. There would be blazing oak-log fires in every room of the London house, night and day, and the garden would be full of fresh, clean snow and pristine icicles. They would go skating on the frozen Hyde Park Serpentine, and on the lakes of Sussex; there would be sleigh rides in the country, bonfires in the city on Guy Fawkes day, a Christmas dinner of goose and hot plum pudding . . . then spring would come, and then another summer, and always there would be Phillip, beside her everywhere, in every season, laughing, talking, loving . . .

The carriage hit a small bump in the road, and they were jolted roughly for a moment before the driver found the proper track again. Jenny stirred sleepily and issued forth a tiny moan, but soon fell still again.

Quietly, almost idly, Elizabeth let herself search out once more the image of the shimmering pool that she now thought of as more truly "Jenny" than was the familiar physical body. With ease, she slipped into that liquid other self, assuming it, owning it. In one smooth motion, she lifted up what was now *her* arm, and put it firmly around Phillip's neck, running her fingers through his long, dark hair. He squeezed her closer, caressing her back through the patchwork quilt, and she lifted her mouth to his. As they kissed, she suddenly felt Jenny stirring from her sleep, and she expertly let the pool of being and control slide back into the other woman's still unconscious grasp. The transition was a smooth one, and Elizabeth was content to relax again in Jenny's sleeping form, still cuddled warmly into Phillip's arms. The movement was simpler every time she made it, she thought with satisfaction: There was no need to extend it into another struggle, no need to risk another seizure; not here, not now. She was already learning, learning fast, exactly how to do what must be done.

Let Jenny sleep, she thought. There will be time enough, and more, for me.

David came home from Buffalo on schedule, but his days and even, sometimes, nights were still a constant jumble of appointments and meetings and planning sessions. He had thought the major work was past when the blueprints were completed, but Bob Rampling was delegating more and more responsibility to him, and he happily accepted the continued work load.

Elizabeth went through the motions of pretending to object to his erratic schedule and his regular nighttime exhaustion, but she herself was totally preoccupied, and secretly glad to be left alone. Now and then she felt a pang of conscience, wishing that they could talk, that she could confide her worries and concerns to him; could even, in some way, apologize for what they'd lost between them, could thank him for the early years. She would soon be leaving him forever, and he would never even know where she had gone. It would be painful for him, certainly: he might be burdened with her in an apparent lifelong coma, or might find her body with the life gone out of it entirely. But there was no way she could warn him without convincing him that she had gone insane. In that event, they would surely blame the electrodes; they would take away the transmitter, and with it all her chances of preventing Phillip's murder. So she kept her silence, much as she regretted having to.

She still had no idea when Jenny would make her attempt. Each time she practiced taking over Jenny's body, she would get a random snippet of the other woman's thoughts and emotions, but nothing organized or concrete. Surely, though, something had to happen soon; Jenny was terrified by what was happening within her mind, and might even accelerate her plans because of it. Elizabeth now made use of every opportunity to take temporary control, whenever Jenny napped or seemed to let her thoughts drift.

Sometimes this still resulted in a seizure, when Jenny's medicine was wearing off or when she managed to work up enough resolve, in the limbo or the stasis to which she was relegated when

Elizabeth had control, to fight back. The fits weren't pleasant for
Elizabeth either, and there was even a possibility that recurrent,
frequent seizures could send Jenny into *status epilepticus*, a condition of uncontrollable, unending seizures that might well be fatal.
To avoid that possibility, Elizabeth now tended more and more to
draw her own limits to the time she spent in command of Jenny,
gliding quickly out of her position of dominion whenever the pressure on Jenny's brain seemed about to be unbearable.

Most of the time, she waited until Jenny was alone before she
practiced. In the four or five days since they had returned from
Sussex, Elizabeth had thoroughly explored Jenny's boudoir on her
own, had inspected and mentally catalogued every painting in the
London house, and had picked the last remaining flowers in the
garden. None of these actions were strange enough to completely
unnerve Jenny, the way that Elizabeth's name on the mirror had;
but she still knew that, each time, Jenny was fully aware of losing
control, though to what or whom she would have no way of
knowing.

Only very occasionally did Elizabeth dare to override Jenny's
self-control in the company of other people, and then never for
more than a few seconds at a time. She didn't want Jenny to become so disconcerted that anyone might suspect Phillip's wife to
be deranged, nor did she want to provoke any more seizures in
front of guests or servants. If the prescribed dosages of bromide
were increased, their effects might somehow backfire; and, once
Elizabeth had taken full and permanent occupancy of Jenny's person, she didn't want to have to deal with such a serious background of epilepsy that a sudden "cure" would seem implausibly
miraculous.

Once, she had tried to speak with Jenny's mouth and vocal
cords, just to order another glass of wine at dinner; but the effort
required was more than she'd expected. She could sense Jenny's
rising panic, and nothing more than a muted squeak came out.
She had tried to cover it with a cough, and then immediately re-
linquished her control.

One nagging problem still disturbed her, even assuming that
she would be successful in the take-over: What might Charlie
Ferrara do when "Jenny" backed out of the plot and did not communicate with him again? Of course, it was unlikely that she
would encounter him on the streets of London—she certainly

never planned to make any more trips to Soho—but what would she do if he contacted her? Naturally, she would deny any knowledge of him or anything he claimed; but he probably possessed some proof of Jenny's background: signed letters, maybe, or even photographs. If such documents or pictures did exist, they would be more than merely compromising: In this society, with its attitudes toward status, sex, and women, they would be devastating. It was a problem that she knew she'd have to face, but for which she had, as yet, no answer.

She was also painfully aware of the other disadvantages inherent in irrevocably forsaking her own century. Because of the Currans' social and financial station, many of them would never directly touch her: child labor, malnutrition and widespread starvation, lack of winter heat or summer ventilation, slavelike conditions in those very factories whose hellish despotism had been Marx's inspiration . . . but certain other negative aspects of the era would be unavoidable, in spite of social class or riches. The worst, of course, were medical in nature. From what she'd seen and heard so far, Elizabeth knew that the time was at least post-1850, so there would be no problem in waiting for the discovery of ether's anesthetic qualities; but even so, any type of surgery would be an unpleasant and dangerous proceeding. Jenny had no scars on her body, so her appendix was still there; and as life wore on, there would be the risk of gallstones, cysts, cataracts, thyroid trouble, cancer . . . Elizabeth was not a morbid person or a hypochondriac, but the prospect of dying from something as simple as an appendectomy would suddenly become an awful, realistic fear.

Even if her organs stayed intact and healthy, there were other worries that she'd always thought of as archaic: typhoid, smallpox, cholera, trichinosis, polio, tuberculosis . . . even influenza was a major killer then, as was childbirth; and there would be no simple, effective means of birth control available.

Pollution, too, would be a problem: The air and water might seem pure and clean, devoid of all the many-lettered chemicals with which modern man had dirtied his environment; but, if anything, the nineteenth century was worse. The burning of bituminous coal was then widespread in London, filling the air with more noxious gases than even modern-day Los Angeles; public sanitation was primitive, and the food and drinking water were crawling with all manner of foul and perilous organic matter, both dead and living. There would be no gasoline fumes, of course; but equine energy had its own pollutant by-products, the evidence of which Elizabeth had already seen and smelled in astonishing quantity during Jenny's exursions outside the house.

Then, too, there were the social realities and the minor or major inconveniences to be expected: Sadly, Elizabeth realized that she could never work again, despite the multitude of London theaters and the inflated importance of Victorian stage design. To follow such a pursuit, *for pay* to boot, would be a literally unthinkable breach of etiquette and even morals for a woman of Jenny Curran's position. No matter what Elizabeth might feel or think, she had to face the fact that she, alone, could never make the slightest dent in the sexiest mores of an entire age and nation. She would have to be content with reading, and shopping, and decorating, and amusing herself at home by dabbling in the minor arts. Thinking of this made her realize just how much she really would miss movies, and late-night TV, and the New York *Times,* and records, and FM stereo, and the constant flow of brand-new books and magazines.

She was fortunate that Phillip's business involved a fair amount of foreign travel; she would manage to finagle her way along on as many of his trips as possible. As pleasant as that might be, she knew that she would be aware of the imposed limitations on world travel: Rio would be a distant, minor port, Acapulco wouldn't even yet be developed, and skiing would be something that a few barbaric Swiss were forced to do to get from place to place. Transportation would be slow and undependable: Steamships would be new, experimental, risky, and require close to a month to cross the ocean. It suddenly occurred to her that she should try to locate as many old almanacs and record books as possible, and memorize a list of great disasters, such as fires and sinking ships, to be avoided.

Those were the arguments against the life change: a loss of modern comforts and conveniences, and the taking on of certain extra health hazards. On the other hand, she would be entering a quiet world of serene simplicity, in which she would know wealth and tasteful luxury . . . and a world in which she would have Phillip. For that alone, she was more than willing to exchange nuclear missiles and gasoline fumes for smallpox scares and horse manure. She wasn't backing out, and she didn't think she would regret her choice.

In any case, by the second week in March, it was apparent that she had no time for second thoughts. Jenny had obviously realized that her periods of odd, unwilled behavior seemed to come most often when she was sedated by the bromide, and she was gradually decreasing her daily dosage on her own. Elizabeth wasn't sure how difficult it might be to make that final, total leap of consciousness and domination if Jenny was in a state of full alertness.

Also, Jenny had been behaving rather curiously in the past few days. She had surreptitiously tossed two of her favorite necklaces, both quite costly pieces, into the Thames as her coach was crossing Westminster Bridge; and the day after, she had secretly buried a valuable diamond tiara behind a hedge in the now-barren garden.

Elizabeth had no idea what these illogical actions might indicate; but she did know that the days were slipping by with unceasing speed. The ultimate, crucial test might come at any place and time. Until then, there was nothing more that she could do but wait and watch.

The meal had been superb, as usual: an almost endless cornucopia of truffles and asparagus and duck *à l'orange* and creamy, thick desserts. The Currans were giving a dinner party for a delegation of Scandinavian trade officials and the local diplomatic representatives of their respective nations. Elizabeth had thoroughly enjoyed the feast, and had let Jenny dine in peace.

Phillip was in an excellent humor, having closed two major deals. With Norway and Denmark out of the way, he was now concentrating his attentions on the Swedish group, most of whom were themselves concentrating on Jenny's neckline. Elizabeth had noted with amusement, and grudging appreciation, the skill with which Jenny played her part in Phillip's various negotiations: an image of demure obedience for Spanish guests, witty flirtatiousness for the French, a boisterous sense of humor for Italians, and plenty of skin for the Scandinavians. Elizabeth's feelings were slightly mixed about assuming those hostess duties herself; she was worried that she might make some odd slipup, might inject a confusing reverse anachronism into some crucial conversation. She hated to imagine the reaction of, say, the Russian consul if she absentmindedly referred to the Bolshevik Revolution, or the astonishment and iciness with which her true opinions on, and knowledge of, the history of colonialism would be met. It would all take getting used to, and she would have to watch her tongue. Even literary conversations would be fraught with elements of danger: It might be hard to remember who had written what yet, and she didn't want to arouse anyone's curiosity by knowing exactly how the latest Dickens serial would end.

The coffee was finished now, and the party was going through its usual division: menfolk to the drawing room for brandy and cigars, and ladies huddling together to discuss the men. Elizabeth could do without that, and she was just about to switch off the transmitter when Jenny excused herself from the group of women for a moment and headed up the stairs.

A crackling fire was already going in the bedroom fireplace; now that the weather had turned cool, the servants would build one early every night and keep it freshly ablaze until she and Phillip finally retired. Jenny stood staring at the burning logs for a moment, then turned away from the flames with a sigh, and walked directly toward the closed French windows that led onto the bedroom terrace where they often took their breakfast. She moved with a steady, purposeful step, and Elizabeth tried unsuccessfully to recall whether or not Jenny had taken her evening dose of bromide. Perhaps, because she was expecting guests, she—Jenny was unlatching the windows, opening them. That would let all the accumulated heat out, Elizabeth thought. What on earth was she doing that for?

The windows were completely open now, and a stiff, cold wind was blowing through, billowing the curtains and dimming the fire. Jenny stepped out on the gusty terrace, seemingly oblivious to the biting chill. A massive, orange full moon hung over the garden like some bloated, out-of-season fruit about to fall from the denuded branches of the tree that stood next to the terrace. Jenny looked briefly at the moon, then turned her attention to the stark black outline of the leafless tree. One heavy branch protruded just above the terrace. Jenny reached up and touched its underside, running her palm against the crusty bark. Her eyes followed the branch's length to where it joined the indistinct mass of the tree's broad trunk, and Elizabeth watched from within as she gazed downward to the spot where the tree cast out its thick roots into the garden soil. Then she looked back at the moon again, and Elizabeth felt her smile, and sigh, and then abruptly turn and walk back into the bedroom. The fire still fought against the wind from the open windows, which she made no move to close.

Elizabeth was thoroughly confused now; why had Jenny come up here at all, she wondered? And why didn't she close those windows, before—suddenly, Jenny began to shriek as if in panic, calling for Phillip. The screams took Elizabeth completely by surprise. She hadn't made any move to take control of Jenny's mind. There was nothing she could think of that could have frightened her like this; but the screams only increased in intensity, and then, with two swift motions, Jenny reached up and ripped open the front of her own dress, exposing her breasts, and then very deliberately smashed one of a priceless pair of Ming

vases against the wall, shattering it with a loud crash. In a sickening rush of awareness, Elizabeth knew exactly what was going on,
and she wasn't ready for it.

The screams, the torn clothing, the open window and the tree
next to the terrace, the jewelry that Jenny had disposed of the
past few days . . .

"*. . . I only came upstairs to freshen up, and when I came into
my room there he was, wearing a mask of some sort, with my jewelry in his hand. I cried out, and he attacked me, and when
Phillip came to help he . . . he . . . took out a pistol . . ."*

Already Elizabeth could hear Phillip's footsteps, bounding
heavily upon the stairs. Jenny was still screaming, but even as she
did she was opening the sewing box where the pistol lay, on top
of all the multicolored scraps of cloth. Behind the screams and
the running footsteps, Elizabeth could hear and feel the blood
that pounded in her brain, or Jenny's brain, or both, and she knew
this was the time, that everything she'd planned must now be
done and done successfully in six or seven seconds, no way back or
out, no stalling, no time for any preparation or delay . . .

Find the pool, Elizabeth thought. The pool of light, find it fast.
Ignore the rest, ignore these other thoughts and sounds, just leap
into that familiar shining pool, leap for the last time, absorb it all,
drain it of its glow, assimilate it, take it, own it, use it, *be* it . . .

Jenny held the pretty little pistol in her hand now, and Phillip
was flinging the door to the bedroom open, shouting Jenny's
name; yet it seemed as if the door was inching apart, moving as
sluggishly as if it had been under water, and Phillip's voice was a
long, deep, unintelligible roar.

In unbearable slow motion, Jenny's eyes moved upward, focused on the mirror above the dresser, and locked there, looking
at themselves, looking at Elizabeth inside them. Elizabeth could
feel the struggle, feel the fear, as Jenny's presence slipped away
into oblivion. Her fingers—Elizabeth's fingers, now—moved stiffly
open, and the pistol seemed to fall with stately leisure toward the
floor. She watched it fall, and then she felt the tears well up, felt
her hands and shoulders start to tremble in exhaustion and relief.
Phillip was coming to her now, his arms outstretched, his face a
mask of anguished grief for all the pains he'd never understand, in
spite of all the life they'd have together. Together!

She turned to meet him, turned to fall into the comfort of his

loving arms . . . and then she felt a painful inner wrench from
out of nowhere, felt a clutching hatred seize her brain, sensed the
sorrowed trembling escalate to full-scale tremors, and her hand was
Jenny's hand again, grotesquely twitching on the dresser top until
its groping fingers found the scissors, and her arm was moving in a
savage spasm, up and down, up and down, the hard edge of her
hand striking Phillip in the face. Her first thought was that she
might hurt him, that her jerking hand might bruise his flesh; and
then she saw the sharpened points protruding from her tight-
gripped fist, saw the scissors penetrate his cheek and neck and
throat, saw the well-honed blades sink deep into his deep brown
eyes, open in amazement to the very moment that the blood
came gushing from them, reddening and soaking her hands and
arms and breasts. He fell away from her, his arms still reaching
out, his pierced brain dead too soon to even spark the reflex that
would pluck the embedded scissors from those blood-drenched
holes that had been his eyes, his eyes, his eyes, his eyes, his
eyes . . .

PART FIVE

She woke up screaming, first, but they were there with the Demerol right away.

The next time, they brought her out of it more gradually, easing her awake by slowly altering the mix of Demerol and Thorazine. She was crying, but she couldn't yet remember why. When she did, the screaming started all over and they had to put her out again.

. . . by the lake, and the horses waiting patiently. Daisies bright as sunlight all around, and Phillip opening the wine . . .

". . . expect a breakdown in a case of this sort . . ."

". . . never *been* a case of this sort . . ."

. . . soft gray silk tufting against her head, and other carriages in the street outside, on their way to Regent Street or back again . . .

". . . insanity is not the issue, simply an overload on her nervous system . . ."

. . . ambassador's bald head shining underneath the brilliant chandelier, and Phillip winking as he notices it, too . . .

". . . shock therapy might perhaps . . ."

". . . more than enough damned shocks already . . ."

. . . bathing her stranger's sleek nude body reflected in the mirrors, bathing and caressing it, anointing it in preparation . . .

". . . legal responsibility was terminated when she signed this waiver, though of course the hospital will be more than willing to . . ."

. . . bursting fireworks brightening the summer night, and Phillip's arms . . .

". . . your fault this happened to my wife, you and your goddamned experiments . . ."

. . . a trip together someday soon, shopping in Florence for another Tintoretto, and moonlight on the Grand Canal of Venice . . .

". . . just no way that we could predict this . . ."

. . . *early morning in the London bedroom, Phillip's body next to hers, Phillip's hand upon her breasts, Phillip's gentle eyes in quiet communion with her own, Phillip's eyes, his deep brown loving eyes, his eyes, his eyes, his eyes* . . .

"Mrs. Austin? Are you awake now?"

Her eyes were fully open, but Dr. Garrick couldn't catch her gaze. She seemed to be staring at a point some distance beyond the opposite wall of her isolated private room. Her pale and shrunken body seemed an ephemeral presence, only barely breaking the smooth lines of the sheet that covered her. Lois Beatty sat on the other side of the bed, tenderly holding the young woman's limp right hand. On Garrick's side, her left hand was strapped to the side of the bed, an IV taped into the wrist, dripping its thick soup of vitamins and glucose.

"Mrs. Austin? Elizabeth? Can you hear me?"

It was April outside, even in New York. The sun was shining brightly through the open window. There had been rain until a day or so ago, and there would probably be more next week, but today the sky had all the look and feel of May. Outside the city, it would even have the smell of May.

"Elizabeth, this is Dr. Beatty. Remember me? Lois Beatty? We talked a lot last summer and fall, before . . . before your operation. We've been waiting here for you to wake up, and Dr. Garrick and I just want to make sure you're feeling better now. Can you tell us how you feel?"

The traffic sounds from the street below were muted, but still there. On a day like this, Lois thought, there should be crickets, not distant horns. She wondered if Elizabeth could hear the horns, if they were disturbing or confusing her.

". . . eyes. No more eyes."

The young woman's mouth had barely moved, and her stare remained fixed on its one directionless direction; but she had definitely said something, or whispered it, and she hadn't started screaming. Yet.

"Do you mean you're having trouble seeing, is that it? Is your vision blurred?"

". . . Dead. She did it. After everything, she did it."

Dr. Garrick shook his head and sighed, frowning slightly at

Lois. The patient was talking gibberish, something apparently related to the hallucinations or imaginings that Peter had told Lois about in California, after the conference. It might be impossible to get anything at all rational out of her about her condition, if she had thoroughly internalized and accepted those fantasies; perhaps even permanently imprinted them, somehow, in connection with this breakdown. The old worries that Peter had secretly shared with Lois, alone at night in the Beverly Hills Hotel, came back now with a vengeance: It might still be necessary to have the Austin woman committed, and if that happened the entire story would soon be pieced together by . . . outsiders. Even if it were never made completely public, Peter would unquestionably be removed from his position at the hospital, and his research funds would dry up like a Kansas cornfield. Reporting strange results was one thing, but once a coverup of them became known, and it came out that records had been burned, tapes erased . . .

". . . really did. She did. I did. Her hands, mine, together . . . in his *eyes!*"

She was crying now, not sobbing or hysterical, but just quietly weeping, the tears falling slowly and unnoticed down her expressionless face.

". . . never saw his eyes, did you? No, of course you didn't. . . . Only me. But they were very nice. Like all the rest of him. No eyes now, though."

She had turned her head and was looking directly at Garrick. His breath stopped short. Maybe she was coming out of it; maybe she could be reasoned with, after all, made to understand that she had been suffering from a minor hallucination, nothing worth mentioning to anybody else.

"Would you mind repeating that, Mrs. Austin? I didn't quite hear you, but you were speaking to me, weren't you?"

She looked straight at him for a moment or two, uncomprehending; then she looked away again, and closed her eyes. They kept on talking to her for several minutes after that, asking her questions about how she felt and if she knew who she was or where she was; but she never answered them, and finally they went away, shaking their heads and frowning.

Maybe tomorrow, they told each other. Tomorrow, or the day after.

They let her go home the second week in April. The apartment was full of flowers, one splendid bouquet after another, from all her friends and theirs. It struck her that a "nervous breakdown" seemed to bring a greater outpouring of expressed sympathy than her operation had. Perhaps brain surgery was just *too* foreign, too remotely abstract; whereas an emotional catastrophe was closer to everyone's reality, a more tangible personal threat that called for stronger symbolic sacrificial offerings than did something so inconceivable, and hence less frightening, as neurosurgery.

Her friends were hungry for details, but their curiosity, whether tactful or blatant, went unsatisfied. Just a case of nervous exhaustion, she told them, nothing more. No, there were no specific problems involved. She and David were getting along just fine, thank you very much. No, she didn't feel the need to talk it out any further; it was all over now, she said, and she was already feeling much better.

It had taken a while, but she had finally emerged from her semicatatonia and her periodic bursts of hysteria enough to tell Dr. Garrick and Dr. Beatty what had happened. There had been sympathy in their faces, particularly Dr. Beatty's; but that was secondary to their obvious, though unstated disbelief. Oh, they'd believed that she had lived through everything she told them; but their expressions made it plain that dealing with a patient's reported hallucinations was nothing novel in their experience. Elizabeth's, they plainly indicated, were just a little more well organized than most.

They'd seemed relieved to see her make a full recovery to lucid consciousness, and also measurably comforted by her assurance that she had no plans to repeat her experiences to anyone. There was no reason that she should, anyway, and she'd been a little surprised when they worriedly brought that up again, particularly since she'd long ago decided that Dr. Garrick's hints about government secrets were a lot of bull. Whatever, that was their con-

cern; if her own doctors didn't believe her, Elizabeth wasn't about
to try to convince anyone else about what she'd been through.

There had been another aspect to their relief, one that
Elizabeth kept in her purse: the familiar transmitter, now half
gutted and looking like a robot amputee without the oblong yellow button that had once controlled the activation of electrode
12. Dr. Garrick had been unable to conceal his satisfaction at having been presented with an excellent, even compelling, reason to
take away her ability to stimulate that troublesome site.

Elizabeth herself had offered no objections to the removal of
the circuitry. For days after her initial recovery, she could associ-
ate the transmitter only with that final, hideous act that had
brought on her collapse. Her nightmares, both waking and sleeping, had only gradually diminished in intensity and frequency. As
they receded slowly into a raw but hidden memory of blood and
anguish, she had been sure that to return again to that once-
familiar world would only cause the painful images to unbearably
resume. Better, she had thought, to nurse her ruptured senses and
to forget as much as possible.

Now that she was home again, though, now that that mon-
strous scene had played itself upon the stage of her remembrance
so many times as to be numbingly familiar in its unpleasantness—
now, with the shock, if not the grief, somewhat abated by the
passing days, other thoughts obsessed her. She had begun to regret
her easy acquiescence to Dr. Garrick's wishes.

Phillip was immutably, irretrievably dead: both in the present
time/space and in the other one that had somehow been opened
to her perception and, toward the end, participation. That much
she knew, and knew she must accept. But what of Jenny?

Lying in the hospital, drugged and emotionally spent, Elizabeth
had considered Phillip's death the ultimate, awful end to everything she had experienced since that November day in Dr. Garrick's testing room, when she had found herself at a piano, playing
Mendelssohn. In the months that followed those first tantalizing
visions, her presence in that other world seemed inextricably involved with her relationship with Phillip. Now he was gone. But
what remained? Was it possible that the entire thing *had* been
just a fantasy, an extended wish-fulfillment of idealized romance?
If so, then the electrode site might be completely blank now, or it
might contain a whole new world of fantasy; Phillip's death could

have spelled the dissolution and evaporation of the whole complicated structure.

If that were the case, then even Garrick should be interested; it
would prove he had been right all along.

But if he *hadn't* been, if the world she had been taking part in
was rooted, impossibly and inexplicably, in objective reality . . .
then it still was going on, had been going on continuously for
three weeks now since Phillip's murder. As she regained her mental strength and her emotional composure, Elizabeth was seized
by a desire to either verify or disprove this assumption, and by
something more: a passionate wish, a *need*, to find out what the
aftermath had been. Elizabeth had lost consciousness in the middle of the bloody act; there was no mistaking the fact that Phillip
had been killed, he could never have survived those vicious, dreadful wounds. But what had happened then? Had the dinner guests
come in to find her standing over Phillip's body, the bloody scissors in her hand? Or had she had the time and the presence of
mind to dispose of them, to toss them on the floor or out the window and to ad lib her way through some hastily amended version
of her original story, claiming that an unknown thief had attacked
both her and Phillip, and had then escaped out the already open
window? Jenny was beautiful, wealthy, and above all, female; the
police and courts of Victorian England would be strongly
disposed to believe whatever tale she might concoct, particularly
with Jenny's skillfully cold-blooded portrayal of the frail, bereaved
young widow in a state of shock. No one, not even Phillip, had
ever had a moment's reason to suspect that she had loved him less
than totally.

Even in the unlikely event that she had been caught red-
handed, Elizabeth realized there would be a ready out: Jenny's
supposed epilepsy. The killing could, with a combination of physician's reports, Jenny's tearful testimony, and an expensive lawyer,
be ascribed to the unfortunate but blameless results of a seizure.
That she was periodically taken with fits was well established,
even a certain topic of gossip and sympathy among the members
of London society, many of whom had personally witnessed one
or more of her attacks. It would not be the first time that epilepsy
had been used as a legal defense for irrational and otherwise inex-
cusable actions, up to and including murder. In fact, there was
one rare form of the condition, diencephalic epilepsy, that *did* ex-

press itself in uncontrollable attacks of violent rage; there were even, Elizabeth recalled, two or three fully verified cases that had actually ended in murder. A Victorian judge and jury would be much more easily swayed by this sort of thing, and the available medical evidence would, at best, be inconclusive and contradictory.

She could really pull it off. Even if she had had time to do nothing more than drop the murderous scissors at her feet, nothing could be proven: Criminology was much less than a science then, and fingerprinting, even if it might have been invented, would be primitive and most likely inadmissible in court. There would be no Sherlock Holmes. The preponderance of evidence, not to mention public sympathy, would be on Jenny's side: the missing jewelry, the open window, her "known" devotion to her husband . . .

Elizabeth's horror and her mourning began to be replaced by anger and a sense of outraged justice. The thought of Jenny blithely escaping punishment for her coolly premeditated murder was an unbearable possibility; and the idea of her sharing the spoils of her crime with Charlie Ferrara was even worse. Elizabeth was the only one who both knew the truth, and cared what happened; justice, or revenge, was in her hands. Somehow, she knew, it would be satisfied.

The sun was hotter than it had been during the long English summer, hotter than the concrete-trapped and reflected heat that soon would plague New York; hotter even than the broiling afternoons that Elizabeth remembered from her southern childhood. This was a truly tropical heat, its intensity made even more stifling by the postwinter humidity that was beginning to coalesce in the atmosphere, harbinger of the constant misty rains and daily thunderstorms that would appear within the next few weeks.

They had been in Mexico for eleven days now, and the house was rented for another ten. Elizabeth would have been content to spend David's vacation time at home, or perhaps somewhere upstate; but he had insisted that they come down here, to someplace lush and warm and foreign, someplace removed from any memories.

The town, Puerto Vallarta, was small, and in the midst of a confused but peaceful coexistence between the elements of old and new. In ten more years, or less, it would become a cheaply flashy copy of its big sister, Acapulco, which lay a hundred miles or so below it on the same spectacular coastline; but now it seemed to offer the best of two worlds, both a sense of sleepy isolation and enough amenities to be considered "civilized."

Elizabeth rolled over on her back, shielding her eyes first from the glint of sunlight on the water in the pool, and then the sun itself. There was a thick, dull plopping sound to her left—another ripened mango dropping from one of the trees in the surrounding garden. She peered over her sunglasses at the leaves on the trees, hoping to see a breeze begin to stir them; but the air was as still as it had been all morning.

The house they'd found was beautiful, if somewhat stark in its cleanliness and pervasive, almost Moroccan whiteness. It was a sprawling, multilevel place, open to the air wherever possible, like all the houses here. It was set on a steep hillside, with three broad terraces overlooking the red-tiled roofs of the town and the vast expanse of the Bay of Banderas beyond, where the sun went through its splendid ritual death each evening. Always the sun here. Even at night: The paintings, the rugs, the clothes, the fruit, all seemed to contain its light, all served as reminders that it would return again, and then again. Always.

"*Perdoneme, señora; quiere usted algun a beber o a comer?*"

"*Sí, yo creo que sí. Una . . . hay de leche de coco en la cocina?*"

"*Sí, señora.*"

"*Bueno, una piña colada, por favor.*"

"*Bueno, señora.*"

So soft, the language. Soft and ripe as the mangoes, the guavas, the papayas. Elizabeth wondered if Jenny had ever spoken Spanish, if she and Phillip had ever walked the sun-baked streets of Madrid, ever ridden horses through the dusty olive groves of Andalusia, ever watched the ever-changing angles of light against the reds and browns and whites of El Greco's hillsides in Toledo. That was what the sloping, clay-tiled roofs of this town reminded her of, she realized; only the endless vista of the Pacific shattered the illusion.

Rosa brought her drink, and Elizabeth sipped the smooth concoction of rum and coconut and pineapple slowly, thinking of Spain, thinking of England, thinking of Jenny. Thinking of Phillip. *His eyes . . .*

She downed the drink in one last gulp and went back in the house. Maybe a walk to town would help. David had gone deep-sea fishing with a San Francisco lawyer they had met in Carlos O'Brian's three nights before. David had been wanting to go fishing ever since they got there, but had hesitated to leave her alone, knowing she had no interest in it herself. Finally, she'd almost had to force him to accept the lawyer's invitation. Anyway, she had the rest of the day to herself, and she didn't want to spend it lying by the pool and thinking.

She stripped off the bathing suit and pulled on a short red-and-yellow sundress and a pair of woven leather sandals. Everything, even her bright new clothes, was in such total contrast to what she'd experienced in the past few months; Why, then, did it seem to call up all the hurtful memories? Maybe the very contrast itself, so striking in its differentness, forced her mind to the opposite, unwanted extremes.

The narrow, rocky sidewalks of the town were almost empty. The few remaining tourists would all be at the beach, or beside their hotel pools. Elizabeth passed a group of nuns all wrapped in black, and a shriveled old man with rotten teeth who was selling *tostadas*. The heat was worse in town, a palpable *something* that she wanted to reach out and push away from her. Sweat dripped down her thighs, and she could feel the thin material of the dress sticking to her back. A group of young Mexicans lounging outside the town square made their senseless clicking/sucking noises behind her back, and she nervously turned the nearest corner, squirming to release her flesh from the sticky wetness of the dress. A small boy was urinating in the street, and three plump women draped in shawls watched her through the screenless window of a barren, two-room house. The neighborhood was filled with the stench of rotting mangoes, like mounds of discarded flesh. Another group of boys, none older than fourteen, galloped past on horseback, as dangerously close as possible. As she stumbled to get out of the way they all clucked and shouted "¡Mamacita! ¡Mamacita!"

Elizabeth turned back to the right and found herself approaching the beach at last. She hadn't brought her bathing suit, but at least she could get a cold drink at one of the *palapas* there. She crossed the tiny bridge that spanned the almost-dry stream in the heart of town, pausing to watch the women soaking their laundry in the tiny trickle of water and spreading it on the rocks to dry. As she watched, an overpowering odor of human feces rose to meet her nostrils, and she moved quickly on, gagging at the smell that mingled with the odors from the hot corn stand nearby. Two older women in white lace hats and printed dresses, Canadians or Americans, passed her in the opposite direction. Each of them was chewing greedily at a corncob dipped in mayonnaise.

Halfway to the beach there was another square, full of crumbling brick constructions: either the ruins of a wrecked building, or the undisturbed remains of one begun but not completed. Beside one of the piles of brick there was an emaciated dog, lying in the shade and panting heavily. It looked up, heavy-lidded and slow, as she walked by. For an instant she had a queer desire to kill it, to smash its head in with a stone.

She stopped at the entrance to the beach, now breathing heavily herself. There was no surf today, and the water of the bay looked brackish, full of seaweed and waste matter. There was a smattering of almost naked bodies lying quietly on the dirty sand, but no one was in the water. She could hear a third-rate rock band playing from one of the *palapas* down the beach, and the cries of children hawking broiled fish chunks on sharpened sticks. Suddenly she felt an arm around her waist and someone breathing warmly against her neck. She jerked away from this unannounced and unwanted presence, and as she did, her sandal caught in the cleft between two of the street's embedded rocks.

"¡Ai, *mamacita!* I surprise you, no? I din' mean to scare you, pretty lady; jus' my way to say hello to someone very lovely like you. Hey, you hurt your foot?"

He knelt in front of her, his hands running smoothly across her ankle and her heel, then lightly up her calf and down again. Nineteen or twenty, maybe, wearing khaki shorts and one of those hideous mesh T-shirts. Thick, too-carefully tended black hair, and fluorescent teeth planted in the middle of a coconut-oil suntan. Handsome in an oily, slimy way, and very much aware of it. Elizabeth tried to withdraw her foot, but he squeezed her calf and held it firmly.

"Hey, be careful, maybe you hurt, pretty lady. You better rest, you know? Better sit down, take it easy. Anyway, you don' wan' to go to this beach here. I gotta Jeep, I take you to a better beach, O.K.? Nice white sand, lotta palm trees, no people. Don' even need no bathing suits, you know? We smoke a li'l dope, lie in the sun, go swimmin' . . . whatever."

"Let go of my leg."

"I got some really dynamite dope, you know? Michoacan, all the flowers in it still. Jus' one toke, you gonna lift right off an' bump you head into the sky, I promise you. Then we go swimmin', you feel the cool, cool ocean all over you skin. You come along, you don' be lonely."

"Let go of my leg and get away from me. Now."

"Maybe you wan' some mescaline, instead? Some acid, huh? I got some really dynamite acid, we watch the whole worl' break up in little pretty pieces jus' for us. O.K.?"

He stood up slowly, grasping her arm just as he released his hold on her leg. His smile was cocky, and his muscular but hairless chest bulged like a rooster's in the ridiculous see-through T-shirt.

"I'm meeting my husband on the beach. Let go of my arm or I'll shout for a policeman."

He grinned amusedly, his straight white teeth shining in the sunlight. "*Ai, querida,* what you wanta do that for? I bet your husban' be tired from all his work back home, he need a rest. You let him lie out in the sun, take a siesta. You an' me, we have a better time. My cousin gotta boat, I take you to Yelapa. We drink *ricea,* swim out off the reef. Your husban', he don' know the difference. I show you everything, show you a great place to go for lobster dinners and for sunsets. O.K.?"

This was his job, she realized: getting pretty gringo ladies to buy him lobster dinners and maybe pass him a wad of traveler's checks or dollars in gratitude or satisfaction. Business must be slow this time of year, and she was one of the few prospective customers around; hence, the hard-sell. She looked more closely at his toothy smile, and for a moment saw not this pushy Mexican beach boy, but Charlie Ferrara, younger. There was the same oily smoothness, the same cocky bravado that passed for self-confidence, the same too-regular features, the same unsubtle promise of sleekly mechanistic sex. Jenny's type. A modern, Latin American version of the reptilian kind of male who might be casually having his way with Phillip's wife, in Phillip's bed, in Phillip's home. Free and clear. No punishment or problems for either one of them, only clucking sympathy for the bereaved but wealthy young widow.

Elizabeth smiled at the brown young boy who held onto her arm, smiled with the passively seductive look of a woman who has at last been won over by irresistible persistence. The boy grinned back, and laughed aloud, pleased and amused at having so easily effected yet another conquest. He let go her arm and motioned in the direction of a battered Jeep parked up the street.

"Hey, yes, now you thinkin' right. You know wha's good, huh, sexy lady? Le's go, I'm gonna show you what Vallarta's all about."

Her arm free at last, Elizabeth reached into her purse. She took out a single peso coin, worth eight cents, and tossed it with a metallic ring onto the rocks at the husky young boy's feet. "Here," she said, "make a down payment on a shirt that doesn't make you look so much like a homosexual."

The boy's surface *machismo* quickly went from preening self-assurance to insulted, animal rage. He seemed about to strike her, but by then Elizabeth had turned away and merged into the crowd of people entering and leaving the beach.

Maybe David would be willing to go home early, she thought.

She would ask him as soon as he got back from the fishing trip this afternoon. And as soon as they were home, as soon as they had left this overheated place that reeked of death and uselessness and exploitation, she would make an appointment with Dr. Garrick, to insist on a replacement for the missing circuits in her transmitter.

Then it would be time to deal with Jenny.

"Absolutely not, Mrs. Austin. I'm amazed that you would even suggest such a thing, after what you've been through. We didn't implant those electrodes just for your entertainment, you know; and certainly not for your possible emotional ruin. If you don't have any respect for your own health, at least consider my obligations as your physician, and don't come to me with ridiculous requests like that."

Garrick sat back in his chair, his mouth tight and his eyebrows scowling. She had expected this to be difficult, but it had gone even worse than she'd thought it might. They'd been arguing for almost half an hour now. Not even arguing, really; just her asking and him refusing, over and over. With no apparent hope of concession or compromise. Now he was getting genuinely angry, which obviously wasn't going to change matters.

Still, she had tried; she had to try. She was consumed with bitter curiosity about what Jenny was doing: whether in the eight weeks since the murder she had managed to erase all traces of Phillip's memory, whether Charlie Ferrara was now living with her openly in the Belgravia house. Elizabeth could imagine the scenes that must be going on there, the laughing, drunken orgies that would be taking place even in the very room where Phillip had been killed. The image was unbearable, and she knew that something must be done to stop the ghoulish celebration. But now, looking at Dr. Garrick's paternally indignant face, she knew that was impossible. She might as well have asked him for an LSD prescription.

Her frustration and discomfiture were interrupted by Dr. Garrick's receptionist, who burst into the room after only the briefest of knocks. "I'm sorry, Dr. Garrick," she said, "but Dr. Winters asked me to tell you right away: Mr. Harold, the patient in 406, has started to hemorrhage."

Garrick's frown deepened, changing character as it did. He jumped up from his chair, immediately preoccupied with this new emergency, and went racing from the room as if Elizabeth had never been there. She had no idea what to do, and looked questioningly at the receptionist, who was still standing beside the door through which Dr. Garrick had bolted. "Should I go, or should I wait?"

The receptionist smiled back sympathetically. "Why don't you hang around for a few minutes, anyway, until we see whether he's going to be tied up with this for a while. Would you like a cup of coffee while you're waiting?"

"No, that's all right. Thanks, anyway."

The receptionist nodded and smiled again, then closed the door of the office behind her. Elizabeth lit a cigarette, feeling vaguely guilty about dirtying Garrick's immaculate glass ash tray. Doctors always seemed to have spotless ash trays, even those who smoked; it was as if they at least wanted to present an image of a good example.

There really wasn't that much point in waiting for him to return, she thought; it was obvious that he wasn't going to change his mind, and she definitely wouldn't be getting the transmitter altered back to the way it had been before.

Her eyes darted fitfully around the room, looking for something to hold her interest and to take her mind off this premature but irrevocable end to everything her life had come to mean in the past seven months. It was really over, all of it, and at the worst point possible.

She leaned over Dr. Garrick's desk, searching for some diversion: a medical journal, a newsmagazine, a book, anything. Then she saw the folder, as if for the first time, though her gaze had wandered over it several times in the past few minutes. Her folder. Her records.

She reached hesitantly toward the thick manila packet, not even lifting it, just turning it around in her direction. When it was facing her, she glanced nervously over her shoulder, expecting Dr. Garrick or his receptionist to come back into the room at any moment; but no one did.

She pulled the folder a little closer and lifted the first sheet. There were photostats of the original reports on her condition, written by Dr. Prentiss; she began reading, fascinated to see, after all these years, the record of all those early tests. There were the tracings of her EEGs during the first terrifying induced seizures, and blasé, totally objective written descriptions of the attacks:

. . . clonic phase ensued, for a duration of
seventy-four seconds. This was accompanied by spontaneous urination, and minor traces of
blood were noted in the spittle. Upon re-
gaining consciousness, subject was unable
to respond to standard questions concern-
ing her whereabouts and current events
("Who is Barry Goldwater?") for approximately fifteen minutes. Internal muscular bruises were apparently incurred
at . . .

She had to force herself to turn the pages, to tear herself away
from these dry reminders of the torments she had suffered in her
childhood. There were regularly updated reports on her prognosis,
then a long series of reports on the debilitating side effects of all
the different drugs they'd tried, then sporadic follow-up reports,
with notes and letters from her high school nurse on fits she'd had
in class, more photostats of her college medical records, a notation
of when she'd gotten married . . . her IQ, she was pleased to
note, was 144. God, there was even a long letter from one of her
art professors, discussing the imagery of her paintings as it might
relate to her condition and her perceptions of it! That one kind of
angered her.

Then the photostats and Xeroxes ended, and most of the rest
was original material, dating from her involvement with this hospital and Dr. Garrick. Dr. Prentiss' letter to Garrick was there, followed by page after page of more test results, more EEG's, more
descriptions of laboratory-induced convulsions. It was like a thick
book, defining her life only in terms of her epilepsy. Reading this,
Elizabeth Austin, née Chandler, seemed to be nothing more than
a troublesome temporal lobe lesion on an otherwise irrelevant
brain.

She flipped through faster, looking for later material. The only
thing she could find about her months of experiences in Jenny's
world was the single, untrue note: "Stimulation of twelfth electrode site caused subject to report brief, unorganized hallucinatory
response. Data insufficient to warrant conclusions at this time."
Her face flushed with anger as she realized there was no mention
whatsoever of all the sights and sensations that she had so meticu-

lously reported, no hint that she had been almost constantly living in another world and time.

The journal she had so carefully edited and typed was nowhere to be found, and there wasn't even a description of those early lab results, the piano and the field and waking up in Jenny's bedroom. They had nonchalantly censored out everything that was important in the whole experiment.

The door opened suddenly, and she jerked her hand back from the folder as if stung. "Dr. Garrick asked me to tell you that he'll only be a couple of minutes longer, Mrs. Austin, and he would like to see you before you go."

"Oh, thank you. Thank you very much." Her face was red, she knew, and her right foot was bobbing up and down in an unconscious display of guilty nervousness. She forced her foot to be still, and hoped the receptionist wouldn't be curious about her blush.

"Are you sure you wouldn't like a little coffee, or maybe a cup of tea?"

"No, I'm fine, really. Thanks for the offer, but I'm fine just sitting here."

The receptionist smiled in a friendly way, and left again. Elizabeth reached back for the folder immediately. Dr. Garrick might come back any second, and she had to hurry if she was going to find out what she wanted to know. She leafed quickly through the other pages, trying to absorb the importance of the myriad charts and graphs and tables of meaningless figures as best she could in hasty glances. She regretfully passed over several reports that, in other circumstances, would have gripped her full attention: discussions of the likelihood that her condition might be hereditary, analyses of the effects that epilepsy had had upon her personality, results of psychological tests of her aptitudes and creativity . . . then, suddenly, she found what she'd been looking for.

It was a long section, forty or fifty pages, beginning with a discussion of micro-electronics and chip circuitry. There were dozens of complex diagrams, the pages crowded with intricately intersecting lines and tiny symbols for capacitors and diodes and who knew what else. And then there was a neatly numbered list, beautiful and almost stunning in its simplicity. Her eyes ran down the rows of figures in a rush, while she listened for the door to open:

⚹ 6—10 Watts at 122.564 Mhz, oscillation 13 Hz
⚹ 7—10 Watts at 124.732 Mhz, oscillation 17 Hz
⚹ 8—8 Watts at 125.687 Mhz, oscillation 15 Hz
⚹ 9—12 Watts at 121.742 Mhz, oscillation 13 Hz
⚹10—7 Watts at 122.870 Mhz, oscillation 16 Hz
⚹11—11 Watts at 125.009 Mhz, oscillation 12 Hz
⚹12—8 Watts at 123.855 Mhz, oscillation 15 Hz

Eight watts of power; frequency one-two-three-point-eight-five-five Megahertz, programmed to oscillate on that frequency at a rhythm of fifteen cycles per second.

Electrode 12. The door to Jenny's world.

The receptionist's typewriter had stopped in the outside office, and she could hear Dr. Garrick talking to her, standing beside the partly opened door. She hastily scribbled the crucial numbers on the inside of a book of matches, closed the folder, and turned it back to its original position, facing Dr. Garrick's leather chair. He came into the office as she was still reaching her hand across his desk, so she furtively plucked an already dead cigarette butt from the ashtray and pretended to be crushing it out. His expression didn't change as he sat down, and he never glanced at the folder.

"I'm sorry about that, Mrs. Austin, but one of my other patients is in very serious condition. I'm due in the OR in five minutes, so I really don't have time to argue this point any longer. As I told you, it's simply out of the question for me to . . ."

"Oh, that's all right, Dr. Garrick, I understand. It was silly of me to ask, I realize."

"Well, you were putting me on a really impossible spot, you know."

"Yes, I know . . . I should have known better, but . . . I guess I was just getting carried away with my—hallucinations."

She glanced up and saw that Garrick was smiling, nodding. Might as well feed him what he wanted to hear.

"They did seem very real, though; if you've never been through something like that, it's impossible to understand how realistic it can seem at the moment. But I guess I'm better off just forgetting about it now."

"Well, I'm glad to hear you say that. You have so much else ahead of you, and I look forward to hearing that you've resumed your work soon. You will keep in touch, let me know how you're doing?"

"Yes, of course. And if anything else comes up, I'll let you know. Thanks again for making me be sensible about all this."

They left the office together, and at the door he gave her a final handshake and a preoccupied smile, then hurried off down the corridor to the operating room. Elizabeth strolled out the front door of the hospital and hailed a cab. She felt more relaxed now than she had in a long, long time, knowing that the pertinent information on how the electrode could be restimulated was safely in her purse. She'd gotten what she came for, and she didn't feel the slightest qualms over the dishonesty of her methods, or anxiety about what to do next. If she'd gotten this far, she could see the rest of it through, somehow. She still had only the vaguest notions of how it might be carried out, but she knew now that she would visit Jenny once again. And, somehow, destroy her.

Billy Joe Watkins shook his shaggy head and smiled, shook his head and smiled some more. You didn't get too many types like that last one, not in a shop like this. Some of the other stores, the big ones on the Upper East Side where they did a lot of retail sales, Sony cassette machines and Panasonic FM radios and Trinitron TVs, stuff like that, Billy Joe bet they got all kinds of great chicks coming in: East Side chicks with their tight jeans and firm asses, all the secretaries and models looking to get their headphones or their clock radios fixed, and maybe looking for a little action on the side, too. But not here, not in this shop.

Down here, way the hell over on West Twenty-third Street, you were too far uptown for the Village trade and too far downtown for the East Sixties trade, and too far west for the Gramercy Park trade. What you got here were a lot of black and Puerto Rican guys who'd blasted the speaker cones out of their big transistor radios, and then you got a lot of beat-up old TV sets and electric typewriters . . . but most of all, you got the hams and the CBers, that was what they'd specialized in here. And shortwave freaks didn't usually have nice bods and long legs. They were all guys, mostly, and more often than not a pretty fucked-up lot: skinny kids with thick glasses, or fat blue-collar types who'd talk to anybody just to get away from the wife and three kids in Queens, even if they lived in Nome, Alaska, and didn't really have anything to say except how was the reception. Lonely people who talked and talked and talked and never met each other. That was who you got in this shop.

But that last one, Jesus Christ. Beautiful. Smooth, too, and bright. Like the kind you see all over the place around Bloomingdale's. What she was doing way the fuck down here, Billy Joe'd never know, but he wasn't complaining. Maybe when she came back next week to pick up her order, he'd try to start up a conversation; she was wearing a wedding ring, but you never knew about those rich bitches, what with all the talk about open marriages electrodes in her brain that were truly irreplaceable, the result of years of research and the most painstaking microscopic assembly.

She ran her fingers lightly over the gray metal surface of the makeshift transmitter, fingering the toggle switch. She'd have to keep this one in her hand, or at least in reaching distance, because it wouldn't automatically shut off when she moved her hand away. At least that would eliminate the need for taping down the button, as she'd had to do before when she wanted to monitor what was happening over a period of an hour or so; once this one was on, it stayed on till she turned it off.

She took a deep breath and stubbed out her cigarette. There was no point in putting this off any longer. Jenny would be waking up at any moment, in that familiar bedroom, beneath the silk sheets that Elizabeth now knew so well. But Phillip wouldn't be there. She would have to steel herself to that fact, not break down in inner tears over something that couldn't possibly be changed. There was a purpose to what she was about to do, and she couldn't let herself forget it.

The toggle switch moved upward with an audible click, and then she

CLEAR

CLEAR

CLEAR

CLEAR

CLEAR

CLEAR

She was standing up, and then she felt herself crumpling loosely to the floor. She had been expecting Jenny's muscles to take over, but they hadn't; she was on her own, she had somehow locked directly into full control without even trying. Everything was startlingly vivid, her perceptions were intensely clear; she waited for Jenny to get up, but nothing happened. She was *here*, it was all up to her; Jenny was nowhere to be found.

"'ere, luv, don't go faintin', now. 'Course it's normal. I've seen many of 'em faint before, but a fine lady like you ought to set an example fer all them ruffians that'll be out there."

Elizabeth opened her eyes and looked around her. She had fallen on a concrete floor, in a small room with no windows. There was a rumpled cot against one wall, and a simple wooden table with a pitcher of water on it. A fire was going, but the fireplace was bare, with no mantelpiece or any of the usually ornate decorations; no andirons, even, just the fire itself and a single iron poker. She tentatively moved one hand and touched her face; it was Jenny's hand, and Jenny's face, but Elizabeth felt as if she were . . . *alone*, the way she'd briefly felt that last night, just before Jenny had come surging back from nowhere to murder Phillip. Where was Jenny now? What the hell was wrong, why was everything so absolutely clear? She shut her eyes again and tried to feel for the toggle switch on the transmitter, tried to envision the living room of her apartment; but it was no use, her perceptions were all here, and now. She felt a rising panic; there must have been something wrong with the damned transmitter, they must have made it much too strong. Could she get back at all, now? David wouldn't be coming home for hours yet. He'd find her then, and he'd turn off the switch; but maybe she was locked in permanently, maybe even turning off the transmitter wouldn't help.

"Come on now, darlin', stand up like a lady, 'ere, I'll 'elp you. 'ave a glass o' brandy now, it'll 'elp, it always does. Don't you fret now, Mr. Calcraft knows his job. 'twas him that done James Greenacre, and Catherine Wilson, too."

Someone was helping her to her feet, a stocky woman in her fifties. Elizabeth had never seen her before, she wasn't one of the usual servants; maybe she'd been hired to take care of Jenny after Phillip's death. But she wasn't wearing maid's clothing, she was wearing some sort of dull gray smock; and which room was this, why was it so barren?

The woman handed her the brandy in a plain metal cup. Elizabeth looked down at it in confusion. It was eight o'clock in the morning, for God's sake. Why were they giving her brandy? And why not in a snifter?

"Go on, now, drink it right down. Give you strength, it will, strength and courage. Not as if you really need it, though, luv, not from the way you've held up through all this. That's what all the broadsides say, 'the resolute and fearless Jenny Curran,' they all call you. An' truth to tell, they're on the mark, leastways as far as that about your courage goes. You've shown a fine, brave spirit, an' never fear: I'll not breathe a word about the faintin'. You'll stand up strong and tall out there, I know you will."

Elizabeth took a tentative sip of the brandy, and almost gagged.

It was cheap stuff, and far too early in the day to take even if it hadn't been. And what the hell was this strange woman talking about, anyway? Elizabeth handed the cup back, still almost full.

"No, thank you. I don't want it."

Her voice! She'd never been able to make Jenny speak before, it had always just come out as a strained and gargled jumble; but now the words were smooth and distinct, the vocal cords and tongue and lips completely under her control.

The old woman's eyes were full of admiration and approval as she took the cup. "I knew it, sure as daybreak. 'Jenny Curran didn't need no brandy,' I'll tell them that asks. 'She faced the mornin' like as if she'd just been off to vespers, that's what I'll say."

Elizabeth looked around the room again, trying to find a trace of something familiar, but there was nothing: no paintings on the thick stone walls, no flowers on the table, no books or knick-knacks. Nothing. Heavy footsteps sounded just outside, and then the door was clanking open with a heavy swing. Another older woman in the same gray smock came into the room, followed by two men. Their faces were impassive, and none of them would look her in the eyes. One of the men was done up in clerical garb, and he held an open Bible in his hands. The other one stepped toward her, carrying a tangled mass of leather straps.

No, she thought. No, it couldn't be.

"Hands together before your waist, please, mum."

No, they couldn't mean it, it couldn't be what it seemed. She could hear the blood pounding in her ears, and she looked down at herself, at the body that had once been Jenny's. She was wearing a fine white dress and lilac boots, and she took a sudden, desperate comfort in this fact. Nobody dies wearing white and lilac, she thought, it isn't proper. This is all something else, maybe some weird treatment for Jenny's supposed epilepsy. Yes, this must be a hospital; hospitals were awful in the nineteenth century, weren't they, as wretched as prisons. O God. O please God, let it be a hospital.

"Hands together, please, let's have no fuss."

He was touching her now, he was taking hold of her hands with his and pressing them together, wrapping the coarse leather around them tightly. She tried to draw her hands back and he clutched them stronger still, hurting a little now . . . like the boy on the beach in Mexico, but rougher.

"Let go of me. I'm going home now, do you understand?"

The women in gray exchanged a look, and raised their eyebrows slightly. Somewhere in the distance, Elizabeth could hear a church bell ringing. No, not ringing. Tolling.

"I'm not ill now, I don't want this treatment. Let go of my hands and send for my carriage immediately, I'm going back to Eaton Place."

The man ignored her. Her hands were securely tied together now, and he began winding the trailing ends of leather around her waist, pinioning her arms close against her body, immobilizing them completely. She could smell the man's stale breath and sweat as he pulled the leather straps taut, fastening their buckles. Like a straitjacket, she thought; a primitive version of a straitjacket. They must be going to try to induce a seizure. She clung to this thought, running it over and over in her mind. A seizure, just another seizure for the doctors to study. The women must be nurses. But why in gray?

The man in the clerical collar was reading aloud now from his Bible, with the distant bell still pealing in the background. "The Lord is my shepherd; I shall not want. He maketh me to lie down in green pastures; He leadeth me beside the still waters, He restoreth my soul . . ."

"Please, stop reading that. I don't want to listen to it. I just want to go home now, just go home."

". . . He leadeth me in the paths of righteousness for his name's sake. Yea, though I walk through the valley of the Shadow of Death, I will fear no evil . . ."

Damn them, damn them, why didn't they stop this? It couldn't be what it looked like, she couldn't let herself think that.

They were leading her out of the room now, down a long and narrow corridor. There were lanterns burning against the walls every twenty feet or so, casting semicircular spots of light on the dusty floor. She hated the dark sections, hated being in between the lighted parts. The man in black kept on reading from the Bible in his dull monotone. He was terrible, he had no sense of inflection whatsoever, all the words sounded just the same. He must put his congregation to sleep in five minutes. Her mind was racing madly, leaping from thought to thought, anything to avoid the impossible but obvious conclusion.

There was an opening in the corridor up ahead, she could see the dim sunlight streaming in. They were taking her outside, the carriage would be waiting. All these straps were just in case she had a seizure on the way, she thought irrationally. She'd go back to Jenny's house now, sit in the garden for a while. David would come back to the apartment later, he'd turn off the transmitter.

Or maybe she could, now. She closed her eyes and concentrated with all her effort on remembering the familiar living room. Television set in the corner. Utrillo print on the left wall. Her sketchbooks in a jumbled stack on one table. Dark blue carpet, light blue drapes. That's where she really was. Not here. There. No white dress, no boots. She was really wearing a halter top and a pair of cutoffs. She was holding a metal box in her lap, and it was making her feel all this.

She tried to make her hand move, make her own, not Jenny's, hand reach out and flick the switch she knew was there; but she could only feel the leather bite her wrists. No box. No switch.

Help me, God, help me.

She stumbled blindly, and opened her eyes again. The two old women at her side caught her, held her up by her pinioned arms. They had come to a small flight of steps, and at the top she could see the place where the light was coming through. The women helped her up the steps. There was a small door at the top, and they led her through. It was raining slightly, just a fine, thin mist, and the sun was obscured behind the clouds, but still its brightness made her shut her eyes in pain after the liquid darkness of the room she'd been in, and the musty corridor.

There was a constant murmur from all around, beneath her and above her, as if she were surrounded by a crowd. She opened her eyes, squinting, and saw them there, in the streets below. Hundreds of them, thousands. Empty eyes and faces, laughing, staring, talking, shouting. At the windows of the buildings around the place where she stood there were other clusters of onlookers, most of these dressed in expensive finery. One group, in a window across the street, was directly level with her gaze: three women and two men, all sipping wine and munching shanks of lamb. The babble of the crowd below was broken frequently by the shouts of hawkers selling oranges and sweetmeats.

God, no, God don't let it be. Mommy, Daddy, David, make them stop, make the whole thing go away. The misting rain ran down her forehead and her cheeks, carrying her sudden tears along with it.

The scaffold was painted all black. There was an iron bar parallel with the prison wall, fixed to the wall about four feet out with iron scroll clamps. Several lengths of iron chain were suspended from the bar, and from the middle chain a noose was hung. The flooring of the platform where she stood was broken in the middle by a square-shaped piece, separate from the rest, and attached by hinges to the wall.

"Jenny Curran, do you now wish to confess?"

It was the cleric, his Bible closed now. His righteous eyes were no longer averted, but looked straight into her own.

It was hard to get the words out, and she almost started coughing. "No, please, listen; I'm not Jenny Curran, I'm not her at all. I know it sounds absurd, but it's the truth. Just let me talk to somebody official, let me explain . . ."

"Jenny Curran, do you confess to the crime of which you stand convicted and condemned?"

"That isn't even my name, my name is Elizabeth Austin, and I . . . I don't belong here, I don't belong anywhere here, I live in New York, I haven't done anything, I tried to save him, please, you've got to believe me, it was her, not me . . ."

The cleric looked away, shaking his head, and a huge, white-bearded man in a plain black suit stepped forward. He might have been a grocer or a tradesman, might be a father or grandfather. There was no expression in his face, but his eyes seemed kind. Elizabeth clutched at that, clutched wildly at the kindness in his eyes.

"You believe me, don't you? You can tell, I couldn't do a thing like that, it was Jenny . . ."

He grasped her by the shoulders and gently turned her to the left, underneath the noose. "I don't want to hurt you," he whispered. "I'll be quick as quick can be. Just look straight at me, and don't listen to the crowd."

There was something stirring at the edges of her ravaged mind, something, someone. Jenny. Jenny waking up, as if gradually recovering from a seizure or a massive shock.

"Give the lady one last kiss, Calcraft!"

"Cor, give 'er one last sumpin' else!"

"Pass 'er down 'ere for a minute, let us 'ave a partin' go!"

Here and there fights had broken out among the crowd, and Elizabeth could see swarms of police moving in with heavy clubs.

The well-dressed people in the window across the street were laughing, and one of the women was looking at Elizabeth through a pair of jeweled opera glasses. One knot of men in the street was singing, loudly and with drunken fervor.

Someone was strapping her ankles together, as the bearded man named Calcraft slipped the noose around her throat, carefully positioning the knot behind her ear. She looked down and saw that her lilac boots were flecked with the sawdust that covered the platform.

The bell was tolling still, and now another, just above the prison gate, began to join it. At the top of the prison wall there was a flagpole, with a pure black flag hanging limply at its lower hoist the flag. Elizabeth's darting eyes caught his for one brief moment, and he blinked and turned away.

Jenny was conscious now, and more: She *knew*. Elizabeth could feel the sudden knowledge, feel the comprehension, feel the total fusion that had taken place between their minds: memories of both their lives, of thoughts, events, emotions—shared, all shared and fully understood by each of them. Everything that either one had ever known, they both knew now.

"All good people, pray heartily unto God for this poor sinner, who is now going to her death, for whom the great bell of St. Sepulchre's doth toll.

"You that are condemned to die, repent with lamentable tears; ask mercy of the Lord . . ."

The bearded man was pulling a thin white cap down over her face. *Their* face. The rain was coming harder now, and it made the fabric stick wetly to their nose and mouth, making it hard to breathe. Through the gauzy cloth, they both could see the dim outline of the other figures on the scaffold, backing slowly away.

". . . ask mercy of the Lord for the salvation of your soul through the merits, death, and passion of Jesus Chist . . ."

"No, please, you don't understand, it's all different now!"

". . . who now sits on the right hand of God, to make intercession for you as you penitently return to Him . . ."

There was a stream of urine running down their legs, and their screams were no longer distinguishable as words. The white cap was sticking to their whole face now, and their hands and feet were sore from struggling against the leather straps. Struggling, for once, together, with a common fear and hopeless purpose.

". . . the Lord God have mercy upon your soul. His son, our savior, Jesus Christ, have mercy upon your soul."

There was a heavy creaking sound beside them and below them, and the oaken flooring dropped away.

It hurt, it hurt, O God it hurt. Their neck was twisted at a sickening angle, but unbroken. The thick hemp fibers of the rope pressed at their throat with awesome strength. Their lungs were filled with air, but the rope was squeezed so tight they couldn't even let it out. They could feel the pressure of the blood inside the head, pressing from behind their eyes. They had to breathe, they had to breathe . . . the tendons in the throat were all crushed together, the larynx was destroyed. O Christ, it couldn't hurt this much, nothing could, O let us breathe . . .

The chest and back were heaving uncontrollably, trying to force the air to come, and still it wouldn't. As they moved, they could feel a multitude of tiny snaps and ripping tissues in the throat. It was impossible, the pain, how could they still be conscious, how could it feel this way . . . one breath, please, just one more, got to have just one . . .

The body that they shared thrashed more strongly still, straining for air, despite the torture that each movement inflicted on the raw and bleeding throat. The arms and legs began to quiver helplessly against the leather straps, and then the whole body was wracked with violent spasms as its cells began to die from want of oxygen. Blind, soaked in urine, rain, and sweat, the two of them together jerked and shook with awful strength, the pain increasing with each spasm.

The final seizure, they both thought at once. And then the spasms, and the thinking, ceased.

The refrigerator was humming, and at first she thought it was blood inside her head. She opened her eyes and could see nothing but blue. Then she realized that she was lying on the floor, her face mashed down against the carpet. She reached one hand up to her aching neck, and ran her fingertips along it in wonder.

The transmitter was on the floor, too, just a few feet away. Carefully, as if learning to crawl, she moved across and picked it up. The toggle switch was flush against the stenciled letters "ON." She pulled it down again, and could feel no change. She flicked it back and forth, off and on, and there was nothing at all: no alteration of perception, no awareness of the current coursing in her brain.

No one else was there. She was alone.

She stood up slowly and made her way to the window. It was a beautiful day, and the sunlit trees in the park below were the greenest things she'd ever seen. There would be people down there, and she knew they'd all be smiling at the summer.

For just one instant her memory began to flash on something awful, but she shut it out. There were things too bad to dream about, let alone remember.

Over. It was over.

She was hungry, she was thirsty, and, for some reason, Jenny Curran was feeling sexy as hell. Once those needs were taken care of, she had a lot of plans to make.